TWISTED REASON

Recent Titles by Diane Fanning

Fiction

The Lucinda Pierce Mysteries

THE TROPHY EXCHANGE *
PUNISH THE DEED *
MISTAKEN IDENTITY *
TWISTED REASON *

Non–Fiction

OUT THERE
UNDER THE KNIFE
WRITTEN IN BLOOD

* *available from Severn House*

TWISTED REASON

A Lucinda Pierce Mystery

Diane Fanning

This first world edition published 2010
in Great Britain and in the USA by
SEVERN HOUSE PUBLISHERS LTD of
9–15 High Street, Sutton, Surrey, England, SM1 1DF.
Trade paperback edition first published
in Great Britain and the USA 2011 by
SEVERN HOUSE PUBLISHERS LTD.

British Library Cataloguing in Publication Data

Fanning, Diane.
  Twisted reason.
  1. Pierce, Lucinda (Fictitious character)–Fiction.
  2. Women detectives–Fiction. 3. Dementia–Patients–
  Crimes against–Fiction. 4. Detective and mystery stories.
  I. Title
  813.6-dc22

ISBN-13: 978-0-7278-6945-6   (cased)
ISBN-13: 978-1-84751-278-9   (trade paper)

All Severn House titles are printed on acid-free paper.

Severn House Publishers support The Forest Stewardship Council [FSC],the leading
international forest certification organisation. All our titles that are printed on
Greenpeace-approved FSC-certified paper carry the FSC logo.

Mixed Sources
Product group from well-managed
forests and other controlled sources
www.fsc.org Cert no. SA-COC-1565
© 1996 Forest Stewardship Council
FSC

Typeset by Palimpsest Book Production Ltd.,
Falkirk, Stirlingshire, Scotland.
Printed and bound in Great Britain by
MPG Books Ltd., Bodmin, Cornwall.

ONE

Eric Humphries stepped out of the shower, inhaling the aroma of brewing coffee drifting up from the kitchen downstairs. As a young man, his list of necessary attributes for the perfect woman never included a requirement for her to be an early riser but he never forgot how lucky he was to have married a woman that was. Every morning, she eased out of bed while he lay there drifting in and out of sleep, half-listening to the small sounds she made as she dressed and got going.

He couldn't imagine starting a day with her energy and enthusiasm. No matter how well he slept or how long, he was always reluctant to break through the inertia and stumble into the shower. His only motivation was the knowledge that Vicki waited downstairs with a smile on her face, a cup of coffee at the ready and the daily newspaper folded beside his place mat.

He put the towel on his head, tousling the dark-brown hair that was losing the battle with the conquering strands of gray. He wiped off the rest of his body and tossed the damp towel on the bottom of the bed. He pulled a T-shirt over his head and stuck one foot into his boxers. Before he could lift the other leg, a scream and the slam of a door echoed through the house.

'Vicki! Vicki!' he shouted as he pulled his underwear up to his waist. 'Are you OK? Vicki?' he yelled as he took the turn on the stair landing, grabbing the newel post for balance. In two more steps, he came to an abrupt stop, staring at his wife.

Her back was plastered flat against the door, her arms stretched from side to side. Her warm brown eyes had lost all signs of their usual calmness, darting about like mice in an overcrowded cage. They widened, shrunk and widened again. Her lips provided the only touch of color in a pale white face. 'Your dad . . .'

'What about my dad?'

'He – he is here,' she wailed.

'Why don't you let him in?' Eric asked as he came down the remaining steps to the foyer.

Vicki sobbed and hiccuped.

'Vicki, please let me open the door.'

She shook her head making her dark curls slap her face, as she straightened her spine and braced against the entryway.

Eric wanted to shove her out of the way and get to his dad. He hadn't seen his father in months. The dementia had robbed the older man of so much and Eric knew he must have wandered to a strange place where he could not remember the way home or even how to ask for help. Eric worried his dad was injured – or worse. What was wrong with Vicki? 'Get out the way,' he insisted, fighting the urge to force her.

Vicki looked up at her husband's fierce eyes and her shoulders slumped. 'I don't want you to see this,' she sobbed before stepping aside.

Eric pulled open the door ready to wrap his arms around his father, but where his dad should have been standing, there was an empty space. Eric looked down and to the right at a pair of feet in freshly shined black dress shoes. He followed the dark-gray legs of the pants up to a belt, moved up the length of a red tie and into the face. His father. Eric dropped to his knees beside him.

He reached out to his dad's neck, desperately seeking a pulse. He pulled at the old man's tie, tore open the shirt with enough force to send little white buttons dancing on to the wooden floorboards. He counted each chest compression as he pushed down with force.

Vicki kneeled, wrapping her arms around her husband. 'Don't,' she sobbed. 'Don't, Eric. It's too late. He's cold.'

Eric shrugged her off and breathed air into the dead man's slack mouth. Eric sat up and resumed the chest compressions.

'Eric, please?' Vicki wailed.

'Either help me or leave me alone.'

Vicki sat back on her heels and pulled a cellphone out of the pocket of her robe, pressing 9-1-1. 'My father-in-law has been missing for five months,' her voice quavered. 'Now, his body is on our front porch. Please send the police.'

'He's not dead!' Eric shouted and bent over to expend more useless breaths into the shell that once was his father.

Vicki sighed. 'Please send an ambulance, too.'

TWO

Sherry stood in the doorway of a room looking out at familiar faces but unable to recall any of their names. 'I want . . . I want . . .' She couldn't remember the word. She could picture it when she closed her eyes: the clear, tall glass with droplets of water clinging on all sides forming little streams as gravity pulled them downward, a light-brown liquid with a foamy top, a straw poking out of the glass. Eddie always gave her one of those bendy straws because she was too short to drink it otherwise. She could taste the rich flavor of the cold concoction slipping down her throat as she sipped. She had to be careful, though. If she drank too fast, the icicle would pierce her head bringing a measure of pain with her pleasure. *But what was that word?*

Most times Betsy would go with her to the lunch counter at Drumfelder's Drugstore and Eddie would put two straws in one glass and they'd share. And sometimes when it was really hot outside, if they could scrape up the extra quarter, they'd split a second one on the same afternoon. 'I want . . .' she said again.

All of the eyes that had turned toward her now shifted back to what they were doing when she entered the room: watching a soap on the television, playing cards with a friend or just staring into space. Sherry was angry with herself for not knowing the word and even madder at those people for not trying to help her find it.

She spun around and walked back outside. She'd go find Betsy. Betsy would know the word. And even if she didn't they could go to Drumfelder's and get one together. She walked away from the building past a row of interconnected one-room bungalows to the path leading into a copse of trees. She walked past oaks, pines and maples, but in their place, she saw the bricks on the street where she spent her childhood. Instead of walking on a dirt trail, as she set her feet down she saw concrete beneath each one and she stretched her stride to avoid the cracks that would break her mother's back.

When she saw Betsy's house, she waited on the sidewalk looking up at the window box filled with bright-red geraniums. Betsy's mom planted them there every spring; there was no way on this line of lookalike homes that you could miss the bright color on her friend's house in the warm weather time. Betsy popped out of the front door with a grin and skipped down the marble stoop.

They walked side-by-side toward Drumfelder's close enough to hold hands but not touching. Betsy sang, 'Maresie doates and dosey doats and little lambsy edivey, a kiddle edivey, too, wouldn't you?'

Sherry never sang that part with Betsy – she just couldn't get it straight no matter how hard Betsy tried to teach her. But she could get the slower verse right and was ready to sing along when a high chain-link fence appeared blocking her way forward. 'Where did this come from, Betsy?' When Sherry didn't get a response, she turned and looked for her friend but couldn't find her.

Sherry put both palms against the fence; it bowed from the pressure but did not give. She stuck her fingers through and grabbed on and shook as hard as she could to no avail.

'Betsy, are you playing a trick on me? And where did you go? Where did this fence come from? We don't have fences this high in our neighborhood. And we certainly don't have one across the sidewalk. I don't know what you did, Betsy, but I'm really mad now!'

Sherry started down the length of the fence looking for where it ended. She was weary long before she reached any sign of it. Now, she did not recognize anything in her surroundings. Her anger morphed into fear. She was lost and didn't know where to find help. Was she in prison? Like maybe one of those works farms? Had she been arrested? She didn't know. Or maybe they put her on a remote island to fend for herself like Dustin Hoffman? She couldn't jump off that cliff like he did to get away. But why did they put her here? She must've done something really bad. But what?

'Miss Sherry?'

Sherry startled with a jump so intense, it nearly knocked her off her feet. She cringed back against the fence.

'Miss Sherry, honey, it's all right. Look at me, sweetheart.

Look at my face. You remember me, right? You remember me. I'm your good friend Don. Remember? I make sure you get a chocolate dessert every night with dinner. And tonight, I'm going to get you a big, fat piece of Black Forest cake. How's that sound?'

Some of the tension slid from Sherry's shoulders. She did recognize his face. She didn't know who he was. She didn't understand why he was here. But she did remember that she did get chocolate when she did what he asked. She peeled her body off the chain-link fence and took two timid steps forward.

'That's it, Miss Sherry. Come on now,' he said reaching out his hand.

Sherry wrapped her fingers around it and looked up at him.

'That's a good girl. Come on now. Let's get on down to the dining room. Before you get your cake, you need to eat your supper and, um, um, it's a good one. We've got some of Brenda's yummy meat loaf and her creamy mashed potatoes and some fresh-picked string beans. It's some real good stuff, Miss Sherry, you'll smell it and your mouth is gonna water like crazy. So let's get a move on, old girl.'

Sherry didn't understand all that he said but the sound of his voice was nice and maybe she'd get one of those things she wanted – whatever they were called.

THREE

Lieutenant Lucinda Pierce was pulling into her assigned parking space at work when her cellphone rang. She grabbed it, leaving the car idle as she answered. 'Pierce.'

'Hey, Lieutenant. This is Jumbo Butler in Missing Persons. Your captain said I could call you for help.'

'In a missing person's case?'

'He's not missing any more. His body's been found.'

'Homicide?'

'I can't say I know, Lieutenant. I just know he's dead and laying on his son's front porch at 834 Jefferson Street. It looks kinda suspicious but I could be overreacting.'

'On my way. And, Butler, call in a forensic team. Until we know it's not a homicide, we need to treat it as if it is,' she said, disconnecting the call and backing out of her parking slot. On the short drive over, she thought about what she was neglecting that morning. She had a major paperwork back-up on her desk but avoiding that task suited her just fine. She'd planned to try to chase down her drive-by shooting suspect again today. She had follow-up work to do on the bar shooting from Saturday night. And, of course, there was the pile of cold cases she needed to review. She wished the captain would start up a cold case unit and put specialists on these old murders, but with the recent drop in the homicide stats, she didn't think that would happen any time soon.

Turning the corner on to Jefferson, Lucinda was pleased she saw no evidence of media presence yet. She knew they would be there soon and appreciated that sawhorses erected halfway down the block would keep them at bay. She pulled in front of the barricade, rolled down her window and displayed her shield in her outstretched hand.

A patrolman jerked one of the sawhorses out of her way and she pulled through, stopping at the curb behind the ambulance. Tipping down her visor, she gave her appearance a once over and sighed at the scars still evident on one side of her face. The damage from a shoot-out during a domestic call had been inflicted in an instant and yet it was taking years and multiple surgeries to try to get both sides of her face to match as closely as possible. It looked better now but she knew no one would think she was normal.

She emerged from her vehicle and took urgent strides across the road to the house, as if she were eager to distance herself from the mirror. She'd never met Jumbo Butler but she was certain of his identity when she spotted a man with carrot-colored hair who couldn't have been more than 5'4" and probably would qualify in the ring as a flyweight. The ironic nickname probably stuck to him in grade school and, not being able to shake it loose, he embraced it instead.

She walked straight to him and stuck out her hand. 'Butler?'

He smiled and gave her hand a hardy shake. 'Hey, Lieutenant Pierce. Man, thanks for getting here so quickly. I sure do appreciate it. Most the times when I have a missing person case that ends up with a dead body, the signs of foul play were evident from day one. But this guy was different. He had Alzheimer's or something like that and everybody thought he'd just wandered off and got lost. At least, I did. And now this.'

'And the body hasn't been moved?' she asked as she walked up the steps to the front door.

'Nope. His clothing's been messed up some by his son and the emergency medical technicians, but otherwise, this is how he was found.'

'What was the son doing?'

'CPR. When I got here, he was having a bit of a stand-off with the EMTs. Apparently when they decided it was too late to do anything, the son went off. He was fighting them to get back to his dad and continue the CPR. I had to get a couple of officers to take him into the house. Then he started hyper-ventilating. The EMTs are with him now trying to settle him down.'

'Is he fit to answer questions?' Lucinda asked.

'You can try but I doubt if anything he says right now will make much sense. You'd do better talking to his wife. She's pretty upset but not hysterical like he is.'

'How have they been throughout the time he was missing?'

'Pretty typical. Called a lot. Yelled at me a bit. Cried a lot. They seem to genuinely want to find him.'

'Let's hope it was genuine. Did you check his financials?'

'Yeah. No activity. Not by him. None on his behalf by the son's family. Not a single account or credit card was used. But he did have plenty of money for a motive as well as a decent life insurance policy that named the son as beneficiary.'

'I'll keep that in mind. Make sure no one else touches the body until the coroner's office clears it. And if a death investigator isn't here soon, let me know and I'll call Doc Sam at home.'

Walking inside, Lucinda passed the paramedics huddled around Eric Humphries and followed the sounds coming from the back of the house. She walked into the kitchen where she found Vicki pacing the length of the room. 'Ms Humphries?'

Vicki stopped in mid-stride. 'Yes. Yes? Are you . . .?'

Lucinda flashed her badge. 'Lieutenant Pierce, Homicide.'

'You think someone murdered my father-in-law?' Vicki gasped.

'We don't know, ma'am. But it sure doesn't look like he just walked up on your porch, laid down and passed away in his sleep.'

Vicki bent her head and moved it side to side. 'No. I suppose it doesn't. I really hadn't thought about it.'

'Because we don't know how he got there, we need to investigate his death as a homicide to make sure nothing is overlooked. When was the last time you saw the deceased?' Lucinda gritted her teeth, knowing she'd picked the wrong word before she finished saying it.

As she expected, Vicki winced. 'Please. His name was Edgar. Edgar Humphries. I called him Dad. You can call him that or Edgar or anything but . . . that . . .'

'When was the last time you saw Edgar?'

Vicki tapped on her forehead with three fingers. 'I know this. I know this. I just can't . . .'

'Relax, Ms Humphries. Take your time. C'mon,' Lucinda said, wrapping a hand around the woman's elbow and steering her toward the kitchen table. 'Let's sit down, OK?'

Vicki allowed herself to be guided across the room and slumped into the age-darkened wood of a Windsor chair. Lucinda sat across from her waiting.

Vicki sighed. 'I can't seem to recall the exact date, whatever it was, but it was just before Thanksgiving. Ten days before. Exactly ten days, on a Monday. Eric and I kept assuring each other that he'd be home for Thanksgiving. He loved turkey. We knew he wouldn't miss it. But he did. The turkey sat on the table growing cold. The surface of the cranberry sauce got all crusty. And still no Dad. We figured he'd be OK without his meds till Thanksgiving. But after that, we were fearful that it could be fatal. All that hoping and praying and nothing.' Vicki brushed the corners of her eyes. 'We need to know what happened.'

'Tell me about the Monday when you last saw him.'

'It was ordinary. I fixed breakfast for all of us. He ate as he usually did. A couple of bites, then he'd stare off into space and one of us would have to remind him to eat. He always beamed when we did that as if we'd given him a surprising and extraordinary gift. Then we both left for work. Dad was sitting on the back porch having a second cup of coffee. I kissed him on the top of the head and patted his arm. He didn't seem to notice.'

'Did you leave him alone every day?'

'For a few hours. We had a woman coming in at midday to fix his lunch and make sure he ate it. Some days she was the only one at the house. Three times a week, we had a nurse's aide who came in to shave him and help him shower. And a nurse who came in once a week to check on his meds and look for any other problems. She was the one who told us in October that we weren't going to be able to leave him home alone much longer.'

'Did you take that seriously?'

'Yes, but we hadn't decided what to do. We'd been visiting homes with Alzheimer's units and also looking into home care. We weren't sure what was best for Dad. We were even considering that one of us should take early retirement and stay home with him. There just didn't seem to be any perfect decision. We put him on a couple of waiting lists to make sure he'd be in line for placement if we decided to take that route – there was one in particular that Dad really seemed to like and we had our fingers crossed. But it bothered us, sitting around hoping for a room to open up – it meant, really, that we were waiting for someone to die. The whole thing was so depressing and we were just floundering. We feel so guilty about that. We have for months. If only we'd made a decision and kept him safe.' Vicki's lower lip quivered and moisture filled her eyes.

'Was he home when the woman came to prepare his lunch?'

'No. That was the first we knew of a problem. She called us. But it wasn't the first time, so we didn't panic.'

'He'd run off before?'

'Not exactly. We'd always find him within two blocks of the house. Sometimes, he'd be raking leaves in someone else's yard. Other times, he'd be picking up sticks that had fallen from trees. Often, we'd find him in his stocking feet. But he never hurt himself and he never wandered far. The woman – Ms Jenkins – checked out his usual places but he wasn't there. My husband and I both hurried home from work and looked again. Then we called the police.'

'And you've not heard from him since that day?'

'No. Not a word.' A tear broke away from one eye and trailed down her cheek to her chin. 'Where has he been?'

'That's what we're going to have to find out, Ms Humphries. How was he with people – with strangers?'

Vicki laughed. 'He was a lover of the world. If you showed the least inclination to listen to his World War Two stories, you were his new best friend. He got so animated recalling his old memories, it was hard to look at him then and remember that he wasn't the same vital man we'd always known.' Vicki sobbed. 'But he wasn't. He'd lost so much. It was so unfair.' She bent forward, collapsing her head on top of her folded arms on the table.

Lucinda stood and placed a hand on Vicki's back. 'I'm so sorry, Ms Humphries. I would like to take his medications with me before I leave if that's OK.'

Vicki lifted her head a few inches. 'Yes. They're all in the little tray next to the toaster. We never moved them.' She dropped her head back down, her shoulders heaving with a fresh round of sobs.

'If you think of anything that might help, give me a call. I'll leave my card here on the table. Anything, ma'am. Anything or anyone that seemed the least bit off, or just unusual.'

Vicki nodded without lifting her head. Lucinda patted her back and walked back to the living room. The paramedics were gone and Mr Humphries was standing with a man helping to hold him up. The two took a few steps toward the stairway.

'Excuse me,' Lucinda said. 'I want to ask Mr Humphries a few questions.'

'I'm sorry, ma'am. But the doctor told me to get him upstairs and put him to bed. He said he'd be over soon to determine if medication was in order.'

'And you are?'

'Pastor Wrigley. From the Grace Street United Methodist Church. The family is part of my congregation. Can I take him up now?'

Lucinda looked into Eric's eyes and saw no sign that he was at all aware of her. *Was he really distraught or was he simply a good actor?* She stepped aside. 'OK. But make sure the doctor knows I need to speak with him before he leaves. And, Reverend, I would like to talk to you, too.'

'Hey, Lieutenant,' a woman shouted from the front porch.

Lucinda stepped through the door and saw the source of

the outcry, Carole Livingston, a death investigator from the coroner's office. 'Whatcha got, Livingston?'

'I don't see any definitive signs of foul play, Lieutenant, but I did find something odd.'

Lucinda tilted her head and raised her eyebrows.

Carole held out a blue-gloved hand and opened her fingers. 'Acorns. Dozens of them in his jacket pockets. Have any idea what they are doing there?'

FOUR

'Forensic geeks reporting for duty, Lieutenant.'
Lucinda smiled at the sight of Marguerite Spellman leading a Tyvec-suited crew into the front yard. 'Always a pleasure to see you, Spellman.'

'We'll start with photographic and videographic documentation here on the porch. Anyplace else we need to do?'

'It's been five months since he disappeared so I doubt we'll find anything useful in the house, but we might as well shoot his room just in case.'

'We'll video all the way there while we're at it. What else do you need?'

'Until we know the cause of death, we won't know whether or not we need to look for a murder suspect. But we do know this: someone violated the law when they dumped his body on the porch. See if you can find anything out in front of the house that might lead to an identification of the person who did that.'

Marguerite spun around and looked at the gaggle of patrolmen on the sidewalk and the police vehicles parked at the curb in front of the house. She turned back to Lucinda, eyebrows raised. 'Really?'

'I know. I know. Do the best you can. Run more evidence tape, shoo out the officers and get those vehicles moved. We've got to try even though the area couldn't get much more compromised if we planned it. And when you have a tech to spare, I'd like someone to come to the kitchen with me and retrieve the prescription meds. We need a tox screen on his body for all of them. He could have had an alternative source while he was away or not having them might have contributed to his death.'

'Give me a minute to talk to the crew and I'll go with you.'

'Lieutenant?' Butler said approaching the porch. He stopped two steps below Lucinda and handed her a plump file. From that vantage point he looked even more diminutive. His head bent back so far, Lucinda thought it looked ready to snap off of his neck. 'I had a copy made of the missing person's case file for the dead guy. It's got contact info for everyone we interviewed including the three people who cared for him during the day.'

'Thick file, Butler,' she said hefting it in one hand.

'Hey, I'll tell ya, I was really worried about the guy. I wanted to find him before he got run down in the middle of the road or rolled by some lowlife. I can add that to my list of failures,' he said with a sigh.

'Don't be so hard on yourself, Butler. Appreciate the file – I don't often get one without requesting it first. Could you help the techs clear out the yard and street in front of the house?'

'Guess I screwed up there,' Jumbo said, a light red flushing his cheeks under Lucinda's gaze.

'No offense, Butler, but if you want to play pitiful, you're going to have to take it elsewhere. I have work to do.'

Jumbo spun around, his whole face now burning bright. He nodded and mumbled at Marguerite as he passed her coming back to the porch.

'Whoa, Lieutenant,' Marguerite said with a laugh. 'He looks a little worse for wear. You giving him a hard time?'

'No need, he was doing a fine job of beating himself up.'

They walked in the front door across the gleaming wood floors to the tiled surface of the kitchen. Vicki hadn't moved from the position she'd assumed when Lucinda left her earlier. Her head bowed over the table rested on folded arms. Lucinda pointed to the tray by the toaster and as Marguerite followed the direction of her finger, Lucinda placed a hand on Vicki's back. 'Ms Humphries?'

Vicki raised her head and looked at Lucinda with red, wet and vacant eyes.

'Are those all the medications your father-in-law was taking?' Lucinda asked pointing to Marguerite who was bagging up the prescription bottles.

Vicki blinked her eyes several times, furrowed her brow and nodded her head.

'Did he have any spare bottles of any of those he could have taken with him?'

Again she made multiple blinks before answering with a shake of her head.

'Did he take those medications on his own or did you need to give them to him?'

'I . . .' Vicki struggled to force her tongue down from the roof of a dried mouth.

Realizing Vicki's problem, Lucinda placed a hand on her shoulder and said, 'Wait. Let me get you a glass of water.' She pulled a tumbler off of an open shelf and filled it from the ice-water dispenser on the front of the stainless steel refrigerator.

Vicki took two greedy swallows before placing the half-empty glass on the table. 'Sometimes he'd think to ask about his pills but he never could remember whether or not he'd already done so. I'm sure he wouldn't have taken them with any regularity if I hadn't given them to him.'

'Thanks, ma'am,' Lucinda said, turning to leave the room. She spun back and asked, 'Ms Humphries, can you think of any reason why your father-in-law would have dozens of acorns in his pockets?'

'Acorns?'

'Yes, ma'am.'

'Acorns? I have no idea.'

Lucinda and Marguerite were at the front door when they heard steps on the stairway behind them. The two women turned to greet the person descending. A corpulent man, in khaki pants, a brown tweed jacket, white shirt and golden tie, breathed heavily as he made his way down. A clump of blond-gray hair straggled on his forehead, revealing a balding head. He clutched a black bag in his left hand.

'Were you the doctor caring for Mr Humphries?'

'Yes.'

'Your name?' Lucinda asked.

'Dr Nelson. Dr Harry Nelson. And you?'

'Pierce, Lieutenant Pierce,' she said with a quick flash of her shield. 'I'd like to speak to your patient.'

'You're a bit late for that, Lieutenant. I gave him a strong sedative. Reverend Wrigley is sitting with him until he's sure Eric is asleep. But even if he is awake, he'll be too groggy for a grilling. Now if you'll excuse me, I have patients waiting in my office.'

'Do you normally make house calls, Doctor?'

'No. This was an extraordinary circumstance, don't you agree?'

'Certainly, Doctor. But why did you give him a sedative?'

Dr Nelson pulled back his chin and looked at her as if she was a specimen. 'He's been through a rather traumatic experience, in case you hadn't noticed.'

'But why a sedative strong enough to knock him out, Doctor?'

'Because, in my medical opinion, that is what was called for. Are you questioning my professional judgment?'

'Just wondering if there was a reason why you didn't want him to answer my questions.'

'You have a suspicious mind, Lieutenant.'

'And you have a diagnostic one. You still haven't answered my question, Doctor.'

'I really need to go,' he said brushing past her.

She grabbed his arm. 'Not yet. Were you Edgar Humphries' primary physician?'

'Of course. I cared for the whole family.'

'What medications did you prescribe for him?'

'I'd have to check his file to know the specific names and doses.'

'Marguerite?' Lucinda asked.

The forensic supervisor stepped forward with the Baggie of pill bottles. 'Doctor, are these the prescriptions you wrote for Edgar Humphries?'

'Yes, yes. You can see my name on them.'

'Is anything missing?' Lucinda asked.

'I don't believe so.'

'Tell me, Doctor; are there any medicines in here that could be responsible for your patient's death if he stopped taking them?'

'Well, stopping the Prozac abruptly could have made him suicidal. Did you see any water bottle near his body?'

'No.'

'He was on two blood pressure medications. That could have taken his life but, in all likelihood, it would take more than five months to do that. I say the most likely problem would be the Plavix. It's a blood thinner and he had stents in his heart. Without that drug, the blockage in his stents could have induced a heart attack.'

'Thank you, Doctor. I'm sure I'll be back in touch.'

'You want records, Lieutenant; make sure you bring a subpoena.'

It was one of those times when Lucinda wished she were still a child – she wanted to stick her tongue out at his retreating back.

When he closed the door behind him, Marguerite asked, 'You think he might have had a reason to shut up his patient?'

'It was a stray thought, but who knows? And who knows why? Just the fact that he made a house call raises a red flag for me. But I don't know. I don't even know if it's a homicide yet.'

FIVE

Lucinda stepped into the living room where elegance struck a perfect balance with comfort. Broad, white crown molding ran around the space with an oak leaf and acorn motif carved into the center board at regularly spaced intervals. A marble fireplace with matching hearth and mantle stood at the end of the room flanked by a pair of built-in bookcases – the edge of each shelf adorned with the same design as the crown molding. The treatment applied to the walls looked more like watercolor than house paint – an abstract rendition of the shallow shoreline along the Caribbean Sea.

Gathered around the hearth, a love seat, sofa and a pair of chairs in a plump, rounded style threw splashes of ocean blue both in a solid color on some pieces and in a delicate floral pattern against an off-white background on others – inviting furniture that promised hours of cozy conversation and relaxation. In a corner of the room next to the hallway, an armless, slip-covered chair stood beside a walnut drop-leaf table with barley-twist legs.

Lucinda selected to settle in that spot because of its good view of the front door and hallway. She sat to an angle in the chair, plopped the file folder on the table and began to read. She'd finished with the statements of the three caregivers when she heard footsteps on the stairway once again. She rose, stepped into the hallway and looked up as Reverend Wrigley descended the stairs with a furrowed brow and a harsh frown. 'Reverend?' she said.

He jerked to a stop with a gasp. 'Lieutenant, you startled me.'

'Sorry, sir. I do need to ask you a few questions.'

'You know, ma'am, as the family's spiritual and marital counselor, I have to hold everything they told me in strictest confidence.'

'So, Vicki and Eric needed marriage counseling.'

'I didn't say that,' Wrigley objected.

'Not exactly. But you did say, and I quote, that you were their "marital counselor". Now, it seems to me, Reverend, that unless they needed help with their marriage, you wouldn't be filling that role.'

'There was nothing wrong with their marriage, it was just that . . . I can't say anything more. Please. No more questions,' he said, holding up open palms in front of his chest.

'OK. Nothing more about their relationship. What about Edgar Humphries?'

'What about him?'

'Did he attend your church?'

'He did when he first moved in with his son.'

'When was that?'

'About two and a half years ago as I recall.'

'So he lived here for two years before he disappeared?'

'Something like that.'

'But then he stopped attending church?'

Wrigley sighed. 'We allowed him to serve the same function in our church as he did in his former church in Nelson County. He was an usher. He was responsible for handing out the church bulletin before the church service and helping pass the collection plates to accept the gifts the congregation bestows upon us in exchange for my spiritually uplifting message. Then one Sunday after finishing the final pew, he just kept walking out the door. Eric found him a couple of blocks away. The collection plate was nearly empty – he'd been handing out the money to the people he met in the street as if it belonged to him and not to God.'

Lucinda swallowed hard to keep a spontaneous laugh from erupting. She didn't think the good reverend would appreciate her sense of humor. 'He stopped coming after that?'

'Not right away. At first, we just took away his responsibilities. But even though we welcomed him into the bosom of our church as a member, not participating as an usher seemed to agitate him. He complained about it each Sunday when he shook my hand after the service but he didn't do anything more. Then during one service, he bolted out of his seat, ran up and down the aisles and tried to forcefully remove the collection plates out of ushers' hands. Coins, bills and checks went everywhere. A couple of kids started crying when they got hit in the face by flying quarters, dimes and nickels. It was so disruptive and, of course, so terribly tragic. God bless that poor man.' He folded one palm across the other and bowed his head.

Something about the retelling of the event and his assumption of the pious pose seemed phoney to Lucinda. She suspected it was how he played his congregation to feed his own ego. Irritation scratched dissonance into her voice. 'Well, did you at least minister to him here at home?'

'He never asked for me, the poor man, not once.'

'That's lame, preacher man. He was a lost soul. You could have responded to that without an invitation,' she sneered. 'Here's my card. You think of anything that can help my investigation, give me a call.'

'I'll pray for you,' he said in a meek tone of voice.

'Quite frankly, sir, a good lead would be far more productive.'

He stared at her with pity-filled eyes. Lucinda feared he'd fall to his knees and break into prayer for her immortal soul right where he stood. Instead, he broke his gaze with a sigh, turned and walked outside without saying another word. She mentally labeled and filed him under 'hypocritical blowhard'.

The card she'd given him lay abandoned on the floor where he stood. She bent to pick it up and became aware of small sounds of movement in the kitchen. She walked into the doorway and spotted Vicki in front of the sink holding a glass carafe.

'Hello, Lieutenant. I'm getting ready to brew a fresh pot of coffee. Want a cup?' Vicki asked.

'That would be nice. Thank you.'

'Have a seat at the table. I'll bring it over as soon as it's ready.'

Lucinda slid back into the chair she'd occupied earlier, but this time, in addition to observing Vicki, she absorbed the pleasant ambience of her surroundings. The kitchen design was different from that in the living room but had a soulful compatibility with it. It was warm, with a sort of south-west feel dominated by earth tones but with splashes of primary and secondary colors everywhere. 'You have a lovely kitchen,' Lucinda said.

Vicki chuckled. 'Thank you. We did this a few years ago after Jimmy, our youngest, went off to college. We were feeling our oats then – free at last, free at last. Just the two of us on our own, living our own life, making a schedule based on what we wanted to do. And being a bit more spontaneous. Sure, we had to accommodate the kids when they came home on break but the rest of the year was ours.

'The weekend after we took Jimmy to Maryland to school, we flew off to the Mexican Riviera to rekindle our old romance. And it worked – oh my, did it work. It was as passionate and intense as was when we first met.' Vicki closed her eyes; a small smile caressed her lips.

'That sounds very nice,' Lucinda said with a smile, reminding her of the weekend she spent with Jake last Fall in the Blue Ridge Mountains.

Vicki opened her eyes, poured two cups of coffee and carried them to the table. After sitting down, she continued, 'While we were there, I bought all of these hand-painted door handles, drawer pulls and wall tiles you see scattered in the backsplash design, along with a few other odds and ends. I wanted to decorate the kitchen in a way that captured the feeling of Mexico and the magic of that weekend. I think I did a pretty good job of it. I love this room – it's where I come when I'm feeling overwhelmed or stressed. It always helps restore my balance and serenity. Except maybe today.

I don't know if anything could work after the way this morning started.'

'I suppose when Edgar Humphries arrived a couple of years ago, it disrupted the unbridled feeling of freedom you and Eric had – like having a child in the house again.'

'Oh worse than a child,' she said pursing her lips. 'You see, it feels right when you tell one of your kids what to do or to wear a jacket or wipe their mouth at the dinner table. But when you have to do those things with someone you respected, admired and adored, it's a nightmare.'

'Did you feel that way about your father-in-law when you married Eric?'

'Oh, no, not at first. The admiration and respect were there but I was too much in awe of him to have any affectionate feelings. He was a physics professor at the University of Virginia – he's actually Dr Humphries. In the beginning, I was intimidated and even a little afraid of him. A gruff voice, a staggering intellect and as blunt as hell. But when Jenny, our oldest, was born, I saw a side of him I didn't know existed.

'When she was an infant, he was soft and gentle with her. As she became more aware of her environment, he learned sleight of hand tricks to keep her amused for the next several years. When her fascination with mathematics became obvious, he spent hours concocting elaborate word problems like ones that involved covering the surface of the earth with peanut and jelly or creating crazy scenarios with planes crashing in New Jersey cranberry bogs and oceans turning into ice cream.

'With Eddie, he found an entirely different way to interact. Edgar spent hours learning elaborate magic tricks to share them with his grandson. He also gave him lessons in light refraction to help him have a better awareness of how to use color and light in his paintings. Eddie is the artistic one,' she said with a smile.

'Jimmy, on the other hand, always wanted to be moving and as fast as possible – snowboards, skateboards, surfboards, scooters – if he could put his feet on something and go, he was happy. But at all times, he harbored an urge to go faster and faster so his grandfather taught him about aerodynamics and how to apply it to the movements he made and postures he assumed. I guess I don't have to tell you that made me pretty nervous. But he always put a lot of emphasis on safety and accident prevention so I couldn't object. He was a wonderful grandfather – a lot more hands on with them, Eric said, than he'd been with his own kids.'

Vicki exhaled a deep sigh with a whimper at its core. 'He was magnificent and to see him turned into a man who couldn't remember how to tie his bow-tie, or balance a checkbook, or find his way home was crushing and the burden of caring for him became heavier every month.'

'Why was he living with you?'

'Where else could he go? Eric has a sister but she was wrapped up in her career well into her thirties before she married and started having children. Now they have four, all living at home including the oldest commuting to college. They don't have room for him physically or emotionally. And he couldn't stay where he was. He just couldn't keep things straight in his life on his own any longer.'

Marguerite Spellman entered the kitchen with two forensic techs. 'We're ready to check out the bedroom, Lieutenant. You want to join us?'

Lucinda nodded and turned to Vicki. 'You don't have a problem with that, do you, Ms Humphries?'

'With looking through his bedroom? No, not at all. I tried to create a cheerful place for him and a helpful place. I tried to make his life here easy. I guess his running away meant I hadn't done a very good job of that.'

'I wouldn't make that assumption, ma'am. We don't know yet how he left or where he's been. It would be helpful if you could you make a list of the facilities you visited with your father-in-law and contact information for the people that helped you, if you still have that information.'

At Vicki's nod, Lucinda turned and followed the forensics crew up the stairs. She waited in the hallway till the photography and videography was complete and then entered. Yellow walls, white curtains with tiny yellow roses on the border, a yellow and white checked comforter; Vicki certainly did design a cheerful bedroom. One wall was filled with photographs – beneath each one a label named the people and locations. Each drawer in his dresser had a list of its contents taped in the upper right-hand corner. A list of important numbers hung from a tiny chain attached to the base of the telephone.

On top of the dresser, dust dulled the shiny surfaces of the coins in a tray, a hairbrush's handle and the top of a wooden box. She slipped on a glove and eased open the lid. Inside were cufflinks, a watch and a rabbit's foot. It made her want to cry.

'What exactly do you want us to find in here?' Marguerite asked.

'Probably most important would be an address book, if he had one. It's possible he left here of his own free will and hooked up with an old friend. We've got to find them. Aside from that, look for any notes – in drawers, in pockets, wherever.'

Lucinda started on the dresser, the two techs went into the closet and Marguerite checked the nightstands on either side of the bed.

Lucinda found nothing in the top three drawers and went down on her knees to search through the bottom one. The other drawers, as labeled, had nothing but rolled socks and folded underwear, T-shirts, and sweatshirts; She pulled the final one out and saw only two piles of sweaters; she lifted the stacks out of the drawer, hoping to find something more.

Marguerite finished with the nightstands and was on all-fours looking under the bed when she shouted, 'I found a billfold.'

'What's it doing under the bed?' Lucinda asked.

'And why is it still there so long after he disappeared?' Marguerite said as she reached long to grab it.

'Is it his? What's in it?' Lucinda asked.

Marguerite pulled her arm out from under the dust ruffle and held up a brown leather tri-fold. 'Let's see,' she said. 'Yeah, I think it's his. There's an expired driver's license with his name on it and an address in Lovingston, Virginia.' She rifled through the plastic sleeve attachment. 'There's a photograph that looks like it was in the wallet when it was purchased, a Visa card, a library card, an AARP card.' She pulled apart the two sides to look at the cash. 'Two, no three, one-dollar bills, and two folded up pieces of paper.'

'What's on the notes?'

Marguerite opened them. 'This one says: "I live at 834 Jefferson Street". And the other one says: "My phone number is 703-197-5791".'

Now, Lucinda felt tears forming. She blinked fast to chase them away.

SIX

Lucinda went down the stairs thinking about her great-grandfather. She was rather young when he died – she never knew him well. She had a vague memory of a funny smell and strange behavior. In retrospect, she wondered if he was suffering through the same kind of deterioration that had destroyed the mind of Edgar Humphries. But she didn't know and probably never would.

Going through the case folder, Lucinda had noticed that Ms Jenkins, the woman who fixed lunch for Edgar, lived just two blocks away. She left the house and went down the sidewalk. It was another Victorian home but much smaller than the Humphries' house. It was faded from the sun and weather, aching for a fresh coat of paint. She pushed open a short wrought-iron gate that wobbled at the hinges. The grass in the lawn was a week or two overdue for a mow.

But the flower beds running around the fence line and next to the sidewalk were immaculate. It was too early in the year for most plants to bloom but crocuses nodded an assortment of small yellow, purple and white heads in every bed. The brass knocker, knob and footplate on the door gleamed and the front porch was swept clean.

The door flew open before Lucinda had reached the top of the steps. A grey-haired, smiling Dorothy Jenkins, with a newspaper folded open to the crossword puzzle in her left hand and a pencil perched on her opposite ear, stood in the doorway. 'What can I do ya for?' she asked.

'I'd like to talk to you about Edgar Humphries.'

'Did ya find him?'

'Yes, but could we please talk inside?'

'Oh, sure, sorry, honey. Where's my manners? Come inta the house.' She directed Lucinda into the room to the left of the front door. 'Ya can have a sit down right in here. Shall I put on the tea kettle?'

'No, Ms Jenkins, I'm fine. Let's just talk,' Lucinda said, as she slid into an upholstered chair with worn arms.

'Okey-dokey. So ya found ol' Edgar? Wonder if that means I got me a job again,' Dorothy said as she sat in a chair perpendicular to her visitor.

Lucinda leaned forward, resting her elbows on her knees. 'I hate to deliver this news, Ms Jenkins, but Mr Humphries is deceased.'

'Damn me. You don't say. How did the old guy die?'

'We don't know yet,' Lucinda said. 'Isn't Mr Humphries about your age?'

'Oh, yeah, sure. We're pretty close in age. But I ain't afflicted with the Old-Timers. Makes a big difference. It ages ya to be confused all the time.'

'I'm sure it does,' Lucinda said thinking that her most confusing cases had certainly taken a toll on her. 'I understand you were the first person to notice that Mr Humphries was missing.'

'Yeah, that were me. I looked all round the house and backyard afore I went walking the neighborhood. Weren't the first time I had to find him to feed him his lunch. I went out up a block, over a block, down two blocks, across another block, up one block and I was back at the house. No sign of the old bugger. Started worrying then.'

'Did Mr and Mrs Humphries seem concerned?'

'Oh, lordie, yes. How they went on! I actually thought they might be a bit relieved, particularly the missus. But no, not quite wailin' and gnashin' of teeth, but mighty close.'

'Why did you think Ms Humphries would be relieved?' Lucinda asked.

'Well, she'd get a bit peckish sometimes – oh, not in fronta the old guy, mind. But sometimes she felt pretty put out with having to take charge of everything, with him not being her father and all. She had to hire the people to come in ta take care of him and trained 'em and responded when there was a problem. Took her away from work quite a bit. Never Mr Humphries. Always her. Think that chaffed her butt a bit.'

'You think she may have had anything to do with Edgar Humphries' disappearance?'

'Aw, nah. She was right fond of him; it was carryin' all the responsibility she didn't like. But it seemed like Mr Humphries finally accepted that his dad needed to go to some sort of home. They were lookin' for one. If they hadn't been lookin' and all, maybe. But, nah, things were workin' out the way she wanted. Even if he hadna disappeared, I'd been out of a job just the same.'

'Do you need to work at your age, Ms Jenkins?' Lucinda asked.

'Can't say I need to, but I'd just as soon have a little job. Keeps me feelin' useful. And helps me afford little extras in my life. Social Security is mighty nice and it pays my bills, but there's nothin' left after that. I almost had another job. Ms Culpepper, over on Lincoln. I was all set up with her to start comin' over and fixin' lunch for her ma during the week. Then, the Monday afore I was supposed to start. Her ma up and disappeared just like ol' Edgar.'

'Really?'

'Yep. Don't think they've found her yet. Hey, is that a glass eye you're sportin'?'

Lucinda wanted to ignore the question but sensed that if she did, it probably wouldn't go away. 'Yeah, Ms Jenkins, I do have a prosthetic eye. Now about this—'

Dorothy tipped her head back and forth like a little bird peering at Lucinda's face. 'Well, if that don't beat all. It's mighty realistic lookin'.'

'Thank you, Ms Jenkins, but—'

'Wonders'll never cease. Whatcha bet one day, they'll make glass eyes you can see outta? Or have they already done that? Can you see outta that one?'

'No, Ms Jenkins. Can we please return to the missing woman?'

'Oh, yeah, sorry, honey.'

'Is her last name, Culpepper?'

'Nah, it's Ms Culpepper's ma. I'm sure her last name's different but I can't recall Ms Culpepper ever calling her by any name but Mom.'

'When were you supposed to start fixing lunch for her, Ms Jenkins?' Lucinda asked.

'Let me think,' Dorothy said, rolling her eyes up to the ceiling. 'It was last year but I can't rightly recall the date. I still got my old calendars, though, let me go fetch it.'

Possibilities rumbled through Lucinda's head. *What are the odds that one woman would be involved with two missing persons? Is she connected to their disappearances? It doesn't seem likely. She's doing great for her age, but really. Could it be someone that knows her? Is she a link?*

'I got it,' Dorothy said as she walked back into the room. 'And here 'tis.' The opened wall calendar curved over the old woman's arm. 'Look it,' she said, pulling the pencil off her ear and using it as a pointer. 'December 8 – that was the day I was supposed ta start.'

Lucinda gathered contact information for the Culpepper family and went back down the street to the Humphries' home. She tracked down Jumbo Butler and asked him about the new missing woman and her concerns about a connection to Ms Jenkins.

'I can get you a copy of that case file. I never saw any connection between the disappearance of Ms Culpepper's mother and Edgar Humphries but then I didn't know about the overlap with a caregiver, probably because Ms Jenkins hadn't started working there yet. Anything else you need?'

'I read the statement you got from Jenkins when Edgar Humphries first went missing so I know what she said. But how was she? How did she strike you back then?'

Jumbo squinted his eyes and rubbed his thumbs and forefingers together. 'As I recall, she was rather distressed about Edgar's disappearance. She seemed to like him and like her job caring for him. In fact, I remember her saying, "Nothing says love like a warm biscuit straight from the oven." Made me think of my grandmother,' he said with a smile. 'Edgar apparently liked those biscuits a lot. And she wasn't hopeful from the start. I remember her saying something about poor, old Edgar having eaten his last biscuit. She was certain something terrible had happened.'

'What about the Humphries?'

'They were pretty optimistic in the beginning. But the doubt set in pretty early on, though, considering his mental condition. But like most loved ones of missing persons, the not knowing made them a bit crazy. Not that I blame them.'

'Did you get the impression that either one of them knew where he was or had anything to do with his disappearance?' Lucinda asked.

'Eric Humphries sure didn't. He was ambivalent about his father going into an assisted living facility and wasn't really convinced it was the best thing for his father. Vicki on the other hand was eager to place him. I guess out of everyone, she had the strongest motivation to get him out of the house. But I can't see her killing him.'

'That might not have been part of the plan but something may have gone wrong. Was there anyone else – someone who might have made you suspicious or even uncomfortable?'

'Yeah, now that you mention it – one of the sons. Can't remember which one it was. But when he was here, he was a problem. No matter what I asked Eric or Vicki, he'd jump in with a defensive response as if I were attacking his parents. I passed it off as anxiety, but who knows?'

'Do you have any other unsolved missing senior citizens cases from this past year?'

'Yeah,' he said nodding, 'I believe I have quite a few. I'll need to go back to the office to check that out.'

'We're pretty much done here,' Lucinda said. 'The forensics team's finished and until the sedative's worn off and Eric Humphries is fit to answer questions I don't think there's anything else to do. Why don't you tear down the tape and send everyone on their way before you go. And don't bother copying any other files just now. I'll look them over when I get there and see if I need anything.'

Lucinda headed round the corner and down a couple of blocks to Lincoln Avenue. She enjoyed the short walk; the air smelled like spring, the trees flashed tiny, bright-green, new leaves, and the forsythia was in full bloom. The homes on Lincoln were statelier than those on Jefferson Street. Lots of big columns and broad staircases led up to the front doors. The Culpeppers' house was even more ostentatious than most – a tall wrought-iron fence ran around the property. She pushed on the gate at the driveway but it was locked. A keypad on the right waited for the entry of a password she did not have. She pressed the call button beside a speaker box but got no response. She'd hoped she'd at least be able to stick a card in the door with a 'call me' note on the back. She settled for slipping it into the black mailbox mounted beside the gate on the other side.

She ran through questions on her way back to Jefferson Street. *Are the disappearances of Ms Culpepper's mother and Edgar Humphries connected? Or is it just a coincidence?* She winced at the thought of that last word. *If they linked together, are the other unsolved cases part of a bigger crime? But why would anyone want to abduct senior citizens with dementia unless they intended to demand ransom? But the Humphries never received a note, or did they? One more thing to ask the Humphries – wonder if I'll get an honest answer?*

SEVEN

After a morning of back-to-back patients and a quick lunch at his desk, Dr Evan Spencer walked out the rear door of his office to drive over to the hospital for a surgery. A metallic bang and a woman's moan drew his attention to the back of the building. He rushed around the corner and saw a man slam a woman into the side of a dumpster and then shove her to the ground. 'Hey! Cut that out!' Evan shouted.

The man looked in Evan's direction for a moment then turned and kicked the woman in the small of her back.

'Stop it!' Evan yelled.

The man didn't listen; he drew back his leg to kick again. Evan grabbed his shoulder, spun him around and punched him square in the nose.

The man's chest heaved, his fists clenched by his side. 'You son of a bitch,' he snarled as he swung a roundhouse punch in the direction of Evan's head. The doctor ducked, pulled out his cell and said, 'Get out of my parking lot or I'm calling the police.'

'This is none of your damned business. I needed to teach her a lesson,' the man said, wiping at the blood trickling from his nose.

'Not here. Not now,' Evan said, pressing the 9 and the 1 buttons on his phone. 'One more digit,' he said, wiggling a finger in the air above the keypad.

The man sneered and spat on the pavement. 'Fine. She's your problem now,' and ran down the street.

Evan kneeled beside the brutalized woman. She was older than he'd thought from a distance – probably in her late seventies. The man who attacked her was a lot younger. Evan reached

out his hand. The woman pushed up on her hands and scrab-
bled backwards, whimpering as she went.

'Ma'am, I'm not going to hurt you. I'm a doctor, I want
to help you.'

But her irises contracted and her pupils darted around all
over the place like crazy red ants.

Evan stepped back a couple of paces. 'OK, OK. I won't
come any closer. I'll get help.' He called a nearby ambulance
service. 'This is Dr Evan Spencer. I have someone in need of
transportation to the emergency room. And please make sure
at least one of the paramedics is a woman. The victim's just
been knocked around and won't let me get near her – it could
be because I'm male.'

'Right away, Doctor. Should be there in three.'

Evan leaned his back against the wall of the building and
slid down to a crouch. He wanted to do something for the
poor lady but all his staff had left for lunch and he knew if
he approached her again, she'd panic. Two and a half minutes
oozed past as they waited for the emergency vehicle.

An athletic woman bounded out of the truck in navy-blue
scrubs, her ponytail swaying in rhythm with her walk. 'What's
your name, sweetheart?' she asked the woman on the ground.

The woman looked up at her as if she didn't understand
the question.

'Oh, that's all right. We haven't been formally introduced
yet, have we? That's OK; we'll take care of that later. You
want to go into the ambulance on a stretcher?'

The woman made tight, hard shakes of her head.

'Well, how about if I help you to your feet then? Will that
work?'

The old woman nodded her head slowly. The paramedic
slipped an arm under her elbow and eased her up. 'Is that
OK, sweetie?'

The victim nodded again.

'Alrighty, darlin'. Now who did this to you?'

The battered woman lifted an arm and pointed her finger
at Evan.

He put up two open palms in a defense posture. 'No, no,
no, no. She is confused.'

The paramedic looked at him through slitted eyes. 'You'd
best follow us over to the hospital, Doctor.'

'I'm heading there anyway. I have a surgery scheduled this afternoon. I'll come down and see how she is as soon as I'm through.'

'I know who you are, Doctor. You'd better be there.'

Evan watched the ambulance pull away, wondering what he'd done to deserve that. He climbed in his car and followed the emergency vehicle down the road.

After the surgery, Evan felt chipper. The procedure went well, no complications, no sweat. He left the surgical suite and ran right into two beefy patrolmen with their arms folded across their chests.

'Dr Evan Spencer?'

'Yes,' Evan said.

'Turn around, sir, you're under arrest.'

'Excuse me? Under arrest? For what?'

'Sir, just turn around and let me cuff you. You don't want to make a scene.'

'What's the problem, officers?' he said as he pivoted.

'You forgot that little old lady you beat up already?'

'I did no such thing.'

'Save it, Doctor. Our orders are to bring you in. Period.'

Red flushed Evan's face from his neck to his hairline as he was escorted past nurses and doctors with open mouths or querulous brows. He flashed a weak smile every time he met someone's gaze but they all averted their eyes from him when he did.

EIGHT

The day was rolling into late afternoon by the time Lucinda entered her office and was surprised to see Sergeant Ted Branson there talking on her phone. He turned in her direction. 'She's here now. Hold on.' Ted put his hand over the receiver and said, 'It's a deputy down in the jail – someone they arrested wants to see you.'

She took the phone from his hand. 'Pierce.'

'Lieutenant, Deputy Turner here. I know this sounds

unbelievable but the police department just brought in a guy who'd rather speak to you than to an attorney.'

'Who did he kill?'

'I don't think he killed anyone, Lieutenant.'

'Then I can't be of any use to him.'

'Wait, Lieutenant. He said he knows you.'

'What's his name?'

'Spencer. Evan Spencer.'

'You locked up the doctor?'

'Yeah, we've got him on an assault charge.'

'Assault? Dr Spencer?'

'He was right there next to the woman he knocked around and she's pressing charges.'

'A woman? He attacked a woman? Are you sure about this?'

'We've got her statement right here. She's still in the hospital. Just 'cause he's a friend of yours, Lieutenant . . .'

'Did he admit to the assault?'

'Oh, c'mon, Lieutenant, they all say they didn't do it.'

'I'll be right there,' she said and hung up the phone. 'Ted, I have to go over to the jail . . .'

'Charley's father's been arrested for beating up a woman?'

'Something's wrong here, Ted. I'll let you know what it is when I straighten out this mess. Do you mind babysitting my line while I go figure it out?'

Ted nodded.

'If anyone calls with information about the Edgar Humphries case, take it down and call me on my cell.'

'You got it, Lucinda,' he said to her back as she strode out of the office.

She turned around. 'Ted? Were you in my office for a reason? Were you waiting for me?'

'Yeah,' he said. 'But it can keep.'

She went to the elevator, pressed the down button but quickly grew impatient and took the stairs down two floors. She took a right, then a left into the tunnel that ran under Third Street connecting the new Justice Center with the older building housing the jail and the Sheriff's Office. A flash of her badge and she bypassed security at the underground entrance. In minutes, the deputy was leading her down the cell block and unlocking the door to the narrow room holding Evan Spencer.

'Am I glad to see you. I didn't think I'd ever convince them to give you a call.'

'Evan, you probably need a lawyer more than you need me.'

'But, Lucinda, I didn't do anything wrong.'

'Yeah but they all say that, Evan.'

'But . . .' he sputtered.

Lucinda held up a hand. 'Save it, Dr Spencer. Just tell me what happened.'

Evan told her about coming to the woman's rescue and the indignity of being blamed for hurting her. 'I told the officers, I told the deputy. No one believes me.'

'Like I said, Dr Spencer, everyone says that. They don't believe anybody. Let me see what I can do to get you out of here.'

'Deputy Turner,' Lucinda shouted down the hall.

Turner pulled away from the wall where he was leaning and let her out of the cell.

'I need to get Spencer out,' she said as they walked back up the hallway.

'Not up to me, Lieutenant. You gotta take that up with the judge.'

'Can you get me in front of him before he adjourns for the day?'

He turned his arm to look at his wristwatch. 'I'll call the clerk and see what I can do.'

In a few minutes, Lucinda and Turner headed back the way they came, this time cuffing and retrieving Evan Spencer. They entered the Justice Center through another tunnel far less wide and welcoming than the public one Lucinda used earlier. They went up to the ground-floor courtroom in a secure elevator.

Turner put Evan in the holding cell next to the courtroom and waited for the bailiff to call his name. When she did, Turner escorted his prisoner before the bench and Lucinda took her place at his side. The deputy recited the charges to the judge and introduced Lucinda.

'What's a homicide detective doing here on an assault case, Lieutenant?' the judge asked.

'Your honor, I became involved with the Spencer family when I investigated the murder of Dr Spencer's wife about two years ago. I have continued to have a relationship with the young daughter of the accused – kind of an informal Big Sister type of relationship, your honor.'

'What's your relationship to Evan Spencer?'

'He's Charley's father, your honor. He allows me to visit her.'

'No romantic involvement between you and the good doctor, Lieutenant?'

Lucinda clenched her jaw and bit off the angry words she longed to speak. If it were anyone but a judge, she'd let them fly. 'No, your honor. None at all.' She glared at Evan daring him to contradict her.

The judge turned to Evan and asked, 'Is that correct, Doctor?'

'Yes, yes, sir, your honor. I tried . . .' he said with a shrug.

Lucinda rolled her eyes. 'Your honor, I have not—'

'Lieutenant, you're not the accused here. What do you want me to do?'

'I'd like you to release Dr Spencer on his own recognizance. I have serious doubts about the validity of the charges brought against him. And he is an upstanding, law-abiding citizen, deeply connected to his community, your honor.'

'How about if I release him and hold you personally responsible for seeing that he returns to court?'

Not exactly what she wanted, but Lucinda wouldn't quibble. He'd be able to go home to his two girls and that was all that mattered. She nodded and said, 'Yes, your honor.'

'See the clerk,' he said and tapped down his gavel. 'Next case, bailiff.'

Turner unlocked the cuffs to allow Evan to sign his name under Lucinda's signature. Evan and Lucinda walked out to her car.

'I sure hope you don't have any missions of mercy outside of the country planned in the near future.'

'No. I haven't been doing much of that. I've mostly been recruiting other doctors for Doctors without Borders but, with one exception, I haven't been out of the states since Kathleen died. I need to be here for the girls.'

'Charley said Ruby was showing signs of improvement.'

'Yes, well, she still sucks her thumb but her psychologist said a little emotional immaturity is to be expected after what she's been through,' Evan said with a sigh.

'Seems to have had the opposite effect on Charley.'

Evan laughed, 'Tell me about it. Sometimes she seems more like my mother than my daughter.'

On the drive to Evan's river-front condo, they talked about Evan's predicament and what needed to be done the following day. Lucinda promised to talk to the district attorney as soon as she could catch up with him. As Lucinda brought the car to a stop, Evan asked, 'You want to come up and see Charley, maybe stay for dinner?'

'I really have to get back to the office. I left some loose ends there when I came to your rescue.'

'Another time, then. And thanks – you look great astride a white horse. You need a white hat?'

'Nah, I did a Texas thing last year and it didn't work out too well and besides, I wanna keep the bad guys guessing,' she said, putting her car in gear and driving out of the parking lot and back to her office.

Walking through her office door, she said, 'Oh, jeez, Ted. I didn't mean you had to wait until I got back. I thought you'd mind the phone until five and then head out. Any calls?'

'Nothing that mattered. What are you going to do now?'

'I've got to write my preliminary report, organize my notes and make plans for my course of action tomorrow on this possible homicide I picked up today.'

'OK, I'll get out of your hair, but once you're past the first 48, I'd like a few minutes of your time.'

'I can make time for you now, Ted, if it's important.'

'Nah. I'll catch you later.'

Lucinda watched Ted's retreating back and wondered what was on his mind. His demeanor with her seemed more subdued than usual. It was almost as if he were saying goodbye. An instant of alarm forced her to her feet with thoughts of following him down the hall. She reconsidered the impulse, sat back down and got to work.

NINE

S herry dressed for dinner. She pulled on her stockings, shoes and a skirt but before putting on a blouse, she reached for her silver locket. It wasn't where it should have been. She looked everywhere for it. She threw underwear and socks out of the top drawer of her dresser. As the items piled up on the floor, she muttered, 'Where is it? Where is it?'

She slammed the top drawer shut and opened the second one for the third time that evening. The first two times through the dresser's contents, she'd shuffled through the clothing. Now, it was panic time. T-shirts and sweaters flew out and joined the other clothing sprawled on the tile.

When it was empty, she shoved it in and jerked out the bottom drawer. Normally, it took a lot of effort for her to get down on her knees, but now she was fueled by desperation and she dropped down totally unaware of the pain. An involuntary 'oof' escaped through her lips before she continued her non-stop mantra of 'Where is it? Where is it?'

The noise drew the attention of the nurse walking past the bungalow. She knocked on the door. When Sherry didn't respond, she cracked it open. 'Miss Sherry? Miss Sherry? Is everything OK?'

Sherry popped to her feet. 'No. It's not. Did you steal it?'

'Steal what, Miss Sherry?'

'You did, didn't you? You steal from me all the time, don't you? Now give it back,' Sherry said, thrusting out an open palm.

'What's missing, Miss Sherry?'

'My locket, damn it. My locket. The one my Henry gave me. Now give it back!'

'Miss Sherry, I don't have your locket, hon, but I'd be glad to help you look for it.'

'Somebody stole it! If you didn't, it was somebody else. And I want it back,' Sherry pushed the woman aside with a strength no one suspected she still possessed. She hit the door and fast-walked down the path toward the dining room.

'Miss Sherry! Miss Sherry!' the nurse shouted. 'You forget your blouse, hon. Come back, get dressed.'

Sherry didn't slow her pace. Her bosom heaved as she barreled in through the double doors of the dining room. 'Who stole my locket?'

A few forks clattered to the table as all eyes turned to the entrance.

'I want it back. Whoever took it, give it back now!'

A few of the diners tittered like school children. The woman sitting closest to her hung her head and sobbed out loud.

Sherry, fists clenched tight by her sides, stepped up close to the sobbing woman and glared down at the top of her head. 'Stop your sniveling and give me back my locket.'

The woman shook her head violently and cried all the louder.

'I know you took it,' Sherry said, flexing her fingers in and out. 'Now give it me or else.'

Don, who never failed to calm her, raced across the dining room and put an arm around Sherry's shoulders.

She shrugged it off and glared at him. 'She stole my locket. I want it back.'

'The locket Mr Henry gave you?'

'Yes. Yes. That's the one. You make her give it back.'

'Listen, Miss Sherry,' Don whispered in her ear. 'You forgot to put on your blouse, doll. Let's go back to your cottage and put one on. Then, we'll get your locket back, OK? And after that, we have chocolate chip cookies for dessert.'

'Chocolate chip?'

'Yes, ma'am. C'mon now, let's get you dressed for dinner.'

While she selected a top to wear and buttoned it up, Don searched through the small bed and bath. He found the necklace on the back of the toilet. 'Lookee here, Miss Sherry. I found your locket.'

'You stole it!'

'Now, Miss Sherry, you know better than that. Your good friend Don would never steal nothin' from you. Come here, I'll fasten it round your neck.'

Sherry turned her back to Don. When he finished, she stepped up to a mirror, smiled at the image of the locket hanging on the bare skin between the two sides of her V-neck. She spun around, still wearing the smile that no longer touched her eyes. 'Time for chocolate now?'

Don offered his elbow, she slid in her hand. He patted it.
'Now, Miss Sherry, let's go have a bite of dinner and a few
of those yummy chocolate chip cookies.'

'With walnuts?'

'Yes, indeed, Miss Sherry. Wouldn't make 'em any other
way.'

'I have some walnuts,' she said pulling away and scurrying
over to her nightstand. She reached in the drawer and grabbed
at something inside, thrust her arm at Don and opened her
hand. 'See!'

Don looked down at the acorns piled in her palm. 'Yes,
ma'am, Miss Sherry. But those aren't the eatin' kind.'

Sherry clenched her hand over her treasures and brought it
to her chest, covering it with the other hand. 'They're mine.'

'Yes, ma'am, they sure are. Put them away now and let's
go on to dinner.'

TEN

Lucinda read through her report on the computer screen,
stopping from time to time to correct a spelling or clarify
a statement. She printed it out and looked it over again,
checking her notes to be sure she left out nothing of importance. She answered her phone before the first ring ended.
'Pierce.'

'Jumbo Butler here, Lieutenant. I've been pulling records
and getting more bothered with every few files I read.'

'What's bothering you, Butler?'

'Well, first I went back twelve months. Then, I went back
twelve more. And I'm seeing a pattern here. There are more
missing elderly in the last year and a half than I remember
ever before. I need to dig some older data out of the files to
be sure but I think it's more than just an increase in the ageing
population.'

'Why not? What are you seeing?'

'Lieutenant, I've been working missing persons for more
than a dozen years. Most the missing old folks we have turn
up wandering around somewhere nearby. Or we get a call

on a Silver Alert because somehow some old guy managed to get a bit farther away from home than anyone thought possible. But most of these cases are wrapped up in a day or two – maybe three. Then, about half of the remaining cases, we find their bodies within a week. Usually dead because of an accidental fall or exposure to the elements – but that usually only happens in the dead of winter or in a bad heatwave.

'The rest, with a few exceptions, show up in an emergency room without ID, or are spotted by someone who knows them. We have had one old lady who disappeared on a Sunday. As many meetings as there were at the church that week, no one saw her or if they did, didn't realize anyone was looking for her. It wasn't until the next Sunday morning that she was found snoring in one of the pews in the sanctuary. She'd been in the church the whole time.

'But now it appears as if we've got a lot more elderly people that just plumb stay missing. That's my perception anyway. I'm going to have to go back further in the records to be sure, but it just doesn't feel right.'

'You don't have stats on this?'

'We've got great numbers on missing kids and missing adults but beyond that any details require a file by file search.'

'So, you have no idea how many of the missing elderly have dementia issues?'

'Not a clue, but I'll find out. I can get some admin help with the search in the morning. I'll keep at it until I realize I'm imagining things or I have some hardcore data for you.'

'Thanks, Butler. Keep in touch,' Lucinda said, ending the call. She picked the receiver back up and called the Culpepper house. When a woman answered, Lucinda said, 'Ms Culpepper?'

'Yes, this is Joan.'

'This is Lieutenant Lucinda Pierce. Did you get my card and message?'

'Yes, ma'am. I did. It's just I forgot to call; I . . . oh, I won't lie. I saw "homicide detective" on your card and I was terrified that meant you'd found my mother's body and well –' Joan sniffled – 'I just hadn't gotten up the courage to call.'

'Oh, no, ma'am. We haven't found your mother. I'm sorry I distressed you. It was Edgar Humphries that prompted me to contact you. You did hear about Mr Humphries, didn't you?'

'Oh dear Lord, yes. I've been checking my front porch constantly half expecting to find my mother's body there. I don't know how I'll sleep tonight. I'm afraid to leave the house in the morning because I'm afraid I'll stumble over her.'

'I'd like to talk to you about your mother. Could I come by tomorrow afternoon?'

'The morning would be better.'

'I'm sorry but I have to be . . .' Lucinda stopped mid-sentence. She didn't want to tell her that she'd be in the autopsy suite watching Edgar Humphries' body being cut up. 'I . . . I have a prior commitment in the morning. I'm sorry.'

'How about the following day, then?' Joan Culpepper suggested.

Lucinda certainly did not want to postpone this interview but she didn't want to bully the woman when she needed her cooperation. Her mind raced trying to come up with a response that would work. Joan beat her to it.

'Oh, I guess you need to get on this right away, don't you? How about tonight? I know I won't be sleeping any time soon.'

'Thank you, ma'am. I'll be there as soon as I can.'

The porch light burned bright by the front door when Lucinda pulled to a stop in front of the old Victorian home. Joan flung the door open before the detective reached the top step. 'Good evening, Lieutenant. Come on in. I've put on a pot of coffee and made some herbal tea. Your choice. I'm going with the tea, although in my state of mind, I think caffeine is the least of my worries. But, then, oh dear me . . . Unfortunately, I probably could prattle on about coffee and tea for an hour to avoid talking about the reason you're here. So, just tell me what you want and I promise I won't say another word.'

Might not be the easiest interview, Lucinda thought. 'Coffee would be wonderful, ma'am.'

'I've got half and half. Oh dear, I said something else about coffee.'

Lucinda laughed. 'Not a problem; I'd love some real cream in my cup.'

'Sugar?' Joan asked and slapped a hand over her mouth.

'Relax, Ms Culpepper. No thanks, no sugar.'

In less than two minutes she returned with two mugs in hand. Lucinda took a sip and was delighted. 'Oh, this is good.'

'I make it a bit strong. That's how my husband always liked it and I got used to it that way. Hope that's OK.'

'It's how I like it, too,' Lucinda answered with a smile. 'I understand that the last time you saw your mother was December 8. Is that right?'

'Actually, it was December 7. I went out to church and when I came back, she was gone. I was away from the house no more than an hour and a half. I thought she'd be fine. I should have known better. I should have asked Ms Jenkins to come in that morning – she was starting the next day. I'm sure she would have come. I'll never forgive myself for that.'

'Why did you choose Ms Jenkins?'

'She needed work and the Humphries said she was terrific with Edgar. And she wasn't there when he disappeared – I asked about that, of course. I just needed her to be here when I was out – I have a lot of commitments: I'm on the executive committee of the Women's Mission League, then there's the Garden Club, lunch with friends at least twice a week, I visit sick church members in the hospital and shut-ins at home, and I volunteer for a couple of charitable organizations. Honestly, I am busier since I retired than I ever was when I was going to a job each day. Ironic, isn't it? Anyway, I just left her long enough to go to the morning service and then Ms Jenkins would start on the Monday and I'd never leave her alone again. And I already had her on waiting lists for assisted living facilities, although she seemed to be going downhill so fast, she might not have been able to handle that much independence by the time something opened up.'

Interesting. 'Could you make a list of the places you were considering for your mother?'

'I have it right here,' Joan said, pulling out a drawer in the end table and extracting a piece of paper. 'You're welcome to it.'

Lucinda scanned the list of facilities and saw some overlap with the list she'd gotten from Vicki Humphries. *Was it significant?* 'How old is your mother?'

'She's 85. And the funny thing is that I thought we were immune from this Alzheimer's type stuff. Friends of mine had parents that showed signs of dementia in their late sixties or early to mid-seventies. But not Mom. She was still quick with a witty retort, still driving her car, still leading an active social life. Then, came the winter after her 78th birthday. She had a bad fight with a bout of pneumonia. She was in the hospital for a while – I thought I was going to lose her. But then she snapped right back – physically, at least. But, mentally, she never was the same. I don't know if it was her illness, the medication she took – one of them was contraindicated with one of her regular prescriptions – or just being in the hospital itself that caused the downturn in her mental capabilities, but it was dramatic.

'She began having hallucinations in the hospital and they continued to trouble her when she came home. I didn't take her driver's license away – I didn't need to. She was suddenly, inexplicably afraid of driving. In fact, she didn't even like riding in the car. And the witty retorts were gone – replaced by inexplicable bouts of angry mumbling. Most of the time she looked puzzled as if she weren't capable of understanding conversation. She no longer communicated her feelings well so I had no idea of what she was thinking. I just knew that watching her decline was depressing and painful and imagined it must be even worse for her.'

'Before your mother disappeared, did you see anyone that looked out of place in the neighborhood? Any loiterers? Any parked vehicles that didn't seem to belong here?'

'No. I can't say that I noticed anything. To be honest, I don't think I was paying attention. I should have been better at that considering my mother's state. But I wasn't.'

'The facilities you visited, did everyone you talk with seem appropriate? Did anyone express an interest in your mother that seemed a bit off?'

'No. Of course, they all acted interested in her. That's part of their sales training, I'd imagine. But, no, nothing struck me as unusual.'

'Did you ever entertain any suspicions of Ms Jenkins?'

'Oh, good heavens no!'

'Really?' Lucinda asked.

'OK. OK. Yes, I did. Not very charitable of me but I did.

It seemed too much of a coincidence. But I talked to Vicki and talked to the pastor and even to that missing person's investigator from the police department – I don't recall his name.'

'Detective Butler? Jumbo Butler?'

'Yes, that's it,' she tittered. 'How could I forget? He even has his nickname in quotes on the business card he gave me. It made me smile – he's such a little leprechaun of a man.'

'We think alike, Ms Culpepper,' Lucinda said with a smile. 'Back to your suspicions of Ms Jenkins?'

'I dropped them – they seemed groundless. No one else was concerned about her.'

'You haven't seen or heard from your mother since December 7?'

Joan sighed. 'Not a word, not a note, not a message. I kept hoping that one day I'd come home and there she'd be, sitting on the porch smiling. Or down on the ground with the pink flowered knee-pad she used, pulling weeds from the flower beds.' A wistful smile spread across Joan's mouth but faded away as quickly as it appeared. 'Now, I am afraid I'll find her on the porch or in the flower bed, flat on her back, cold as ice. It's not a pretty thought.'

'No, ma'am, I know it's not. I am hoping the Humphries investigation will somehow lead us to your mother and we'll be able to bring her home to you.'

'But, how, Lieutenant?' Tears streamed down Joan's face. 'She certainly won't be the woman she once was. Will she even remember me? Will she know my name? Or even worse, will you bring her home in a pine box?' Joan hugged herself tight. 'Whatever, Lieutenant, whatever – I just want to know. It's the not knowing that makes me die a little more every day.'

Lucinda wrapped her arms around the woman and held her while her body shook. Lucinda knew this was a pain she'd never experience; her parents never made it to old age. But, still, she could feel it. It reverberated in the well of pain that lived inside her ever since the day her parents left her. She struggled to contain her own tears and smother an over-whelming sensation of anguish.

ELEVEN

Back at her apartment, Lucinda fed her gray cat Chester and went into the bedroom to pull off her work clothes and slide into a T-shirt and a pair of sweatpants. Chester was cleaning his whiskers with his paws when she returned to the kitchen. She scooped him up and cuddled him – but he wasn't as affectionate as usual. He planted his paws on her chest and pushed away. She set him down with a sigh.

She plopped on the sofa and invited him to snuggle with her but he was not the least bit interested in that, either. It was almost midnight, she should be sleeping. She needed some sleep before the 6 a.m. autopsy. That cup of coffee was a big mistake. She tried to interest Chester in playing with a jingly catnip-stuffed mouse but he just yawned at her.

She picked up the phone to call Jake but hung up before she finished punching in the numbers. She grabbed a book and tried to read but couldn't concentrate. 'Oh the hell with it,' she said. 'So what if I wake him up.' She could tell by his mumbled response that she had. 'Hey, Jake. Sorry if I woke you.'

'Lucinda? Is that you? Is something wrong?'

'Can't sleep.'

'So you're not going to let me sleep, either? I think that might be a positive step forward in our relationship, in an odd way.'

'I'm sorry, Jake,' she laughed. 'I was hoping you'd be awake. I wanted someone to talk to about a new case. Sorry I bothered you. Go back to sleep.'

'I'm awake now. And I'm curious. What's the problem with your case?'

'Jake, I'm not even sure I have a case.'

'Do you have a dead body?'

'Yes.'

'And you're investigating it?'

'Yes.'

'That sounds like a case to me, Lucinda. No matter the outcome.'

'When you put it that way, sure. But I'm not certain it's a murder.'

'You thinking suicide?'

'Not hardly. Most people don't get dressed, stretch out on their son's front porch and quietly kill themselves without leaving a mess. And it's a little bizarre for a natural death since he'd been missing for months.'

'You got that right. What else is eating at you?'

'The missing person guy seems to think there's been an uptick in elderly disappearances. Are you seeing anything like that on a national level?'

'Not that I'd know but I could ask in the morning.'

'Thanks. That would be great, Jake. I'm also wondering if it has anything to do with the victim's Alzheimer's. There was another woman in the neighborhood with dementia and she disappeared a couple of weeks after my guy did.'

'Could be a coincidence. But before you say a word, I could feel your wince through the phone line.'

Lucinda laughed. 'You know me. My least favorite word in the English language.' Chester chose that moment to jump up on Lucinda's lap and rub his jowl on her face, his purr volume set on high.

'What is that noise?' Jake asked.

'Chester.'

'Ah, how's the old boy doing?'

'He was a bit stand-offish earlier but now that I'm giving my attention to someone else, he's all lovey-dovey.'

'He should be a woman.'

'Jake . . .'

'OK, OK, you're right. He's definitely male. About this case, what are you thinking? Where do you think it might be going? Abduction? Patricide for profit? Caregiver rage? What?'

'I've talked to two caregivers. Both were planning on putting their parents in a facility. Both had obviously been stressed by the situation. But it seemed like they were dealing with it all OK.'

'If we scratch the caregiver motive, that still leaves us with the same perpetrators in patricide for profit. Most kids are

their parents' heirs – and that means it's always a good possibility for motive.'

'Just doesn't seem to fit here.'

'Don't blind yourself to the possibility, Lucinda. Some of
the nicest seeming people are hiding a lot of narcissistic darkness inside. But you don't need me to tell you that. I get the
feeling, though, that something else is bothering you about
this case. What is it?'

'It's me.'

'You?'

'Yes. My reaction to it – it's not as professional as it
should be.'

'Not professional? Lucinda, you're always professional.
What are you talking about?'

'I can't get my parents out of my mind. They keep creeping
into my thoughts.'

'You probably never will get them out of your mind. That
was a traumatic event and you were only a teenager.'

'Exactly. It was a long time ago. Ancient history, Jake. I
should be able to let it go. It shouldn't be bothering me now
– at least not in the middle of a case.'

'Ease up. You saw your mother shot to death. You heard
the gunfire when your father committed suicide. And now
you're talking to people about their parents. What do you
expect?'

'I expect myself to be professional at all times – just like
you expect the same of yourself.'

'Lucinda, I've worked with you on more than one case.
I've never seen you be anything but a professional. This last
year has brought your past to the surface – two deaths in the
family, the problems with your sister. Thinking of your parents
now just means you're human – it doesn't mean you are any
less professional.'

'If you say so, Jake.'

'Oh, blow me off one time. Jeez! I don't hear an ounce of
conviction in your voice.'

'You're too easy on me, Jake.'

'And you're too hard on yourself.'

'I have to be.'

Jake sighed. 'Listen, I'll see if I can get some information
together for you tomorrow about the elderly, dementia and

disappearances. But while I got you on the phone, when are we going to get together again?'

'I don't know, Jake.'

'It's almost apple blossom time. The Blue Ridge beckons.'

'Let me get a little further along with this investigation and we'll see.'

'Hey, wait too long and you won't see – apple blossoms wait for no one.'

'Call me this weekend, OK? And thanks, Jake.'

Lucinda set the phone in the receiver. She was still disappointed in herself but nonetheless, just talking to Jake made her relax about it a bit. She fell asleep on the sofa, running her fingers down Chester's back.

TWELVE

Sherry woke up before dawn and her thoughts felt clearer than she could remember in a long time. With the clarity came the knowledge that she was not supposed to be there. She wasn't sure where she was but she was positive that it wasn't right. She was certain she should be at her daughter's house. But where was it? And how could she get there?

She closed her eyes and tried to remember her daughter's address. She could see the house but not the number and not the street. She squeezed her lids tight. Still, the address didn't come. She had to find it. She had to try anyway.

Something was wrong with her brain. She accepted that, but still, it sometimes made her angry – horribly angry. She often wanted to beat her head against the wall. But she had to make sure she never did that. That old guy did. He had blood running down his face when they stopped him and took him out of the rec room. She hadn't seen him since. Or had she and just couldn't remember? 'Oh, damn it. Damn it, damn it, damn it.'

Stop. Stop now! Anger doesn't help. Anger makes it harder to think. Deep breaths. Calm down. I need to think. Think.

My purse. I need my purse. It has my driver's license and

that has my address. Where is my purse? She stumbled around
in the dark room, reaching into drawers, feeling for her
bag. She went to the closet and felt along the floor. Only
shoes. She looked in the bathroom cabinet but it wasn't
buried in the stack of towels. Then, she remembered. She had
asked Don for her purse. He said she didn't need one here.
That everything was free so she didn't need money or credit
cards.

Don said he was her good friend. But if he was, wouldn't
he have given her the purse back? She did need it. She needed
her license and her address book. And why don't any of the
phones work? Don told her not to worry about it. It was like
that in the country a lot, he'd said. But that's during storms.
There aren't storms every day. Was Don lying to her? Hiding
something from her? Or was that just crazy talk?

*No. It's not crazy talk. I am not crazy. At least, not right
now.* She knew something was wrong. This place was wrong.
They called it her cottage, her bungalow, her home. But it
was just an old motel room in an arcing string of temporary
shelters. The exterior was designed to imitate the outside of
a brick house but it was all show. Inside, it was just a shabby
room with a bed, a nightstand, a lamp and a dresser – there
wasn't even a television. Just this space with a small bathroom attached. No kitchen like a real home. No living room.
What am I doing here?

She didn't have an answer and she didn't know where she
would go. But she knew she had to leave. She got prepared:
brushing her teeth, combing her hair and putting on a pair of
khaki slacks, a blouse and a heavy cardigan. She sat on the
end of the bed to tie her walking shoes.

She was ready. *No. I need my purse.* She got down on all
fours and looked under the bed. It wasn't there but she spotted
it under the nightstand. She laid flat stretching her arm long
to pull it out.

She sat on her bed, her purse clutched to her lap. She waited
for first light, praying her mind didn't fade with the rising of
the sun. She wasn't sure if she had any control over her mind
at all but she would try to focus it – she would do everything
she could to hold on to this gift of awareness and not let it
go.

But when the first signs of dawn crept through the blinds,

Sherry was gone where she sat. She didn't move. She simply stared. She did nothing at all until she heard the knock at the door and the cheery voice calling, 'Rise and Shine, it's break-fast time.'

She stood up, walked out the door and followed the others to the dining room.

THIRTEEN

Chief Deputy Larry Hirschhorn tried to be optimistic about this morning's search for five-year-old Hannah Singley. The temperature had stayed well above freezing the previous night, making him confident she would have survived the weather even though she was last seen wearing lightweight pajamas and bunny slippers.

Still, there were a lot of other dangers out there. She could have fallen down a hill, into a stream, or tripped over a branch and struck her head on a rock. She could have been attacked by a wild animal – or even by someone's dog overzealous to protect his territory.

Then there were the two-legged predators. Even out here in the peaceful countryside, they seemed to be everywhere, watching, waiting, seeking the opportunity to pounce. They recognized their prey in a heartbeat and reacted to it faster than you could turn your head.

He was worried about the parents, too. They were acting like normal parents: concerned, helpful, distraught. But so had the infamous Susan Smith who, it turned out, had falsely claimed her two young sons had been abducted by a black man after she killed them both herself. It was always possible that it was just an act: two people mimicking the behavior of concerned parents. Their actions the evening before had been lackadaisical and troubling before they noticed the disap-pearance. They had sat Hannah in front of the TV with a bowl of macaroni and cheese and then didn't check on her for more than three hours. *What kind of parenting is that?* He bristled at the thought of it.

The searchers gathered before him in the road that ran past

little Hannah's house. Every single deputy had reported – even the ones who had got off duty just minutes earlier. The volunteer fire department was there in force, too, as well as a troop of trained Explorer Scouts. Daylight had clawed its way through the curtain of the night. It was time to go.

They stretched out, arm's length apart and trudged into the woods across the road from the Singley home. When searchers spotted anything the least bit suspicious, they called out and Hirschhorn ran over and stuck in an orange flag. For a while, nothing merited more than marking for later gathering. Then, a cry edged with panic echoed from the far end of the line. Hirschhorn followed the sound to an Explorer Scout.

'Whatcha got?'

Speechless, the young man pointed. Hirschhorn followed the length of his finger down to the ground where he spotted a splash of pink. He moved closer and saw the rabbit ears flopped over in the weeds: one pink bunny slipper.

Hirschhorn cursed himself for leaving the camera in the truck. The scout pulled out an iPhone and offered it to the deputy. 'I don't need to call. I just need to go back to the truck and fetch the camera.'

'Why bother? You can take a picture with this. I can show you how to work it.'

'Better yet, why don't you take the pictures? It'll save some time.'

After looking over the photos and deeming them satisfactory, Hirschhorn pulled a pair of gloves and a bag out of the satchel carrying the orange flags and secured the slipper. Before they moved on, he marked the spot. He and the scout lagged only slightly behind the rest of the search line. He took care not to hurry the boy along to catch up. Every inch needed a careful look. With each outcry from someone in the group, Hirschhorn rushed forward, hoping and dreading the find of another slipper – or the body of a young girl.

He'd planted another half-dozen flags before the pond came into view. He exhaled noisily. He certainly didn't want to find a drowned child but he knew from the start that it was a possibility. He walked a few yards forward when he saw it – a flash of fabric among the reeds on the edge of the water. He broke into a run.

He saw the tendrils of hair floating on the surface and

shouted out, 'Hannah!' before realizing that the body was too long for a child. He knelt in the mud and pulled the head out of the water, flipping an elderly woman – obviously deceased – on her back.

Hirschhorn knew it was time to call in the state boys. The pond would have to be searched, both for evidence in the case of the dead woman and the possibility of locating Hannah. Drained, dredged or dived, that was the state's purview. He placed the call.

He selected a few deputies to stay with him to conduct a perimeter survey of the pond and secure the crime scene. He sent the rest of the group on to continue the search for the little girl. He hoped they would find her far away from the pond; if she was here, the news would not be good.

He divided up the men with him into two groups of three and headed them off in opposite directions around the body of water. They poked poles into the reeds that ringed most of the pond and jabbed them into the muck a few inches into the water. He was grateful it was early in the year – a few months from now and they'd all be welted from mosquito bites. The searchers were about two-thirds up each side when someone opposite Hirschhorn called out, 'Found another one!'

'Hannah?' Hirschhorn asked.

'Nope. This is a man. Gray hair. But not much of a face left. ID ain't gonna be easy.'

Hirschhorn clumped around the far end of the pond, scanning the water's edge as he went. He looked down at the body and its animal-ravaged face. He couldn't recall any open cases of missing elderly in the county – not any that would have been gone long enough for that much damage. He'd have to call back to the office. For that matter, he'd have to check with the city, too. It wasn't too far a drive from there to dump a body here.

They finished up the perimeter search and strung the tape, tree to tree, around the whole area. He'd called his administrative assistant. She was checking their files, would call the city missing persons department and report back.

There was nothing to do now but wait for the state folks to arrive. And hope when they got here, they didn't find a third body. And if they did, to pray that it wasn't Hannah.

FOURTEEN

Lucinda pushed her arms through the turquoise, knee-length lab coat and tied it behind her. She secured her hair at the back of her neck and put on a surgical cap. She slipped into booties, slid on rubber gloves and donned a pair of goggles. A mask hung around her neck, ready to be raised when the cutting started.

She pushed through the stainless steel swinging doors into the autopsy suite. The room smelled funky but not nasty – they worked on the really bad cases in an isolated room with its own separate ventilation system for which Lucinda was eternally grateful. Poor Edgar Humphries' nude body lay on the stainless steel, buttocks up, as Dr Sam performed his external examination. He raised his eyes as he saw her approach. 'Pierce.'

'Doctor,' she responded.

'This is a sorry thing for a man to endure at the end of a decent life,' Dr Sam said. 'Hope the good Lord lets me die of natural causes in front of a busload of doctors and a barrelful of nurses. Anything to spare me this final indignity. Autopsies are dreadful things.'

'But Dr Sam, I've always appreciated the way you've insisted on respect for the deceased. There's never been anything out of order in your morgue.'

'Respect is all well and good, Pierce. But look at what I do every day. It's nothing but desecration of a corpse. Sanctified, legal and necessary, of course. But desecration it is.'

'I never knew you felt that way, Doc.'

'Well, you should have. And after I die, I want to be cremated – don't want some mortician combing what's left of my hair or piling make-up on my lifeless face making me look like a kewpie doll from hell, either. How do you think he died, Pierce?'

'Don't have a clue, Doc.'

The doctor grunted. 'Well, that's a first,' he said as he and the tech flipped the body on its back. He pulled out his scalpel and got to work.

Lucinda hid a smirk by raising the mask over her mouth.

It was noon before Lucinda finally left the morgue. Cause of death was a heart attack. They'd have to wait until toxicology came back to find out if a lack of medication was a factor. *And where had he been for five months? Who had taken care of him? Who placed him on the porch? And does that person bear responsibility for his death? Am I wasting my time on a natural death? No, it may be a natural cause, but the means of death had a sinister cast to it – too many questions remain unanswered.*

Lucinda took the elevator to the fifth floor hoping to catch District Attorney Michael Reed before he went to lunch. She wanted to get Evan Spencer's case closed or at least stalled for further investigation.

She knocked on the sill of Reed's open doorway. 'Got a minute?'

'Yeah. But just a minute. Make it quick. I'm meeting my wife for lunch.'

'The assault charge against Evan Spencer?'

'What about it?'

'I think it's groundless.'

'And why is that, Pierce?'

'Because he told me what happened. And he didn't do it.'

'Oh. And so now you believe him. A couple of years ago, you wanted me to arrest him and charge him with murder. You blocked his departure from the country on a mission of mercy. And now, you believe him.'

'I came to believe him back then, if you recall, Mr Reed. His cooperation led us to his brother.'

'I can't keep track of all your flip-flopping, Pierce. I run for office every six years and I flip and flop less than you. Forget about it. Charges are filed. The victim is pressing forward. We'll let a jury decide.'

'Sir, at least take the time to thoroughly investigate the woman's claim before doing anything further.'

'Right now, my staff is busy with more important things – like murder. You want to look into it, fine. But I can only give you one week.'

'But, sir, I am in the middle of—'

'That's not my problem, Lieutenant. You want to look into it, look into it. But bring me something conclusive in seven days or leave me alone. Now if you'll excuse me, my wife is waiting.'

She watched his back as he walked down to the hall and stepped into the elevator. Turning around to face forward, he saw her looking at him and gave her a toodle-oo wave as the doors closed. She knew he was a good prosecutor but sometimes she wanted to kick him down all five floors of stairs and out the front door.

She walked down the two flights to her office and in the center of her desk she found a note weighted down with a tape dispenser. 'Come see me as soon as you can. Interesting developments. Jumbo.'

The message light was blinking on her phone. She decided to play them back before going down the hall to Jumbo Butler's office. One of them was from Vicki Humphries: 'I have some information you wanted, Lieutenant Pierce. I'm at work now but feel free to call me here.'

Lucinda flipped out her notebook and punched in the numbers to Vicki's direct line.

'Vicki Humphries.'

'This is Lieutenant Pierce, Ms Humphries, returning your call.'

'I overheard what Dr Nelson said to you yesterday so I went by his office and got a copy of my father-in-law's medical records for you. I thought it might save you some time and trouble.'

'Thank you. I really appreciate that. I hadn't gotten around to making a request yet for a subpoena – this is really a time saver. Can I come by and pick them up this evening? Will you be home?'

'Yes, Lieutenant. That would be fine. I'll see you then.'

She hung up and walked down to the Missing Persons division. 'Hey, Butler. What's up?' she called out as she stepped through the door.

'Back here, Lieutenant,' Jumbo shouted.

Unlike the new cubicle layout in her work area, the city hadn't gotten around to redesigning this department. New desks and file cabinets had just been set up in any space available making the path to anywhere full of more twists and turns than a rabbit warren.

She maneuvered through the maze, reaching Jumbo's office at last. He introduced her to Karla Dunbar, the administrative staff who'd assisted him with his file by file search. With her wire-rimmed glasses, short skirt and wide Afro, the young woman seemed as if she'd escaped from an earlier decade.

'I was right, Lieutenant. We went through five years of files. There's been a real uptick in missing elderly in the last 18 months that's disproportionate to the increase in population in that age group,' Jumbo said.

'OK. And?'

'And?' Jumbo asked.

'And, Butler, you said you had new developments – with an s.'

'Oh right. I forgot I hadn't told you yet. Early today, I called the Missing Persons division at the state police. I told them about my concerns. They said that they'd already been a bit alarmed by the numbers coming out of my office recently and said they'd red flagged us to do a follow-up investigation but hadn't gotten around to it yet. Anyway, the captain there told me to keep her informed on what me and Karla found in our file search.

'Then about an hour and a half ago, she called me back and said that two unidentified bodies of elderly folks were found in Dinwiddie County that morning. No missing people in the county matched the descriptions but since we were the nearest major city, they just might belong to us.'

'Really? Are the bodies here?'

'Nope. They're in Norfolk.'

'Why's that? We're a lot closer – and Dinwiddie is in our district, isn't it?'

'Ah, I guess you didn't hear the news. There was a massive explosion followed by a fire at a large apartment complex in the south of town just minutes before noon. Doc Sam's not accepting any out of town bodies until he can deal with the fatalities that are pouring in to the morgue as we speak. So they transported the two Dinwiddie bodies down to the Tidewater district. Can't ever make it easy for the investigators, can they?'

'Doubt if they give us a thought.'

'Anyway,' Jumbo continued, 'me and Karla have been going through the files of the last year and a half. Here's how we've divided them up. This bin –' he said, laying a hand on a blue plastic crate – 'has all the files of missing elderly where there is no report of dementia.' Moving on to the red container, he said, 'And this one has all the files with dementia.' He moved over to the third crate. 'Here we separated out the files from this past month – most of the files are from the past few days, probably folks that are just lost and will be found any minute now.

'The captain said that if we can bring down dental records for any possible matches, they can have a forensic odontologist there this evening.'

'So what are you waiting for?' Lucinda asked.

'We were just getting ready to cull the herd a bit. We know the dead woman is 5'2" and the dead guy is 5'11". Figured we'd pull out any folks that aren't within an inch or two of those heights and I'd take the rest down to Norfolk.'

'I'll help and drive you down there if you like.'

'You sure? We'll probably hit some dense drive time traffic.'

'I've got lights in the grille of my car. And I'm not afraid to use 'em.'

'Great. Let's get through these files and get going,' he said with a grin.

Lucinda couldn't help thinking he looked even more like a leprechaun when he had a smile on his face.

They pulled all the documents they needed and double-checked to make sure the dental records were enclosed. As they headed for Lucinda's car, she remembered her promise to visit Vicki and pick up the medical records. She called Ted who agreed to pick them up for her and offer apologies.

She pulled on to the highway wondering if she was investigating three homicides or going on a wild goose chase driven by the ghosts of her past.

FIFTEEN

The traffic grew much denser as they approached Norfolk, both because of the higher population and the timing of their arrival in the area. But, true to her word, Lucinda was not shy about using her lights and forcing their way through the bottlenecks. At just under two hours on the road, she pulled into the parking lot; Lucinda was pleased – just a few minutes over the MapQuest-indicated time.

Inside, the odontologist had not yet arrived and the forensic pathologist was still busy with the bodies. They paced the floor outside the autopsy suite waiting for one of the two to be available. The doctor greeted them first.

'What were the causes of death?' Lucinda asked.

'The John Doe died as a result of cerebral edema – brain swelling – brought on by a skull fracture from blunt force trauma. He had contra-coupe injuries to the back of his skull but the real damage was to the front. And here's the thing that doesn't make sense to me yet. There is repeated trauma to his forehead – but all in approximately the same spot – and it seems to have been caused by a flat surface, like a floor or a wall. Now, I've seen someone beaten to death that way but you usually find other indicators: bruising on the arms, shoulders, or neck and strikes that land on the sides of the skull because the victim struggled. But this one's strange – either he was unconscious when he was beaten or he did this to himself.'

'In other words, no clear signs of foul play?'

'You got it. But considering where he was found, there had to be foul play. Someone must have dumped the body – he's too far from a wall or floor out there to have injured himself that badly and then gotten to the pond by himself, where he just happened to stumble and fall into the water. Besides, there's no water in his lungs so he couldn't have been breathing then.'

'Are you doing a tox screen?'

'We'll run the standard toxicology but unless we learn who he is, we don't know what else to look for.'

'Hopefully we can help with that. What about the woman?'

'The Jane Doe did die from drowning. However, once again, I'm suspicious because of where she was found. On the other hand, there are no signs of the bruising you'd expect if someone held her underwater. Still, the water in her lungs bothers me.'

'How so?'

'I put some of it on a slide and looked at it with a microscope, comparing it to the water sample retrieved from the site where her body was found. There are different organisms in the two that troubled me. But that isn't my area of expertise. I sent samples off to the FBI lab to see what they can determine. And before you ask, my response to the tox screen is the same. I suspect you asked because you had something in mind. Care to enlighten me?'

'Of course, Doctor. We're investigating a case where we suspect that a heart attack was brought on because the victim didn't have access to his medications for five months. I'm wondering if these two had been cut off from their prescriptions as well. And if that played a role in their deaths.'

'Well, Dr Tooth should be along soon and maybe you can get an ID.'

'Dr Tooth? That's his name?' Jumbo Butler asked.

'No,' the pathologist said with a laugh. 'That's just what I call him. And, look, here he is now.'

'Hey, Dr Guts,' the newcomer shouted up the hall.

'See, the nickname I gave him is thoroughly justified,' the pathologist said to Butler and Pierce. 'Dr Tooth, welcome to my parlor.'

'Did you remember to do X-rays for me this time or are you going to make me stick my hands in dead mouths?'

'I won't even dignify that remark with an answer. Here are the detectives. They're all yours.' He nodded his head, turned and walked away. He stopped just before leaving the room and said, 'Lieutenant, there was something odd. It probably doesn't mean anything but I thought I should mention it.'

'Yes, Doctor?'

'The man – his pockets – they were full of acorns.'

'Thank you, Doctor. I don't understand it either but it's not the first acorns we've run across in this case,' Lucinda said.

After the pathologist left the room, the forensic odontologist said, 'To set the record straight, my name is Dr Krasnik. What have you got for me to examine? How many files?'

Jumbo held out the folders. 'We've got six women, nine men.'

'You couldn't narrow it down more than that?'

'Sorry,' Jumbo replied with a shrug.

'Well, have a seat. This may take a while. At least the state pays me by the hour, so I can't complain too much.'

Lucinda and Jumbo chatted about the department, working conditions in the separate divisions and people they both knew. They ran out of conversation long before they had answers from Dr Krasnik. They were both dozing in the hard plastic chairs when he finally emerged from the back.

'The good news is that I made positive identification on both the bodies. The bad news is that two of your people are dead – and I know those family notifications are a bitch. Can't say I envy you.'

'Thank you,' they said in unison. 'We really appreciate your time,' Lucinda added.

Jumbo took the files and they walked out to Lucinda's car for the long ride home. Lucinda turned on the overhead light and Jumbo read to her from the documents. The woman, Adele Kendlesohn, had been missing since Halloween day. The man, Francis DeLong, hadn't been seen by his family since last summer. Both suffered from dementia. Additionally, DeLong had shown symptoms of psychosis off and on for decades.

'It'll be eleven or so by the time we get back to town,' Lucinda said.

'After all this time, no sense in bothering the families tonight, is there?'

'First thing tomorrow, then?'

'First thing? Like seven, seven thirty?' Jumbo asked.

'Let's make it six thirty. I'll meet you in the parking lot behind the Justice Center.'

SIXTEEN

Sherry sat on the edge of the bed with her arms folded tightly across her chest and her right index finger tap-tap-tapping a spot on her arm just above her left elbow. 'I already had supper, they said. Humph. Not likely. I would have remembered eating supper,' she said out loud to the empty room. 'And, oh, that Don, all nice and sweet, he sidles up to me, with his bag full of tricks and make nice and says, "You already had two chocolate puddings, Miss Sherry. You can't have any more tonight." Ha! As if I wouldn't remember eating chocolate. I'm not that stupid. Sonsabitches. They were trying to starve me to death. That Don, he's the worst of all of them. And is he gonna pay. I'll see to that.

'Or maybe they're trying to drive me crazy. Gaslight me like they did to that pretty Ingrid Bergman. She saved herself from that bastard – and you better watch out, I will, too.'

Underneath this layer of outrage and paranoia toward others, Sherry harbored a more intense anger and frustration with herself. She remembered that she was supposed to do something that day. She recalled waking up with a plan. But she was certain that she hadn't followed through with it. Worst of all, she had no recollection of what it was she planned to do. *I should have written a note. I should make lists like I used to do.*

She dug around in drawers until she found a pad of paper and a pen. But then she didn't know what to do. It went beyond not knowing what she wanted to write down. It was far more elemental. She looked at the paper. She looked at the pen. And she couldn't remember how to bring them together to put words down. She turned them both around in her hands, looking at them from every angle. But nothing came to her. She threw them both as hard as she could. The pen bounced against the wall, the pad fluttered its pages in the air and fell to the floor before making it halfway to its destination.

Fat teardrops formed in her eyes and plopped on to her cheekbones before traveling down to her chin. She wiped angrily at them as they hung there, mumbling her irritation with the itching sensation they caused. *Maybe I told someone what I wanted to do. Maybe if I asked, someone would remember.*

At that thought her tears dried – now she had something to do. She placed a hand on the bed on either side of her hips. She tried to push her body up but the mattress was too soft and her arms too weak. She placed her palms on her knees, leaned forward, and straightened into an upright position. A proud smile crossed her face as she walked to her front door.

She turned the knob and pulled. It didn't open. She leaned

backwards, putting her weight into the task but the door would not yield. She turned the lock on the doorknob and repeated the process but still had no luck. She beat on the door and yelled. But no one came.

She kicked the door until she was aware of the growing pain in her foot. She sat on the edge of the bed, removed her shoes and saw blood on one big toe. She hobbled into the bathroom, got the box of bandages and limped back to the bed with her big toe raised up away from the floor. She covered the injury and slumped in defeat. *The door was locked. I'm a prisoner. They locked me in to keep me from getting food. The window . . . I'll climb out the window.*

The thought of grabbing the cord and pulling up the drapes never occurred to her. Instead she fought with the fabric, tugging on it, pulling at it, fumbling with the folds until the gap revealed itself. She tunneled her way behind it but the big picture window defied her. It had no ledge to grab and lift, no seams to exploit. She thought about breaking the glass but the fear of a bad cut stopped her. She slapped the glass lightly as if she thought she'd hit a magic spot and slide through to the other side like Alice through the looking glass.

The bathroom window popped into her thoughts. Instead of pulling backward and letting the drapes slide over and off of her head, she fought with them, panicking when it seemed they were holding her captive. The fabric brushed against her face like bird wings. A vision of Tippi Hedren in Hitchcock's *The Birds* filled her vision, cruel beaks pecking at her scalp, wicked claws grabbing for her face.

Sherry closed her eyes and flapped her hands around her head trying to chase away the imagined feathered demons. She squirmed in terror and, without knowing how she managed it, she broke free. Nothing touched her face, the birds' screams faded away. For a moment, she dared not move – she stood still, panting and trembling. Slowly, she opened her eyes. The birds were gone. She scanned the room fearing she'd see one perched on her headboard, on a lamp, on the frame of a door. But not one was in sight.

The bathroom window. She took a step in that direction and stopped. *What if the birds are in the bathroom? Waiting to attack me? But it's my only way out.* She pressed her palms hard against her thudding heart. She took one tentative step after another until she reached the doorway. She peered around the room but saw no sign of them. *What if they're hiding behind the shower curtain?*

Cautious, she placed one foot after another until her shins touched the edge of the tub. She reached out one hand, grabbing the plastic covering. She inhaled deeply, held her breath and jerked back the curtain.

She choked out a sound halfway between a laugh and a cry. No birds. She steadied her breath and stepped one foot after the other over the edge of the tub. The window was set up high – she had to stand on tiptoes to reach the latch. She flipped it open, grabbed the ledge and pushed up but it wouldn't budge.

She tried again and again – veins popping out on her neck, face flushing bright red – until her arms ached from the effort. She tried to wriggle her fingers around the sill and slip them under the sash but the gap was far too narrow.

She leaned forward pressing her hot forehead against the cool tile on the wall and sobbed. She slid down slowly, crumpling into a defeated heap. She lay on her side, curled up and cried herself to sleep.

SEVENTEEN

Lucinda pulled into the driveway of the house belonging to Adele Kendlesohn's son and daughter-in-law. She curled her lip in disgust. Another huge brick monstrosity with pompous two-story columns that she felt looked more like an institution than a home.

Lucinda and Jumbo walked on to the porch and rang the bell. Dogs barked in response, while a fluffy black cat slunk up to the glass and stared through the side pane at the people causing all the commotion. A scowling Eli Kendlesohn opened the door, the cat darted away and the dogs bit at the air as they snarled.

'I recognize you,' he said, pointing at Jumbo. 'But I don't think I've seen *you* before.'

Lucinda flapped open her badge and said, 'Lieutenant Pierce, sir. We would like to talk to you and your wife, please.'

'She's not even downstairs yet,' he objected.

'Sir, it's about your mother.'

'Oh, of course it is.' His face lengthened forming deep furrows downward from both corners of his mouth. He seemed to age before their eyes. 'I guess I can assume this isn't good news.'

'Sorry, sir.'

'Let me put these dogs out in the backyard so they don't drive us all crazy.' He walked away with a Corgi, a Scottie and an unrecognizable ball of fluff at his heels. When he walked back up the hall, he stopped to shout up the stairway. 'Honey, the police are here. It's about Mom.'

He opened the door and invited Lucinda and Jumbo into the house. The ostentatious crystal chandelier hanging in the foyer annoyed Lucinda even more than the exterior façade. The scent of lemon furniture polish overwhelmed her nose causing it to crinkle and squirm involuntarily as if trying to escape her face.

Eli guided them into a formal living room with a grand piano in one corner by the entrance and a large, impressive oriental vase in the other. He stopped before a fireplace with a walnut mantle and slate hearth. Above the mantle hung an enormous oil painting of a woman in an evening gown smiling smugly down at one and all.

'Have a seat, please,' Eli said. 'I'm going to get a cup of coffee; can I get some for the two of you?'

They both accepted the offer and when Eli vanished into the kitchen, Lucinda brushed off the back of her skirt before easing down on the stark white cushions of the sofa. Jumbo followed her lead, contorting his body to try to see if he missed anything before he, too, took a seat on the other end.

Eli returned bearing a tray laden with four steaming mugs, a pitcher of cream, bowl of sugar and four spoons. As he set it down on the coffee table, his wife stepped into the room. Lucinda looked from her to the portrait and noticed the resemblance. Not a good omen, she thought.

'Help yourself to the cream and sugar,' Eli said, picking up one mug, slurping and giving a satisfied sigh. Turning to his wife, he said, 'You remember Sergeant Butler, don't you, dear?'

'Of course, I do! How could I possibly forget our Jumbo, working so hard to find your mother,' she said extending her hand and offering a condescending smile that looked very much like the one in the oil painting.

Jumbo stood and shook her hand. 'Hello, Rachael. Sorry to bother you so early.'

'Think nothing of it,' she said before looking over at Lucinda. 'And this is?'

Lucinda lifted up from her seat, leaned forward and stuck out her hand. 'Pierce, Lieutenant Pierce.'

'Do you work for Sergeant Butler?'

'Darling,' her husband interjected with a chuckle, 'she's a lieutenant.'

'As if that means anything to me – I suppose, though, that means the answer is "no".'

'They've come with news about my mother. I'd like to hear—' Eli began.

'Eli, please! Be a little patient. We aren't in your board-room. We can't just get right to business – why, that would be rude.' She smiled at her visitors as if she knew there was no doubt in the world that they would agree with her. 'We need to understand everyone's place in this tableau first. Now, don't we? So what brings the two of you here together? And what are your roles in this case?'

'Mrs Kendlesohn, we are here because of your mother-in-law. We have some news and a few questions. If you'd please—' Lucinda started.

Rachael spun around as if she hadn't heard a word Lucinda said. 'Eli! Where are Ginger, Scottie and Dandy?'

'I put them out so they wouldn't bother—'

'Bother? They are wonderful little dogs.' She leaned forward and peered from Lucinda's face to Jumbo's face and back again. 'You do like dogs, don't you? I can't say I trust people who don't like dogs. And what happened to your face, Lieutenant? Are you a burn victim? In a car accident? Or were you actually born that way?'

Lucinda rose to her feet, straightening to her full height of 5'11", and quite grateful she wore heels that morning because it helped her tower even more over the shorter woman. 'Sit

down and be still, Mrs Kendlesohn. Or leave the room. We
have important news to deliver to your husband. This is not
a social visit.'

Rachael jerked her head back, pulling her chin into her
neck. 'Eli, did you hear her?' she said in an outraged tone.

'Rachael, please . . .' Eli entreated.

Finally, even the ever-patient Jumbo had his fill. 'Cut the
crap, Rachael, and sit down.'

Rachael pursed her lips and slowly descended into a nearby
chair. 'Sergeant Butler, I am so disappointed in you. And you,
Lieutenant, make sure you leave your badge number with me
before you go.'

Lucinda ignored her. 'Mr Kendlesohn, we found your
mother. Unfortunately, she was deceased when we located her.
We are so sorry for your loss.'

'Where did you find her?'

'Down in Dinwiddie County. Do you have any idea why
she'd be there?'

'I don't think we know anyone in that area. Do we, Rachael?'

'Of course not. It's all just army bases and wilderness down
there.'

'Have you heard from your mother since Halloween?'

'No, of course not,' bristled Rachael.

'No, we haven't, Lieutenant,' Eli said. 'How did she die?'

'She drowned, sir,' Lucinda said.

'Drowned? An accident? Was she swimming? She hasn't
gone swimming in years.'

'Considering where she was found, sir, I doubt she was
swimming. But beyond that, at this point, we just don't
know.'

'You don't know? What do you mean, you don't know?'
Rachael snapped.

'Rachael, please,' Eli urged.

'We're still investigating, Mr Kendlesohn. I'm not sure
when we'll have the answers. Every possibility is under
consideration.'

'Every possibility?'

'Yes, sir.'

'Accident? Even suicide?' Eli asked, wincing as he said the
last word.

'Yes, sir.'

Eli's eyes widened. 'Murder? Someone may have killed my mother?'

'That's a possibility, sir. I'm afraid we're looking into that as well.'

'I can't imagine why anyone would want to kill my mother.'

Rachael made a rude snort.

Lucinda glared at her. In that moment, her distaste for the woman turned into loathing. 'It doesn't always make sense, Mr Kendlesohn. We're trying to figure it all out but we do need your help. Tell me, did you have any plans to put your mother in a facility before she disappeared?'

'Well, I really didn't like the idea all that much, but . . .' He faltered mid-sentence. 'I'd considered it but although it might be a safe environment, it seemed so cold, so cruel, after all she'd done—'

'But I insisted,' Rachael interrupted. 'Go ahead, tell them. Your dreadful wife just couldn't stand that batty old woman around the house anymore.'

'Rachael, don't—' Eli began.

'It's true. You might as well say it. She roamed around in the middle of the night. She forgot where to put her tooth-brush, her dentures – found them once in the refrigerator on top of the butter. And those flashes of anger she'd have. I had her on a half a dozen waiting lists. I was at my wits' end.'

Eli flushed bright crimson, but didn't say a word.

'I'll need a list of those facilities, Mrs Kendlesohn,' Lucinda said.

'Why? She never stayed in any of them.'

'I just do, Mrs Kendlesohn,' Lucinda insisted.

Rachael sighed long and loud. 'If you insist, Lieutenant.'

'I certainly do, ma'am,' she said and turned back to Eli. 'Did your mother take any prescription medications?'

'She did take a few but despite the loss of her mental capabilities she was in very good shape physically.'

'Do you still have those prescription bottles by any chance?'

'Yes, I'll get them for you,' Eli said as he rose.

Before he could walk away, Rachael said, 'You have them? I told you to throw them away months ago.'

'I know, Rachael, but I couldn't. I was still hoping she'd come back one day.'

'Oh, really, Eli? How unrealistic.' She shook her head in disbelief.

'Mrs Kendlesohn,' Lucinda interrupted, allowing Eli the opportunity to escape the room. 'The facilities list? When can I get that from you?'

'I suppose you'll want contact names and numbers, too.'

'That would be quite helpful.'

'I think I can find the time sometime this week.'

Lucinda stood again and leaned over the seated woman, resting her hands on the arms of the chair. 'You will find the time this morning. Someone will pick up the list at noon. Make sure it's ready.'

'Your badge number, Lieutenant.'

Lucinda whipped out her badge, flipped it open and said, 'There it is. Memorize it.'

'I – I – I can't. Not just like that.'

Lucinda pulled a pen and a pad of paper out of an interior suit pocket. 'Here I'll make it easy for you.' She jotted down the digits and ripped out the sheet of paper. She was delighted to see the woman cringe at the harsh tearing sound. Lucinda flipped the page into Rachael's lap.

Eli returned to the room holding a paper bag. 'Here you go, Lieutenant. They're all in here.'

'Thank you, sir. You can contact your funeral home and let them know that your mother is down in Norfolk. They'll know where to go to get her. If they have any questions, they can call me. Here's my card. Once again, sir, I am so sorry for your loss.'

'Thank you, Lieutenant. Thank you for your time. And you, too, Sergeant. I appreciate all you've done.'

As they walked down the sidewalk to the car, Jumbo said, 'Boy, I sure feel guilty.'

'Ah, c'mon. We had to tell him about his mother's death, Butler.'

'No, not that, Lieutenant. I feel guilty for leaving him alone with that woman.'

Lucinda laughed. 'Can't argue with you there.'

EIGHTEEN

The next stop for Jumbo and Lucinda was the home of Heather and Mark McFaden, the daughter and son-in-law of Francis DeLong. They pulled up to the curb in front of a long ranch with stone running up to the window-sills and white siding from there to the roof. Heather was in the front yard, hose in hand, watering a flower bed. She stared at them with a furrowed brow and pursed lips.

As soon as Jumbo emerged from the car, Heather's mouth flew open, she dropped the hose and ran toward the car. 'You found Dad, Sergeant Butler? You found Dad?'

'Yes, Mrs McFaden. We found your father,' Jumbo said with a sigh.

'Is he OK? Where is he? When can I see him?'

Jumbo jerked his eyes away from the woman's pleading face. 'I'm sorry, Mrs McFaden. So sorry . . .'

'What happened? Is he hurt? Is he sick? Oh my heavens! He didn't finally hurt someone, did he?'

Lucinda put a hand on the woman's shoulder. 'Ma'am, can we go inside and talk, please?'

The furrows deepened on Heather's forehead; it seemed to Lucinda that she was perplexed by her presence and hadn't realized that Jumbo wasn't alone until that moment. She darted her eyes between the two detectives and nodded. Her head hung low as she dragged her feet toward the front door – each step exaggerated as if she were pulling her feet out of sucking mud.

Inside, Heather waved her left hand toward a seating arrangement in front of a stone fireplace and stepped into the edge of the hallway. 'Mark. Mark. Sergeant Butler and – and – uh, somebody else are here about Dad.'

She walked into the living room, sat in a chair and straightened her spine rather than sinking into its comforting arms. She folded her hands in her lap. 'Mark will be here as soon as he can. He was dressing.'

'I'm here, I'm here,' Mark said, limping into the room –

one foot wearing a shoe, the other clad only in a sock. He sat on the arm of his wife's chair and reached protectively around her shoulders.

'Mrs McFaden, we are very sorry to have to bring you this news. But—' Jumbo began.

'He's in jail isn't he? Or is he in an insane asylum?' Heather cried.

'Easy, sweetheart,' Mark comforted her. 'Let's hear what they have to say before you start jumping to conclusions.'

'Actually, it's a bit worse, Mrs McFaden. And we are both terribly sorry for your loss,' Jumbo said.

'Loss? Loss? What do you mean loss? Are you saying? No. No. He can't be dead,' Heather shrieked.

Mark slid to the floor on his knees and wrapped his arms around his wife, pressing his forehead against hers. 'Sssh, sssh, sweetheart. I know it's hard but we'll get through this together.'

When Heather's shoulders stopped heaving, Mark released her and resumed sitting next to her on the arm of the chair. 'Apologies, detectives. Heather really loved her dad. The last nine months have been hellish for her.'

'He'd been living with you when he disappeared, correct?' Lucinda asked.

Heather nodded her head.

Mark added, 'He's been living with us off and on since we were married – and that was nearly thirty-five years ago.'

'Off and on?' Lucinda queried.

'Yes, you see, Francis had more problems than his most recent struggle with Alzheimer's or dementia or whatever it was.'

'He was a good man – Dad was a good man,' Heather protested.

Mark patted her arm and said, 'Yes, he was a good man at heart, Heather.' He turned to the detectives. 'Sometimes, though, he'd have a really bad psychotic episode and we'd have to commit him to an institution until they could regulate his medication again.'

'What was the nature of these episodes?' Lucinda asked.

'He was never violent – not to us, not to anyone, except himself,' Heather said, her voice cracking as tears fell.

Mark gave her a one-armed squeeze and planted a kiss on top of her head. 'He did hurt himself – sometimes rather

badly. That was why we had to have him put away several
times for his own protection. He heard these voices. He was
never clear to us about what they said to him. He claimed
there were literally little people in his head, yelling at him.
When it got really bad, he'd bash his head against the wall
or the floor, the dashboard of the car – any place that was
handy. He said he wanted to kill them or at least make them
move out.'

'That had to be difficult to deal with,' Lucinda sympathized.

'Yes, but more than that, it was just flat out sad,' Mark
said with a sigh. 'And Heather's right – when his psychosis
was kept in check by the anti-psychotic drugs, he was a
sweet old guy and a great storyteller. But when the chemical balance went haywire, it was like an alien had taken
over his body.'

That comment brought on a huge sobbing wail from Heather.
'I was wrong. I was so wrong.'

'Wrong about what?' Lucinda asked.

'I – I – I didn't – I – I,' Heather stammered.

Mark patted her arm again. 'Hush, sweetheart. I'll explain.'
He cleared his throat. 'The doctor suggested that we put him
in an Alzheimer's unit because he'd started wandering a lot.
It was really hard to believe how crafty he could be about
slipping out of the house. We visited a couple of places but
they just broke Heather's heart. As much of his life as he
spent in institutions already because of his mental illness, she
just couldn't bear locking him up in one of those places for
good. And I just couldn't stand to force the issue. We thought
we'd try caring for him at home a little longer and then, he
was gone. I guess we both erred out of misguided gestures
of kindness.'

'And you haven't heard from him once in the last nine
months?' Lucinda asked.

The couple shook their heads.

'Could you give me a list of the facilities you visited?'

'Sure, no problem,' Mark said.

'What about medications? Was he taking any at the time
he disappeared?'

'Oh, yeah, lots of them. Two drugs for high blood pressure, one for high cholesterol, but the one that worried us the
most was his anti-psychotic medication. He'd been doing well

on it for a long time – but without it, there's no telling what would happen. The first two weeks we were more concerned about the lack of those meds than anything else.'

'Did he suffer?' Heather asked.

Jumbo and Lucinda winced.

'Oh, it was awful, wasn't it? I can tell by the look on your faces,' Heather moaned.

'He died from blunt force trauma. It appeared as if his head had violent contact with a flat surface. That injury caused him to die slowly, but in all likelihood, he was unconscious and unaware of any suffering throughout most of that ordeal,' Lucinda said.

Heather wailed out an inhuman sound and Mark pulled her to her feet and wrapped her in an embrace. Over his wife's shoulder, he looked at the detectives, jerked his eyes toward the door and mouthed 'one minute'.

The detectives expressed their sympathy once again and stepped out the front door. Five minutes later, Mark joined them carrying a list and a clear plastic bag filled with prescription bottles. He handed the two items to Lucinda and said, 'Thank you. I had a couple of questions I didn't want to ask in front of Heather. First, if he did kill himself by beating his head against the wall, will his death be ruled a suicide?'

'I doubt that, sir,' Lucinda said. 'Not unless there are other indications of suicide and from what you're telling me that doesn't seem likely.'

'Good. A suicide ruling would tear Heather up. Where did you find him?'

'That's the odd part, Mr McFaden. We found his body in a pond out in Dinwiddie County. You have any idea of how he would have wound up there?'

'No, but, in a pond? And he didn't drown?'

'No, sir, it appears as if his body was left there by someone else. He did not drown.'

'It seems like I should have a dozen more questions but I can only think of one: how do we get his body back for a funeral?'

'Just tell the funeral home that his autopsy was performed in Norfolk – they'll know where to find him. And, Mr McFaden, you're not going to want your wife to see his body. There was extensive damage caused by scavenging animals.'

'Oh, dear Lord,' Mark moaned.

Lucinda handed him one of her cards. 'Don't hesitate to call me if you think of any more questions.'

Mark stared at her card. 'Homicide? You think someone murdered him?'

'We thought it was a possibility, Mr McFaden. From what you told me this morning, it seems less likely now but I've got to keep investigating until I know that with a certainty.'

After Mark went inside, Jumbo asked, 'You still think it might be murder?'

'Somebody dumped his body in the middle of nowhere, Butler. There must be a reason for that. And I won't rest until I know who did it and why.'

NINETEEN

Two blocks from the McFaden home, Jumbo's cellphone blurted out a reggae beat announcing an incoming call. When he disconnected, he said, 'That was a woman whose husband, I believe, just up and left here a few months ago. She's been reluctant to accept that possibility but now, it seems, she's stumbled across a hidden stash of love letters. Would you mind stopping by her place for a few minutes? It's on our way.'

'Not at all. I'll just wait in the car and make phone calls and think some things through.' Lucinda called Ted after Jumbo slipped inside the modest ranch home at the end of a cul de sac. She explained the situation with Mrs Kendlesohn.

'Sounds like she'll need a little on-site encouragement to get the job done,' Ted said. 'I'll head right out there.'

Doubts about her motivations in this case of missing and deceased senior citizens took over Lucinda's thoughts. That, in turn, took her back to that awful day – the sound of gunfire, the smell of the powder in the air, the slow-motion drop of her mother's body on to the stairs. The roar of the shot that followed and the thump as her father's body hit the floor in the hallway. She blamed herself. She shouldn't have hidden at the top of the stairs. She should have come down when she heard her father's voice. He wouldn't have shot her mother if he knew she was watching. Or would he? She would never know and because of that she had never been able to grant herself absolution for her inaction.

Is that why I'm meddling in a natural death, an accidental suicide and a drowning? Is that why I am trying to find other reasons? To make someone responsible for their deaths? Or is there really something there? Her musings traveled in circles. A half-hour after Jumbo went inside, her frustration pushed her to try to derail her train of thought.

She lowered the visor, slid open the mirror and contemplated her face. Rambo said he wanted to work on her nose next. She doubted he could ever make the damaged side look anything like the original. But she'd probably let him have a go at it anyway.

She sighed deep and long. She'd been in the wrong place at the wrong time for just a brief moment. And it was taking years to deal with the aftermath of that tiny bit of time.

The passenger door opened, drawing her out of her ruminations. 'Sorry about that, Lieutenant,' Jumbo said. 'If I'd known it would take that long . . .'

'You don't need to say another word, Butler. I'd have busted in there and dragged you out if needed.'

Jumbo gave her a sidelong glance. 'I'm still not sure when to take you seriously and when you're just jerking my chain.'

Lucinda laughed and pulled away from the curb.

A note from Ted lay in the middle of Lucinda's desk: 'Here's the list I picked up from Mrs Humphries last night and the one I got today from Mrs Kendlesohn – surprised she survived your visit – what a B!'

Lucinda chuckled, lifted the note and scanned the lists. She pulled out the two others she'd gathered, laid them side-by-side, and cross-checked the names. She made a separate list, prioritizing the facilities that made it on to all four lists, working down to those that were on only one. She got on the Internet and went to Google maps where she planned the most efficient route for visiting the places highest on her list.

Ted interrupted her, 'Ah, you found them?'

'Yes, thanks for running those errands for me.'

'OK, tell me the truth: were you really tied up this morning or were you avoiding seeing that woman again?'

Lucinda laughed. 'I really was tied up – missing a visit with Mrs Kendlesohn was just one of those rare and welcome perks. Hey, you said you wanted to talk. So, what's on your mind?'

'It might take a while – I don't want to take you away from more important things.'

Lucinda shrugged. 'Aside from visiting these senior residential units, all I have to do is wait for toxicology results or a miracle. And I doubt I'll find answers at any of the facilities, but still, it is something that needs to be done, but not this red-hot minute. Let's go across the street to the coffee shop – I need a latte.'

Ted nodded and they left the office. In the elevator, Lucinda asked about Ted's children. Ted shared a brief update on school grades and sports activities but she could tell he was holding something back. She knew whatever was on his mind, it obviously would affect his kids – and that probably was an area of serious concern.

The coffee shop wasn't one of those tidy, cookie-cutter places like Starbucks or Seattle's Best. This was a funky hangout with strange artwork on the walls, piles of magazines, community newspapers and tattered paperbacks on occasional tables and conversation areas of comfy furniture in the rear as well as a section of prim café tables and wrought-iron chairs up front. The counter was overloaded with plastic-wrapped brownies, glass jars filled with biscotti and contribution cans for half a dozen causes.

The barista who greeted Lucinda and Ted was actually the owner. His long gray hair cinched into a ponytail that hung down to the middle of his back making him stand out from his much younger employees. He prepared Lucinda's latte and Ted's cup of dark roast with practiced, efficient moves that made him appear as if he really had three or four hands instead of just the two visible ones.

Lucinda led Ted back to the far corner of the shop where she slid into one overstuffed chair while Ted sat diagonally across from her. 'So what's up, Ted?'

'I'm thinking of making a major change – moving out of town – soon.'

'Won't you want Pete and Kimmy to finish up the school year first?'

'That's just it, Lucinda, I wouldn't be taking them with me – I'd leave them with their mother.'

'Whoa, back up, Ted. I thought you were living with Ellen and the kids again and I thought you were getting along well.'

'Yes and yes.'

'Well, then, why are you thinking about leaving them?'

'It's my dad. He's been going downhill since he lost Mom six months ago. He's not up to caring for the house and yard but he can't bring himself to sell the place – it was where Mom grew up. I need to go be with him and help him take care of things.'

'I remember that house, it's huge. Your whole family could fit in there with room to spare. There's something else happening, Ted. Spill it.'

Ted took a sip of his coffee and looked away.

Lucinda sat patiently; if she had learned anything from interrogations, it was that if she waited out the periods of silence, the pay-off often was useful information.

Ted did not disappoint. He turned his head back, staring into his coffee mug. 'Ellen and I are getting along fine – in fact we've never gotten along better. But it's not like a married couple – it's more like a sister and brother. I sleep on the sofa 'cause it feels like it's wrong to share a bed with her.'

'Is this that tired old place, Ted, where our high school romance is coloring your perception?'

Ted snorted. 'Listen, I deserved that – and I don't blame you for thinking that way. But Ellen and I talked about it. She brought it up – she was the first one to say she deeply valued our renewed friendship but she just didn't feel that way about me any longer. She hasn't even mentioned you except to express her gratitude for your support in the courtroom and her mortification at pulling a gun on you.

'I've got to admit it was a relief learning that she lacked any passionate feelings for me, because I sure didn't feel that way about her. When I think about making love, you are on my mind.'

'Ted . . .' Lucinda bristled.

'I know, I know – you're not ready to go there until I resolve my family issues. At least that's what you've been saying all along. Lately, though, I've been thinking that's just been your nice way of saying, "No way, Jose". But I've accepted it. And my dad needs me.'

'I know your dad's place is only a couple hours away but the kids are still so young – you won't be able to see them all that often, not with working and taking care of your dad. And for that matter, where will you work?'

'The work part is easy. I already have a job offer with the Regional Computer Forensics Lab . . .'

'Congratulations. So those courses you've been taking the last couple of years were worthwhile, despite your many doubts.'

'Yes. And thank you for not saying, "I told you so",' Ted said with a laugh.

'But the children, they need you.'

Ted sighed. 'I'm not convinced that they do.'

'Oh, c'mon . . .'

'Seriously, Lucinda. When I come home from work, I often feel like I'm intruding on a tight family unit where I don't belong. It's as if the three of them have moved on without me. I mean, the kids still love me and they're glad to see me, but it's not like they really miss me when I'm gone.

'I just don't get it. It hurts – a lot. I was there for them while their mother was in the hospital for more than a year. And yet, now, it seems like she's the only one that really matters.'

'Ted, they're kids. They take you for granted. They're just making up for lost time with their mother – it's temporary, nothing more.'

'I don't know, Lucinda. I just don't know. I've got to make a decision by next week to accept or reject the job offer. I'm taking all the time they are giving me, but I don't know how I can turn it down – it's a terrific opportunity and my dad needs me.'

'Have you talked to Ellen about this?'

'No. No. I don't want to make her feel forced into moving with me or anything like that.'

'Ted, talk it over with her. Tell her what you're thinking. So maybe she doesn't want to move into the same house with you up there but maybe she'd want to move nearby – for the kids' sake. Or, after all she's been through, maybe she'd like to move somewhere new to get a fresh start.'

'I hadn't considered that – maybe I should talk to her.'

'Maybe? Oh good grief, Ted. Maybe? Even though you're not sharing a bed, you're living in the same house with this woman – you have to talk to her. You can't just slip out the door and not come back.'

'I wouldn't do that. I would've said something to her at some point.'

'You mean on your way out the door?' Lucinda said with an exaggerated eye roll. 'Man up, Ted. Talk to Ellen. Do it tonight.'

Ted held up his hands, palms facing out. 'OK, OK, I'll do it. Do I need to bring in a note tomorrow to verify that I did?'

'Shut up, Ted,' Lucinda said with a shake of her head. 'Are you busy this afternoon or would you like to ride with me to the senior living facilities, for old times' sake. I could use your puppy dog eyes and schmoozing talents with the ladies. It always seems to make gathering information a whole lot easier.'

TWENTY

Lucinda and Ted stopped first at River's Edge, the one facility on all four of the lists provided by the families of the three dead and the one still missing. It was far more upscale and stylish than either of them had imagined. A vast foyer spread out just inside the entrance of the main building. The centerpiece of the room was a round inlaid table topped by a huge vase filled with a dazzling array of flowers.

Lucinda's heels clicked on the highly polished floor as the pair walked to the information desk. Between the four victims, there were three contact names at River's Edge. Lucinda introduced herself to the perky receptionist and requested to speak to all of them. A young man, wearing a suit and a look of compassion and weariness usually associated with funeral home staff, and a middle-aged woman, with a bounce in her step and an eternal smile on her face, met them at the desk;

the third person was not at work that day. 'I'm Jenna and this is David,' she said. 'It's a pleasure to meet you. It's such a lovely day. Why don't we talk out in the garden?'

Lucinda smiled as she thought that this woman was so full of sunshine, she would think it was a 'lovely day' even if the wind was howling, lightning striking and hail pounding the top of her head.

Jenna led the way to a large enclosed courtyard with white wooden furniture scattered in conversation groups among the bushes, small trees and flower beds. She patted her legs and said, 'Now, what can we do for you?'

Lucinda asked about the three families who visited the facility. Neither one of them remembered anyone but Mrs Kendlesohn. David winced at the memory. 'Not a very pleasant woman and a bit too eager.'

'Too eager?' Lucinda asked.

'Yes, definitely. Most children and their spouses visiting here for the first time are reluctant, hesitant, worried about making the right decision, but not that Kendlesohn woman. She would have dropped her mother-in-law at the doorstep and driven off if it were possible. She was asking to be added to the waiting list long before we got out of the lobby.'

Lucinda raised her eyebrows, pleased to hear affirmation that she hadn't been too harsh in her judgment of Mrs Kendlesohn; she was as bad as her first impression and merited further investigation.

'I'm so sorry we don't have anything more to offer,' Jenna apologized. 'But we do have a constant stream of people in here day after day. Perhaps we could offer a tour of the facilities?'

'It might be useful,' Lucinda said. *And who knows what we might learn?* 'Another thing that would be of tremendous value would be a list of disgruntled former employees who left in anger or were fired for cause.'

'I'll pass that request along to the Human Resources department,' Jenna said, 'but there's no one that comes to my mind right away.'

While touring the assisted living area, a gray-haired, wrinkly-faced woman's smile reminded Lucinda of her mother's and how much she wished she could see it again. She went on a flight of fancy, imagining visiting her mother here, taking her out for lunch, meeting her friends.

Her thoughts were interrupted when Jenna and David came to an abrupt stop in front of a pair of doors. 'The people in this area of River's Edge are free to go where they want to go – out to the courtyard, down to the club, the swimming pool, out for visits off the grounds – but that is not true for this next part of the facility we will visit. We will be going into the Alzheimer's lockdown facility. It's not just for Alzheimer's patients but for those suffering from any form of dementia. Be careful when we enter – and when we leave – there is a woman who tries to slip through the doors all the time.

It was here that Ted fell quiet as he dwelled on darker thoughts about his father and the possibility he would end up in a place just like this one. Looking into the drawn faces and vacant eyes of so many of the inhabitants, he recognized his dad's ultimate fate and cringed from it. He saw a man in the corner with a small group of people gathered around him. The man waved his arms and seemed engaged in enthusiastic story-telling but even that man's eyes reflected an emptiness that betrayed his energetic performance.

They stopped in the recreation room and watched a staff member lead a few women and two men in a child's memory game. Seeing their difficulty to do the simplest task horrified Ted. He wanted to scream out the answers. Instead, he turned around and fast-walked back up the hallway to the exit, his gaze not once lifting from the carpet beneath his feet.

As he punched in the code, he was not aware of the little lady standing patiently beside him. He did not realize she slipped out the door with him until a staff member shouted out, 'Marie is out, again.'

A small army emerged from the lockdown unit and other parts of the building. They mobilized to surround Marie. Each one of them moved slowly and talked softly. Marie dodged about as if seeking escape from the closing net. Finally, a male aide got close enough to her to offer her his arm. She gave him a coy smile and slid her hand into the crook of his elbow. 'My, my, Miss Marie, it's a fine day for a stroll, isn't it?' he cooed as he led her back through the doors.

Ted apologized profusely to David and Jenna.

'No harm done, sir,' Jenna said. 'You were obviously moved by your experience in there and your mind was on other things. It's understandable – the lockdown unit is a powerfully sad place.'

Lucinda wanted to visit at least two more facilities that afternoon but wondered if she should take Ted back to the Justice Center first. They climbed into the car but Lucinda didn't turn the key in the ignition.

Ted didn't say a word, didn't look in her direction and gave no indication that he was aware that she hadn't started the car. She waited two minutes, then three. Finally, she broke the silence. 'Ted. Ted.'

Ted shook his head and looked over at her.

'What is it?' she asked. 'What bothered you so much back there?'

Ted hung his head and shook it slowly from side to side.

'C'mon, Ted. Spit it out.'

Without lifting up his face, he turned it in her direction. 'I – I don't know.'

'What do you mean you don't know what bothered you?'

He inhaled deeply and straightened his spine. 'It's not that. I know what bothered me. I just don't know what to do.'

'Is it your dad, Ted? Is that what it's about?'

'Yeah, I just realized that I've been in denial. He's worse off than I thought.'

'How? What happened?'

'I call him nearly every day, Lucinda. Most days he says, "Hi there, son. Long time since I've heard from you." He's slipping. And I saw his future in that lockdown unit and it tore me apart. I really do need to get up there and the sooner the better.'

'You need to talk to Ellen tonight.'

'Yeah, that'll be fun.'

'What, Ellen and your dad don't get along?'

'Oh, heck, that's not it. The two of them get along better than I often get along with either one of them. They love each other. When Ellen was in the psychiatric hospital, he drove down here to visit her every month.'

'Then what is it?'

'In there, I realized I need her help with Dad and I'm afraid she won't be willing to give it to me.'

Eli Kendlesohn spoke to the funeral home and made arrangements for his mother's body to be transported back for her service and burial. He agreed to meet the man on the phone the next morning to select a casket and take care of other details including the financial matters.

Rachael walked into the room in the middle of his conversation. When he returned the receiver to the cradle, she said, 'Why are you going to all that trouble and expense?'

'Rachael, what do you mean? We can't just leave Mother at the morgue and pretend she didn't exist.'

'Don't be an ass, Eli. What I mean is: why are you wasting all the money transporting her body and buying a casket?'

'What do you want? You want me to bring her home in the trunk of my car and bury her in the backyard?'

'Oh, God forbid!' Rachael snapped. 'You'd spend every moment you were home, moping by her graveside. If you hadn't been so attached to that batty woman, we could have sent her away months ago and not have to deal with all of this now.'

'But we do have to deal with it, Rachael. And it *will* cost money. There is no way to avoid that. But, don't worry, there's no need for you to curtail your spending habits.'

'Of course it will cost money, but it doesn't need to take that big of a chunk out of your inheritance. Call them back. Tell them you changed your mind. Have her cremated in Norfolk and they can ship the ashes back here – or just dump them in the ocean.'

'You are heartless!' Eli exclaimed.

'Heartless – not hardly. I'm sensible. Practical. Something you, with all your fancy business titles and Italian suits, never have been. Speaking of practical, have you called the life insurance company yet?'

'OK, Rachael, you want practical. How's this? There is a double stone where my dad is buried and the spot next to it – already paid for – is intended for my mother. The marker is even engraved with her name and birth date – all it needs is the date of her death. Some of what might have been my inheritance was spent on that tiny piece of property and the plaque – we sure wouldn't want that to go to waste, would we?'

'You're ridiculous, Eli. Bringing her back here for burial is just throwing good money after bad. It's a waste. And I expect your darling sister won't want to pay any of the expense and yet will expect a share of the estate.'

'Of course, she will. She is entitled to half of it and she'll get it.'

'Oh, fine. We sacrifice our freedom, our privacy, our everything to give your mother a place in our home. Your sister? She flies in for an occasional weekend and then whisks off to some remote corner of the world to have fun and adventure. Now she expects to be paid for being so negligent!'

'Negligent? Fun and adventure? She's doing her job, Rachael. She's an international news correspondent. She can't do that from down the block.'

'Well, what she does is a lot more fun than slipping into the yoke of your father's business and working yourself to an early grave. She didn't stay here for that now, did she?'

'But I wanted to take over the business; she didn't. I'm glad she didn't. I'm glad she's got a job she loves. I'm glad she's not saddled down with someone like you,' Eli said.

'How dare you?'

'Please, don't say another word. I'm going to the cemetery to visit Dad. Then I'll drive around for a while. I don't know when I'll be back.'

Of course, Rachael did not heed his admonition to be quiet. Her voice followed him to the garage and into his car. He switched on the radio, turned it to a jazz station and tuned out her voice.

But he couldn't tune out thoughts of her. *Maybe that's why a homicide detective came to our house? Maybe they think we had something to do with mother's disappearance and death? I know I didn't. That leaves Rachael. And quite frankly, nothing she would do could surprise me.*

TWENTY-ONE

Lucinda had requested a list of disgruntled former employees from all three facilities she visited that day. She was delighted to see that River's Edge had already sent a fax and one of the others had emailed a response.

She did a background check on the five names and discovered that one was in prison – and had been for nearly a year; another was in Iraq working for a private security firm for even longer – *God help the Iraqis* – leaving her with three people to interview. She printed out the most recent addresses for all of them and left the office less than twenty minutes after her arrival.

She stopped first at the home of Bobbi Reynolds. It was a small but well-kept brick rancher. The sixty-year-old woman who greeted her at the door could have been described in exactly the same way.

When Lucinda asked about her departure from River's Edge, she said, 'It was my supervisor. She and I never saw eye to eye on anything. I really thought that some of the folks in the lockdown unit would be fine for a short visit off the grounds. I took one woman to a shoe store – on my own time, mind you – and she picked out a pair of walking shoes. She said it was the first time she'd had a pair that fit right in two years.

'My supervisor didn't think that was appropriate – didn't care how happy I'd made the woman. She fired me the moment we walked back into the unit.'

'Do you often buck rules?' Lucinda asked.

'Only when they don't make a lick of sense.'

'Does that happen often?'

The woman laughed. 'Yeah, haven't you noticed?'

Although Lucinda agreed with her, she didn't let the other woman know. 'How far would you go to break a rule you didn't think made any sense?'

'What do you mean? Give me a fer-instance.'

'OK. Let's say you were still working at River's Edge and

you thought one of the lockdown residents did not need to be there. Would you help that person escape?'

'There were a few folks that didn't seem like they needed to be there a good part of the day – but then they'd have their bad moments, usually in the late afternoon, early evening. We called it sun-downing. But I don't recall anyone that I was certain didn't belong there at all.'

'But what if you did?' Lucinda pushed.

'I never thought about that. But, yeah, I guess if that were the case and I'd tried the proper channels without getting any result. Particularly if that old bat supervisor said, "It doesn't matter what *you* think" again, I might help a person like that escape. It kinda seems unlikely to me, though. But why are you asking – did something happen at River's Edge?'

'No. No. Just trying to cover all the bases on some missing elderly.'

'Nice story but I know you're lying. I saw your badge; it said "homicide". Just what are you doing? Somebody died, huhn? And they're trying to pin it on me?'

'No, ma'am, no one is trying to pin anything on you.'

'OK, right. I don't think I should talk any more without a lawyer. I think you should leave.'

Lucinda walked out of the house without objection but when she slipped into her car, she put a little star by Bobbi Reynolds's name. *Two possible suspects – and both women. I can't imagine Rachael Kendlesohn picking Bobbi Reynolds as a partner in a conspiracy but neither one of them could have delivered Edgar Humphries's body without help.*

At her next stop, she found a man in a wheelchair. He told her he was angry when he was let go for not being able to do his job any longer. He said he even uttered some nasty remarks that could have been taken as threats. 'But, as you see,' he said with a shrug, 'they were right. I was no longer capable of doing the job. Just six months later and I can't even get around on my own.'

The third former employee, Jeremy Stanford, was the one who Lucinda saw as the most troublesome of the bunch from the start. He got canned for drinking on the job, had been picked up twice for driving under the influence and he had shown up drunk at his former place of employment on a number of occasions – once they had to call the police to get him to leave.

She pulled up in front of a Cape Cod house where the lawn was covered with matted-down tall plant material, gone to seed. The winter's snowfall was the only reason the weeds weren't poking up higher than the chain-link fence. A mockingbird perched on the rim of a dry bird bath singing a long, heady tune filled with sounds borrowed from multiple birds. When Lucinda opened the gate, he looked in her direction, bobbed his tail twice and flew off. She walked up the sidewalk thinking about the snakes, rats and other things that could easily be hiding in the mess on either side.

She rang the doorbell but got no response even though she could hear the blare of a television. She knocked on the door lightly but that didn't seem to stir anyone to action either. She beat on the door with her fist and it creaked open. She called out his name.

The only response she heard sounded like a strange series of animal snorts and snarls. It was hard to hear over the loud noise of squealing wheels and car crashes from the TV. She yelled out again. The animal noise choked off, then started up again, sounding like someone struggling to breathe. *Should I call for backup? Nah, could be nothing. But, then again . . .* She pulled her gun as she stepped across the threshold. She flattened her back against the wall by the archway to the other room. Leading with her gun, she curled around the edge of the wall, her good eye darting into every corner.

At first, it appeared to be an empty room – the only movement was the wild, unrealistic car chase on the large screen on the opposite wall. Then she saw toes sticking up on the raised footrest of a recliner.

She shouted, 'Police. Raise your hands in the air.'

The only response was another grunting, snorting animal sound, which she now recognized as a particularly loud snore. She sighed. Keeping her gun at the ready, she circled around the recliner until she had a full view of the occupant.

An empty bottle of rum was canted sideways in his lap. Drool slid down one side of his mouth. Black bristles sprouted on a pale white chin. She moved closer but the smell drove her back. He stunk of rum and sweat and dirty feet. She slipped her weapon back in the holster.

'Sir,' she shouted. 'Wake up, it's the police.'

His body jerked, his lower lip pulled to one side and bleary eyes squinted in her direction. 'Wha – wha – wha – I din do nuffin, occifer. Jes' mindin' m'own bidness.'

'Does anyone else live here with you?'

'Live here? Wit me? Naw. Naw. De all left me. Long time ago. Ya wanna live here wit me?' he asked, his mouth stretching into a distorted grin.

Oh, good grief, he doesn't look capable of tying his own shoes, let alone taking part in a crime. He probably couldn't get out to the mailbox without help. But, she still had to talk to him and she doubted if he'd get sober without assistance. She hated the thought of putting him in the back seat of her car. She thought about calling for a patrol unit to take him in to sleep it off. But that felt too wimpy.

'Come on, Mr Sanford. Stand up. I'd like to talk to you down at the station. Want to take a ride with me?' She almost cuffed him but thought better of it. Likely, it would be easier coaxing him to her car if she didn't. And as drunk as he was, she knew if he tried to get away she could run him down – he probably wouldn't get more than two feet without falling on his face.

She shivered in revulsion as she wrapped a hand around one of his skinny arms. He let her lead him to the vehicle without causing any problems. Opening the rear door, she put a hand on his head to guide him safely inside.

His body stiffened, turning toward her, his lower lip stuck out further than his nose, and he said, 'You arrestin' me, girly?'

'Mr Sanford, wouldn't you be in handcuffs if I were arresting you?'

His brow furrowed as he blinked his eyes. He held his hands up before his face.

'I just want to take you on a little ride down to the Justice Center. Why don't you slide on in?' Lucinda coaxed.

'Oh,' he said, unlocking his knees and allowing her to ease him into the back seat.

TWENTY-TWO

Ted put his keys in the front door and mentally took a deep breath as he opened it and walked inside his home. He felt more awkward this evening than he'd felt even on his first date with Ellen when he'd had to face her controlling father, the judge.

He found his wife in the kitchen where she was tossing salad in a huge glass bowl. 'Hi, Ted,' she said, shooting him a smile over her shoulder.

'Where are the kids?' he asked.

'They are both spending the night with friends. I thought it would be good if we had some time alone.'

Ted swallowed involuntarily, felt a clamminess on his neck and sensed his testicles pull tight against his body as if trying to slip inside to hide. 'Really?' he said, his dry tongue clacking against the roof of his mouth.

She kept her back toward him and said, 'Yes, Ted. I think we really need to have a long talk and with the kids underfoot, I don't think that's possible.'

'A talk?'

She turned around and looked at him with a furrowed brow and half of a smile. 'Good grief, Ted. What did you think?' She flicked his arm with a red and white checked kitchen towel. 'Neither one of us are ready for anything more right now.'

'Oh,' he exhaled deeply.

Ellen shook her head at him. 'So typically male. Top of your mind is always sex even when you're not interested in having any. Go turn on the grille. I've got a pair of rib-eyes marinating, the potatoes are baking and I just finished with the salad. And before you ask, no, I am not getting out the candlesticks or the white tablecloth – absolutely no plans for a romantic evening, Ted. So you can relax.' She picked up the salad bowl and slid it into the refrigerator.

As he opened the back door, she said, 'Oh, another thing. I didn't say we need to talk because I want to bitch at you

about something. I just want to talk – about the kids, about
the future and about the conversation I had with your dad.'

Ted pulled the door shut and walked across the patio to the
gas grille. Lifting the lid, he sighed. *Relax. Oh sure. She throws
in the kids, my dad and she says 'relax'. And how did she
know I wanted to talk about the same things? She seems
to know what I'm thinking – she could always do that. There
was a time I appreciated it, but now it kinda creeps me out.*

He went back into the house, forcing a smile. 'Grille's
heating up.' He pulled out a chair and sat down at the kitchen
table.

'Good. Could I get you a beer, a glass of wine?' Ellen
asked.

'Yeah, sure. A beer would be great.'

Ellen pulled a Corona out of the refrigerator and poured a
glass of Lambrusco. She stuck a sliver of lime in the mouth
of the bottle and set it in front of Ted with a smile. 'Surprise!'

'Nice. Thanks,' he said but his anxiety level rose up another
notch. Corona was a treat and he wasn't sure of the meaning
behind it. He stared at the bottle watching beads of water
forming on the glass.

Ellen pulled the glass pan with the steaks and marinade out
of the refrigerator and noticed he hadn't touched his beer.
'What? You don't like Corona anymore?'

'Oh, yeah, sure,' he said, sticking an index finger on the
lime and popping it down into the bottle before lifting it to
his lips. He took a swig but the lump of dread in his throat
made it difficult to swallow. 'I'll put the steaks on.' He took
the pan from her hands and walked back out on to the porch.
He hoped he could stay out there, away from Ellen, until they
were done.

He sighed as the door opened and Ellen stepped out, his
beer in one hand, her glass of wine in the other. 'It's awfully
nice out for so early in the spring.'

Ted grunted, accepted his beer and forced down another
swallow. Ellen still seemed cheery. The breezier she became,
the more uptight Ted felt. He wished she would go back inside.
A ding from the timer on the stove was the answer to his
prayer.

'Ah, the potatoes should be ready. I'll poke them and see.
A couple more minutes on the steaks?'

'Yeah,' Ted said.

She went inside and popped back out too quickly for Ted's comfort. 'They're done. I turned off the oven. How about the steaks?'

Ted lifted the lid and flipped the meat. If he left them on another minute, they'd be overdone. He sighed. 'Yeah, looks like they are.' He lifted them on to a plate and turned off the gas.

'Terrific,' Ellen said, opening the door and holding it for him. In the kitchen, she served both of them. They took seats at the kitchen table across from one another. Ellen chewed a bite of salad, while Ted used a fork to toy with a slice of radish in his bowl.

'I called your dad this morning,' Ellen said.

'That's nice.'

'We talked for about fifteen minutes. Well, to be honest, I did most of the talking but he did say he was doing fine and planned on taking a walk in the park.'

'That's nice.'

'I thought so, too. But then, about ten minutes after that call, he called me.'

'Really. Did he forget something?'

'He forgot *everything*, Ted.'

'Everything?'

'Yes. He said, "Sure been a long time since I heard the sound of your voice so I thought I'd give you a call." At first, I thought he was joking. But then I realized that he'd already forgotten the phone call – just ten minutes later. I'm worried about him, Ted.'

Ted's anxiety eased a little. She was giving him the opening he wanted. 'That doesn't surprise me, Ellen. I've been worried about him, too.'

'I don't think he should be living alone any longer.'

'I know,' Ted agreed.

'I think we need to do something about it, right away.'

'You're right.'

'I figured if we were really careful with our spending, we could make it until you found a job or we sold this house – whichever came first.' She split her baked potato in two, added a pat of butter, a spoonful of sour cream and sprinkled on a pinch of chopped chives.

Ted squirmed, realizing Lucinda was right. He should have talked to Ellen weeks ago. 'I already have a job.'

'I know you have a job here, Ted, but I thought you might be able to find a similar position up there with the police or the sheriff's department. Sure, you might have to take a cut in pay – it is a smaller city but—'

'No, Ellen. I've got a job offer up near Dad – in Charlottesville – at the Regional Computer Forensics Lab. And actually it's a pay increase and a better health insurance plan, too, since I'll be a federal employee.'

'And you didn't tell me?'

'I was planning on talking to you about it tonight.'

'How long have you known?'

'Just a few days. I've been thinking. I thought maybe I ought to take it and move up there and take care of Dad.'

Ellen stabbed a forkful of potato and brought it to her mouth. She picked up her steak knife and carved off a piece of her steak and chewed on it as she stared out the window.

Ted sensed the fragility in the air. He dared not say a word fearing it would shatter the evening – and maybe his life.

Ellen set down her fork. 'So, what about me and the kids? How did we fit into your plans?'

Ted ran his hand through his hair, then brought it down, across his mouth.

'Well, Ted?'

'I, uh, I . . .'

'You were planning on moving up there without us.'

Ted hung his head and nodded.

'Have you lost your mind, Ted?'

Ted opened his mouth but could not form a word. He shrugged in silence.

'How did you expect to take care of your father and work at the same time?'

'I – I don't know. Hire someone to look after him during the day if necessary.'

'That is so stupid. I'm not working. I can take care of him.'

But, you and I – we're not – I mean . . .'

'Ted. Listen. In your father's big rambling house, we could each have our own bedroom – that sure beats you sleeping on the sofa like you're doing now. Maybe in time, we'll get back to where we were before we lost the baby. Maybe we won't. Maybe we'll just live like a brother and sister taking care of your dad and the kids. But I love your dad. I want to take care of him. And the kids – they need you.'

'I don't know about that.'

'You think the kids don't need you?'

He shrugged.

'Oh, good grief. Yes, the kids need you. Yes, I enjoy your company. And yes, I want to help you with your dad. So, what is the problem? Oh!' The color drained from Ellen's face. 'Is there someone else? If there is, that's OK. I understand. I can see why—'

'No, Ellen. There is no one else. And before you ask, there is nothing going on between me and Lucinda.'

'Ted, I wasn't going to ask. I'll be honest – if you got involved in a relationship with her – or anyone – it would bother me because I do still have hope that our marriage can be repaired and renewed. But if you've had enough or if we just can't recreate our former bond, I can accept that. In fact, I promise you, I will leave without a fuss the moment you ask me to do so. I just think right now, we need to be there for your dad – and it will take the both of us. And the kids? They don't completely trust me yet. I left them for months. I was institutionalized and had no choice – but they don't understand that – they just know I left them. You are the security in their lives. They need you, Ted, as much as they did while I was gone.'

'You really think so?'

'Yes, Ted, I know so.'

'You're OK with being Dad's caregiver?'

'Aside from the fact that I wish he did not need one – yes, totally. He has been wonderful to me since before we were married. He's a great guy and the children love him, too. It's going to be hard for the kids to transfer in the middle of the second semester at school but I don't think it's wise to leave your dad alone until then.'

'Maybe I can go up right away and you can come up when the school year is out?'

'How would that work?' Ellen asked.

'There must be a way. I'll accept the job – I don't think they want me to start for a month so that solves the problem for a short while. And during that time, I'll look for an adult day care center, home care nurse or nurse's aide, whatever – the solution might be expensive but it'll only be short term.'

Ellen nodded. 'We can do this, Ted. We can make it work as long as we need to.'

'I hope we can. But if I start showing my ass, you'll have to speak up.'

She threw her head back and laughed. 'Oh, that so won't be a problem.'

TWENTY-THREE

Lucinda started her morning in an interview room at the county jail. She sat in a wooden chair on the far side of a metal table. Jeremy Sanford shuffled through the door a few minutes later. He looked better than he had the night before, but even if you shaved his stubble, combed his hair and put on clean clothes, he wouldn't be winning any blue ribbons.

'Good morning, Mr Sanford,' Lucinda said.

Sanford narrowed his eyes. 'Prove it.'

'Have a seat, sir. I just have a few questions.'

'First you answer a few of mine. Last I remember, I was sitting, watching TV in the comfort of my home. Then I wake up in this hellhole. What's up with that?'

'I had some questions for you, Mr Sanford. Asked you to come down to the station with me and you did.'

'Why am I still here?'

'Because, sir, it is department policy not to interview anyone under the influence. So I had to wait until you slept it off.'

'And I couldn't get a private room? You wanted to ask me questions and I had to spend the night with that guy?' Jeremy wiped his hand across his mouth.

'You didn't like your room-mate? Why is that?'

'He wasn't white.'

Lucinda wanted to tell him what she thought of that statement but she didn't want to prolong the interview. The odor wafting from Jeremy's unwashed body had intensified overnight. 'Do you have a job, Mr Sanford?'

'No. Bastards fired me from my last one and they been bad-mouthing me any time I apply for another. I oughta sue the sunsabitches.'

'I thought you were let go for drinking on the job, Mr Sanford.'

'I was. So what? I weren't the only one hit the bottle. Takin' care of those demandin' little biddies rubs on your last nerve.'

'What did you do there?'

'I bussed tables in the dining room. Cleaned up trash in the courtyard. Cleaned up messes wherever they made 'em. But did they ever notice? Hell, no. They just bitched about what I hadn't done yet. Gettin' fired there was the best thing that ever happened to me. A man can only take so much.'

'Then, why did you go back there, Mr Sanford?'

'Not 'cause I wanted my job back but 'cause I just needed a job – and because of them, I couldn't get one. I wanted them to shut up and stop bad-mouthin' me.'

'Did you threaten them?'

'Well, yeah. Wouldn't you? I told 'em to shut the fuck up for I'd be siccin' a lawyer on 'em.'

'Did you ever consider any more drastic action, Mr Sanford?'

'Like what?'

'Think about it, Mr Sanford. You know bad things sometimes go down in the workplace.'

Jeremy laughed, slapped the table and laughed again. 'You mean like, I go in there with an Uzi and start firin' the place up. Now that would be sumthin'. But, nah, I ain't the violent type and I don't like the sight of blood – paper cuts give me the heebie-jeebies.'

'Did you ever meet the folks who brought in an elderly parent to look the place over?'

'Yeah, right. Like they introduce me to the rich folks comin' in there. Nah, see here was the rules: you see visitors, you make yourself scarce. You – the mop, the bucket, whatever – need to be gone, gone, gone. Don't want to let any reality crowd in on the perfect little home for Mom and Dad.'

'Did you know a man named Edgar Humphries?'

'He a patient?'

'No. He was on the waiting list.'

'Don't think so. Sure didn't meet him at River's Edge if he was just visiting. If I met him anyplace else, don't remember. Name don't ring a bell.'

'How about Francis DeLong?'

'Nah,' he said with a shake of his head.

'Adele Kendlesohn?'

Jeremy shrugged.

'Is there anyone you worked with that didn't seem quite right to you?'

'Most of 'em,' he said with a snort.

'Seriously, Mr Sanford. Anyone who seemed inappropriate with visiting families or with any of the residents?'

'The people that didn't seem normal to me is the ones who seemed to like working there. Couldn't figure that out – too much smell of old in the air, too much paranoia from the ones who was losing it, too much end of the road vibes everywhere you turned. You wanna pick somebody who might do something crazy to those old folks, look to one of them fools who're smilin' all the time. Them's the ones who are gonna crack and start shoot the place up or injectin' nasty drugs into folk's arms.'

'You ever hear of any abductions?'

'Abduction? You mean like kidnappin'?'

'Yes, sir.'

'Listen, lady, those folks are in there 'cause their kids don't want 'em around anymore. Now what good would it do to kidnap them? Those kids ain't gonna pay a ransom to get 'em back – they don't want 'em in the first place. So, that's what happened? Old folks gettin' snatched? Damn, you can scratch me off that list. Last thing I want is to bring one of them old codgers home. Can I go now? I'm in serious need of a cure for my hangover.'

'Yes, sir, Mr Sanford. But stay away from River's Edge from now on.'

'Tell 'em to stop bad-mouthin' me.'

Lucinda rolled her eyes and knocked on the glass. *This was a waste of time. Where do I go from here?*

TWENTY-FOUR

The morning felt chilly when Layla DiBlasio stepped outside but after jogging a block, the temperature seemed just right. She hadn't worn her iPod today. She wanted to hear the birdsong and appreciate the flowers rather than get lost in the music.

She'd run half a mile, turned, run a block and took another corner, halfway to home. She was just three blocks from the next turn when she saw her friend Rosemary's mother-in-law, Juliet Szykely, walking out of the house near the end of the block with a man in navy-blue hospital scrubs. *I hope she's not sick.*

She was only a block away from Rosemary's home when Juliet stopped at the junction of the private sidewalk and the public one. She flapped her hands at her escort. He waved his arms around, talking to her. She shook her head back and forth.

The man grabbed her elbow and pulled. Juliet shrieked. Layla broke into a sprint. 'Hey, hey you! What are you doing?'

He looked up at Layla and gave one last tug on Juliet before running to a white cargo van parked at the curb. Layla pulled out the paper and pencil she always brought along on her jogs and wrote down the name of the logo on the door of the van: Franklin Medical Transport. Then she jotted down the license plate number as the driver sped off far too quickly for the quiet residential street.

'Ms Szykely, are you OK? Do you remember me?' Layla asked, approaching the older woman with slow, smooth movements.

The fright drained from Juliet's eyes and she nodded her head. 'You're a friend.'

'Yes, I'm Rosemary's friend,' she replied. 'My name is Layla.'

'I'm not supposed to leave the yard. Jeff said I can stay here if I don't leave the yard unless I'm with him or Rosemary. I didn't leave the yard.'

'I know. I'll tell them – I'll make sure they know. Who was that man?'

Juliet shook her head. 'He said Jeff sent him. He said I needed to go to the doctor. I said I needed to call Rosemary first. He said we'd call with his cell. Then he tried to make me leave the yard. I can't leave the yard. But he wouldn't listen.'

'Well, don't worry about it. Let's go into the house. I need to make some phone calls. OK?'

'Pierce,' Lucinda said as she picked up the phone.

'Lieutenant, you said you wanted to know about anything strange involving elderly people?'

'Sure did.'

'There was an attempted abduction of an old lady over at 907 Dogwood Court.'

'Thanks. Call Sergeant Butler in Missing Persons. Tell him to meet me out in the parking lot right away – or if that's not possible to meet me over there.'

'Got it!'

Lucinda raced down the stairs and to her car. She backed out of her parking space and looked around for Jumbo. She spotted him running out the door as quickly as his short legs would carry him, his red hair flying in all directions. *A harried leprechaun chasing down the last bowl of Lucky Charms*. She stifled a laugh.

He pulled open the door and hopped in the front seat, panting. Lucinda jerked forward out of the lot and over to the quiet of the Green Forest subdivision. The community was designed with curvy roads surrounded by lots of trees carefully preserved during the construction phase. All the streets were named after trees or woodland flowers and shrubs. It wasn't the kind of place where the police were often required.

The house was easy to spot; two patrol cars and an unmarked were in front of it, parked by the curb. She pulled up behind them. She was pleased when she saw Sergeant Robin Colter standing in the front yard. Lucinda had worked with her on other cases and trusted her instincts. After passing her sergeant's exam, Robin worked home break-ins and burglaries most of the time. Both women hoped that she would snag the next opening in Homicide.

Smiling, Lucinda called out to her, 'Hey, Colter. What are you doing here?'

Robin looked up the sidewalk and returned the smile. 'I was just a couple of blocks away when the call came in and ended up being the first one on the scene. And what about you? I haven't seen any dead bodies lying around.'

'I've got three senior citizens who were missing and have now turned up dead under suspicious circumstances. I told Dispatch to put me on the hot list for any crimes against the elderly. Sergeant Butler here is from Missing Persons.'

Robin stuck out her hand. 'Sergeant Colter,' she said.

'Just call me Jumbo,' he replied, grasping her hand in his.

Robin gave Lucinda a sideways glance. Lucinda's lips struggled to subdue the urge to laugh. Robin looked down at the sidewalk, cleared her throat, and said, 'Odd situation here.' She briefed the two detectives on what had happened and directed them into the house where the witness and the potential victim were waiting.

Inside, Lucinda and Jumbo shook hands with Layla and turned to Juliet. The elderly woman blurted out, 'I can't leave the front yard unless I'm with Rosemary or Jeff. I told him that. He just wouldn't listen.'

'I am so sorry about that, ma'am. You never saw that man before?'

Juliet pursed her lips and shook her head. 'Never. Never. I can't always remember names but I don't forget faces. Do I?' she asked, turning to Layla.

'She always recognizes me,' Layla affirmed.

At a jerk of Lucinda's head, Jumbo sat down next to Juliet and started talking to her. Lucinda drew Layla out into the foyer. 'So really,' Lucinda asked, 'how good is she with faces?'

'I'm not sure. She seems to recognize everyone she's known for a while. But can she recall someone she met for the first time last month or even last week? I'm not sure. Rosemary should know better. She's on the way.'

'She's the daughter-in-law?' Lucinda asked.

'Yes. She has more workday flexibility than Jeff – she's the sales manager for a radio station, he teaches high school history. I left word for him at the school but I'm not sure when or if he'll be able to get away.'

Layla recounted her morning to Lucinda. 'I thought maybe

I'd overreacted. Maybe he was supposed to take Juliet to the
doctor and I scared him off? But I called Rosemary and she
said no one was scheduled to come by the house. That's when
I called you guys.'

'We have a bulletin out on the vehicle but the license plate
number you gave us belongs to an older Nissan Sentra. Are
you sure you got the letters and numbers right?' Lucinda asked.

'Absolutely. I was close enough and quick enough to double
check it before he was out of sight. Stolen plates or a computer
glitch?'

'Could be either or neither – we're looking into it. And the
sign on the door of the van? You got a good look at that, too?'

'Yes. It looked like one of those magnetic signs you just
stick on.'

'Do you recall any additional details about the man?'

'No, sorry. At first, I was focused on Juliet. Then when he
got in the van, I was paying more attention to the vehicle
itself than the driver.'

'And you saw no one else?'

'No. But with a cargo van, who knows who could be inside?
But the sliding door was open – he drove off without shut-
ting it – and I didn't see anyone else, but—'

Suddenly, a harried blonde in a dark-gray suit and matching
heels crossed the threshold of the house, shouting out, 'Where
is she? Where is Mom?'

'Your mother-in-law—' Lucinda began.

'Yes, yes, yes. My mother-in-law. Where is she?'

Lucinda gestured into the living room where Juliet and
Jumbo sat with their heads close together. They both turned
toward the noise and a broad smile stretched across the
old woman's face. 'Rosemary,' she said.

Rosemary walked over to Juliet's chair, knelt in front of
her and took hold of both of her hands. 'Are you OK, Mom?'

'Yes.'

'You're sure? That man didn't hurt you?'

Juliet turned toward Jumbo with a furrowed brow. 'No. We
were just talking. About the war. And the rationing. He said
we can have all the butter and stockings we want now.'

Rosemary inhaled deeply and forced a smile. 'That's right,
Mom. No problems with butter or stockings. Well, I'll let you
two chat.' She pushed up on her knees, stood upright and

walked back to the foyer. 'Oh man, Layla, I don't think she remembers what happened,' she said shaking her head. Rosemary gave her friend a hug. 'Thanks so much for coming to her rescue. I don't know what would have happened if you hadn't been here at the right time. Jeff and I are going to have to have a long talk. It's just not safe for her to live here any longer unless one of us stops working.'

'What about that woman you called?' Layla asked.

'Oh, yes, Dorothy Jenkins. I talked to her on the phone and I was seriously considering that possibility. But she's pretty old, too. I thought she would be great social interaction for Juliet, but now I think she could have been overpowered herself if she were here. I think we're going to have to find a placement.'

'Have you and your husband discussed that possibility?' Lucinda interjected.

Rosemary looked over, eyebrows arching as if surprised to see someone else in the foyer. 'And you are?'

Lucinda slipped out her badge, flipped it open and said, 'Lieutenant Pierce.'

Rosemary studied Lucinda, her eyes sliding from side to side as if trying to memorize every detail of her face.

Although uncomfortable with the scrutiny, Lucinda stood without speaking until the stare broke away. 'Ms Szykely, have you visited any senior facilities for possible placement?'

'A few. It just hadn't seemed necessary right away.'

'Did you have her wait-listed?'

'At one place, just because it had such a long list and it was Mom's favorite.'

'And where was that?' Lucinda asked.

'River's Edge.'

Coincidence? I doubt it. The only place where all five are wait-listed. But what could the motive be? An employee with a grudge? A family member with someone further down on the waiting list? But surely that list is not public information.

She realized that Rosemary and Layla were both looking at her with expectant faces. 'I'm sorry. I got lost in thought. Did you ask me a question?'

'Yes. Is there a problem with River's Edge?' Rosemary asked.

'Not to my knowledge,' Lucinda answered.

'C'mon, Lieutenant,' Layla urged. 'What are you holding back? When Rosemary said River's Edge, I could almost see a comic strip light bulb pop up over your head.'

'Just stirred up a random thought – sorry, my mind simply went elsewhere,' Lucinda said with a smile she hoped was convincing. Slipping two cards out of her pocket, she handed one to each of the women. 'Let me know if you spot anything that looks the least bit suspicious in the neighborhood. And think about the last two weeks, try to recall anything that, on reflection, seems odd or out of place.' Turning away from the women, she said, 'Sergeant Butler, you about ready to go?'

Lucinda walked out to her car, punching in Ted's number as she walked. 'Ted, could you contact Jenna in the sales department at River's Edge and let her know that you need a full employee roster. We need to do a background check on everyone who works there.'

'Are we looking for anything in particular?'

'I'm sure we are but I don't know what it is. I do know I have three dead senior citizens, one missing one and the attempted abduction of yet another. And every single one of them – all five – were wait-listed at River's Edge. And when you talk to Jenna ask her about her waiting list. Ask her about confidentiality. Ask her who has access to it.'

'You got it, Lucinda. Listen, I had a great talk with Ellen last night – we've got a plan. I'll clue you in when you get back here.'

'If I get back there.'

'Sounds like you've got hold of something.'

'It may be nothing but I'm going to hang on to it until it turns to dust. Later, Ted – thanks a lot.'

Jumbo slid into the passenger seat. 'Sorry to keep you waiting – Juliet didn't want to let me leave.'

'You sure have a way with the ladies, Sergeant – they never seem to want to let you go.'

'Yeah, my charm works magic with the ladies old enough to be my mother or my grandmother. Women my age or younger look over the top of my head and never realize I'm there.'

'I'm going to head over to the address we have for the license plate on the white van that belongs to another car. You need to get back to the Justice Center or do you have time to track down the owner with me?'

Jumbo pulled out his cellphone and glanced at the screen. 'No messages. Let's roll – I'm a sucker for the unknown.'

'Don't get your hopes up. We'll probably find a ratty little Nissan that's sitting up on concrete blocks.'

TWENTY-FIVE

Lucinda pulled into a sorry-looking street lined with brick terraced houses built in the post-Second World War housing boom. Porch roofs sagged, wrought-iron railings rusted, and assorted junk littered most of the teeny front yards. Here and there, a few residents demonstrated house pride or gardening love with pretty porches and tended flower beds behind short edging. The address they sought was one of the saddest-looking homes in the block.

Jumbo waited on the sidewalk while Lucinda stepped up on the porch and pressed the doorbell by the front door. While she waited, she noticed the mail protruding out of the wall-mounted mailbox. The envelopes yellowed and curled from exposure to the elements. When she got no response, she pulled out the papers secured between the screen door and the jamb.

'Interesting,' she said as she thumbed through them.

'Whatcha got?' Jumbo asked.

'A UPS delivery attempt notice but the date and any other handwritten information that might have been written on the paper is now long gone. There's disconnection notices for the electricity, the gas and the water. And a piece of paper that appears as if it might have once been a note but it's totally illegible now. Doesn't look too promising,' she said before pounding her fist on the door.

A woman, wiping her hands on a red checked apron tied around her waist, stepped out on the porch of the home next door. 'You're wasting your time. Nobody's been in or out of that place since . . . well, I can't remember when. It's been a long time.'

'Did you know your neighbor?'

'Knew him to say "hi", not much more.' She narrowed

her eyes. 'Who are you anyway? Why are you looking for him?'

'I'm Lieutenant Pierce, this is Sergeant Butler.'

'Police?'

'Yes, ma'am.'

'Is he in trouble?'

'No,' Lucinda said, even though it was looking more and more as if he was a serious person of interest. 'It's just that we found his stolen license plate.'

'Well, Gary sure never mentioned that to me.'

'Gary Blankenship?'

'Yeah, I think. I think that was his last name. Like I said, I only knew him in passing.'

'Did he live here alone?' Lucinda asked.

'A grown daughter and son lived here with him.'

'No wife or live-in girlfriend?'

'Not as far as I could tell.'

'Did he have many visitors?'

'There was a guy in his late twenties, I think. He used to come by a lot. I think Gary said that was his oldest son.'

'Do you recall what kind of car he drove?' Jumbo asked.

The woman looked over at Jumbo standing down on the sidewalk. At that lower elevation, he looked even shorter than he actually was. She scanned him up and down and then turned her attention to Lucinda. One side of her mouth curled up in half of a smile. 'So, tell me. How did they manage to pair you two up? Somebody like the Mutt and Jeff look? Or were they fans of the *Odd Couple*? Or did they just think the bad guys would fall down laughing and you wouldn't have to chase them?'

Grim-faced, Lucinda and Jumbo both crossed their arms tight across their chests. 'Ma'am, please answer Sergeant Butler's question.'

'Aw, c'mon. You've gotta see the humor in this – you're not blind. You've got a sense of humor, dontcha? A woman officer with a scarred-up face, tall enough to play professional basketball paired up with a little runt of a carrot-topped guy with cherub cheeks. C'mon.'

'Ma'am. We are conducting an investigation. You have been asked a question. Please answer it,' Lucinda demanded.

The woman sputtered out a laugh. 'Sorry. I forgot the

question.' Her eyes darted between Lucinda and Jumbo. 'Honest, c'mon. What was the question?'

'Do you remember what kind of car Mr Blankenship drove?'

Her brow furrowed for a moment and she said, 'Yeah, yeah, it was one of those little boxy cars.'

'You know the make or model?'

The woman rolled her eyes. 'Yeah, right. Can't say I even remember the color and I'm usually pretty good at that. I do know it was a dark color and usually covered with road dust or splattered with some of that red clay mud. Hey, listen, is that it? I got some stew cooking on the stove; I really need to check on it.'

'Let me give you my card first, in case you think of anything else about your neighbor.' Lucinda walked over to the other porch. As she handed it to her, she said, 'If he comes back here, or if you see any of his kids, call me right away, OK?'

'Sure,' she said, opening her screen door.

After she stepped inside, Jumbo said, 'What now?'

'Damned if I know. Seems like every time I turn around, I've got another thing on my list that requires waiting instead of doing.'

'I'll be glad to help in any way.'

'Tell you what,' Lucinda said, 'I need to follow up on an unrelated case. How about if I drop you off at the Justice Center on my way? First brief Ted – Sergeant Branson – on the situation we found here. Ask him if he can get the paperwork started on a search warrant for this house. Then, there should be a report on my desk about Gary Blankenship. If not, check with Research and see what's holding it up. When you've got it, make a copy of it and give it to Branson – it's bound to have something he can use. Then, look it over and give me a call if you find anything that looks worth pursuing.'

'You got it.'

'And those three kids his neighbor mentioned. See if you can find names and whereabouts for them. That tag was never reported stolen. Either he doesn't even know that it's missing or maybe one of his kids took it and he doesn't want to get them in trouble. There could be an innocent explanation but, at this point, I think it's more likely that we'll find Al Capone, alive and well, teaching Sunday School in Buenos Aires.'

*   *   *

After dropping off Jumbo, Lucinda reached over her seat and into the back, grabbing a file folder containing the documents she had about the woman who claimed Evan Spencer had beaten her up in his parking lot. Her name was Susan Jones and she lived out in the country on a street with a number instead of a name. She hoped she'd been able to find it before sunset.

It was in a tired rural area once filled with small family farms. Many of those families who were still there rented space to trailer homes that sprouted up along the roadside like weeds. Other farm land was running wild, seldom used driveways with tall grasses growing in the middle, houses at the end of them looked bedraggled, unloved, abandoned. There were a few exceptions. None of them appeared prosperous but some looked as if someone cared.

The mailbox with Susan Jones' number was one of them. A thin ribbon of close-cropped green ran up the center of a gravel driveway leading to a farmhouse that could use a fresh coat of paint but hadn't reached the cracking, peeling stage yet. She pulled her car to a stop beside a scarred up Silverado pick-up truck.

As soon as she stepped out of the car, she heard the yelling of a male voice. She hurried up on to the front porch. She rang the doorbell but didn't hear any sound of it echoing in the house. The yelling continued unabated; she could make out a word here and there, most of them profane. She pounded on the door with her fists. The yeller didn't break his stride.

A crash, a thump, a moan. Lucinda turned the door knob but it didn't give. She raced around to the back, pulling her gun. She banged on the kitchen door and the yelling stopped. She looked in the window and saw an elderly woman sprawled on the floor in front of the stove. She cracked open the door and yelled, 'Police!'

She heard pounding footsteps on the hardwood floor. She moved in that direction, her gun up and ready. She heard the click of a dead bolt latch, the creak of the door, more pounding footsteps, but now outside. A motor started, she raced on to the porch, heard a screech as the truck backed up fast, side-swiping her car. She shouted at the man to stop.

He looked back over his shoulder at her as he spun the

steering wheel. The truck jerked and surged forward, sending gravel flying through the air. She grabbed her cell, called in the vehicle description and license plate number, requested an ambulance and hurried back inside.

The woman was now sitting up with her back to the stove, cradling an arm that jutted out at an odd angle. She gave Lucinda a rueful smile. 'I just don't know what gets into me. I'm so blasted clumsy.'

'Clumsy?' Lucinda echoed in disbelief.

'Yeah, just look at that.' The woman nodded her head toward the far wall.

Lucinda turned in that direction. A glob of mashed potatoes slid slowly down the yellow wall leaving a white, lumpy trail with tiny streaks of brown gravy. On the floor lay a shattered white plate with a thin blue line around its edge that appeared worn and old as if it had served thousands of people in a small town diner over decades of use. Lying among the shards was a slice of meatloaf, scattered green beans flecked with bits of bacon and another lump of mashed potatoes topped with gravy.

'Yep. I ran into that wall, dropped the plate and I think I mighta broke my arm, too. I am so clumsy.'

Lucinda saw an empty plate with a fork and knife beside it on the kitchen table. On the opposite side, the utensils lay there alone. Over on the stove, a loaf pan held the rest of the meatloaf, a large pot was half-filled with beans, a smaller pan held still-bubbling gravy and a mound of mashed potatoes with a deep spoonful gouged out of the middle sat in a big bowl beside the stove.

'Who was here with you, Mrs Jones?'

'Nobody.'

'Nobody?'

'I was here by myself.'

'Then who ran through the house when I came in? Who drove off in the pick-up truck and scraped my car?'

Susan cocked her head to the side and said, 'What are you talking about?'

'Ma'am. I know someone was here. I suspect it was your son.'

'I was here, fixing supper, all by my lonesome. I don't know what you're talking about.'

'Mrs Jones, this is senseless. I know you were not here alone. I know you didn't just run into the wall.'

'I don't think you were here when that happened. Did you see the plate break?'

'Look at that plate, Mrs Jones. Look at it! It is shattered. And you expect me to believe you just bumped into the wall.'

'I bumped kinda hard.'

'What the hell were you doing, then? Running as fast as you could and plowing into the wall at top speed?'

'Of course not, silly. I just ran into the wall. People run into the wall all the time.'

Lucinda crouched down beside her. 'What's this, Mrs Jones? You have a split along your cheek line?'

'I got beat up by this doctor. You wouldn't believe—'

'This cut is more recent. As are these fingerprint marks on the upper part of your arm.'

'I'm telling you that doctor beat me up.'

'Why? Why did a doctor beat you up?'

'It was unbelievable. He was mad because we were crossing his parking lot.'

'That makes no sense.'

'I know. I had a doctor's appointment—'

'With Dr Spencer?'

'Oh, no, with Dr Cohle in the next building. But that parking lot was full. So we left the truck a block up the street. So we were just cutting across that parking lot when that Dr Spencer came out and went all nuts on us.'

'You didn't just get all clumsy and run into the dumpster,' Lucinda said, not being able to contain herself even though she knew her sarcasm was a total waste.

'No. Now that's ridiculous. That doctor beat me up and he's going to pay.'

'Pay? You mean like money?'

'Yeah, lots of money.'

'You filed criminal charges, Mrs Jones. The criminal court does not award monetary damages.'

'They don't?'

Lucinda shook her head.

'But, Cal told me . . .' she said then sealed her lips tight.

'What did Cal tell you?'

Susan pinched her lips tighter.

'Mrs Jones, do you know you can be arrested for false charges?'

Her eyes widened but still she did not speak.

'And as soon as we find Cal, he'll be arrested, too.'

'Why are you arresting Cal?'

'You have a broken arm, Mrs Jones. The abuse is obvious. And it is illegal.'

'I told you I just ran into the wall. You can't arrest Cal because I'm clumsy. And besides, no matter what you say, I'm not pressing charges against my son.'

'Under law, Mrs Jones, you don't need to do a thing. I would prefer if you would file charges and testify against the man who has broken your arm and probably brutalized you for years, but it's not necessary. In cases of domestic violence, the courts can act to protect you with or without your consent.'

Susan blinked and a tear trickled down her face.

'C'mon, you can tell me what happened,' Lucinda urged.

Susan's lower lip quivered. 'Nothing happened. I ran into the wall.'

Lucinda exhaled loudly and rose. 'The ambulance will be here soon,' she said. She clenched her jaw with frustration. Cases like this one drove her nuts. She had an urge to grab Susan and shake some sense into her but she knew it would do no good. She could only hope that the county would take the charges seriously and Susan would have enough time away from the bastard to come to her senses on her own.

Lucinda was standing by the front door watching for the arrival of the ambulance when her cellphone rang. 'Pierce.'

'It's Jumbo, Lieutenant. Found the names of all his children. Called their phone numbers. Two were disconnected. One was answered by a wife, Mrs Donald Blankenship – Charlotte Blankenship. She said she filed a missing persons report for her husband nearly two years ago – and, yes, I checked and she did.

'She thought that was why I was calling her. But she told me where her in-laws worked and her husband's brother Derek, sister Donna, and father Gary have not been seen at their places of employment for about the same amount of time Charlotte's husband's been missing.'

'What about their spouses?'

'She said that she never knew her mother-in-law. Family

told her Mom ran off with a man she met in a bar when the kids were little – haven't had a chance to follow up on that yet. And neither sibling was married. Well, her sister-in-law had been for a few months – a real nice guy according to Charlotte – but Donna walked out on him. "Just like her worthless mother," Charlotte said.'

TWENTY-SIX

As soon as the ambulance pulled away with Susan Jones, Lucinda followed it down the gravel drive and out to the highway. Her mind buzzed with the things she needed to do and the problems that needed solutions.

She thought she'd gotten Evan Spencer off the hook on the false charges filed against him but she'd have to find time to talk to the DA. She knew he'd be long gone by the time she got to the office; he was probably already home by now. *But where is this case going? Is the Blankenship clan connected to Joan Culpepper's missing mother, to the death of Edgar Humphries and the bodies of Francis DeLong and Adele Kendlesohn who turned up in that pond?*

What about Rachael Kendlesohn? Something about that woman isn't right. Is she simply a self-centered bitch or is it something more sinister? I'd like her to be responsible. I'd enjoy slapping cuffs on her wrists. But what if she is involved but only responsible for what happened to her mother-in-law? What if none of these cases are connected? Rachael's mother-in-law and Francis DeLong have to be connected. There's no way they would both be found in the same remote spot otherwise.

Could there be a conspiracy between Rachael Kendlesohn and DeLong's son-in-law Mark McFaden? Mark was very solicitous of his wife but what if that was an act, a cover-up of a crime? If he and Rachael acted together, then those two deaths wouldn't be connected to the attempted abduction of Juliet Szykely, the death of Edgar Humphries or the disappearance of Joan Culpepper's mother. But does that make sense?

Maybe there really are two scenarios here: the McFaden-Kendlesohn conspiracy and the other three cases that are all tied to Dorothy Jenkins. Her name popped up again this morning. But why? What motive could Dorothy Jenkins possibly have? She took care of one of them, met another one and only had a telephone conversation with a family member of the third.

Doesn't River's Edge make more sense? Yes. That facility is connected to all five. I wonder how Ted is progressing with those background checks.

I need to be careful. I can't get so caught up in the most recent suspects to forget about all the others. I can't afford tunnel vision. Everything has to be considered. Everyone explained. No possibility ignored, no matter how improbable. It seems impossible to follow all these threads at once, but I have to do it. Someone else might be abducted. Someone else might die.

Lucinda pulled into the parking lot of the Justice Center with no memory of the drive. She'd navigated on instinct, lost in her thoughts about the case. The realization hit her as she stepped out of her car and made her more than a little anxious.

She ran up the two flights of stairs and strode straight to Ted's office. 'Background checks. Anything interesting?'

'Not yet,' Ted said, 'but we're—'

'Search warrant?'

'Two, three minutes more, it'll be ready for the judge.'

'Butler?'

'Sergeant Butler? What about him?'

'Where is he?'

'I don't know. He might be in Research, might be in his office. But he left a note on your desk.'

'Thanks,' she said, spun on her heels and walked out.

Ted stepped into the hallway. 'Lucinda . . .?'

'Later, Ted. Bring me the warrant request when you print it out.'

Lucinda picked Jumbo's note off of her desk and read: 'Got Research looking for information about Charlotte's mother-in-law. Plan to make phone calls on anything they turn up. I'll call if I need to pay anyone a visit. Jumbo.'

Lucinda forced all thoughts out of her mind but the warrant. She had to get it. She reviewed the arguments she would make to the judge as she waited for Ted. True to his word, he popped in minutes later.

'Here you go,' he said. 'Judge Glass is still in his chambers working late reviewing appeals documents.'

'Judge might have a question for you – are you coming with me?'

'Anything, any time, Lucinda.'

As they walked down the stairs, Ted said, 'Actually, Lucinda, what I said wasn't exactly true.'

'What? What's not true?'

'I won't be able to do anything, any time for much longer. I've decided to take the job up in Charlottesville.'

'Really?'

'Yes. But I haven't given notice yet so if you could keep quiet about it . . .'

'No problem, Ted. In fact, right now, I don't have the brain space to even think about it.'

Everything went smoothly with the judge – the warrant was signed; now it needed to be delivered. Lucinda called Marguerite Spellman's cellphone. 'Marguerite, are you in the building?'

'No, Lieutenant. I'm at home. But that's not a problem. What do you need?'

'I've got a search warrant. I need the place scoured for any biological evidence that any one of four different people ever spent any time in there. And if there are any signs of anything suspicious.'

'Do we need a document specialist?'

'Wouldn't hurt. I'm bringing Butler from Missing Persons with me but depending on how much paper is there, it would be helpful to have another pair of eyes.'

'You got it. Anything else I need to know.'

'There's no electricity and no running water.'

'I'll pack the truck accordingly, Lieutenant. Should be able to be on the scene in an hour and fifteen minutes – or maybe less.'

Next, Lucinda called Jumbo. 'I've got a search warrant for the Blankenship place and the crime scene techs are gearing up to meet us at the house. I'm assuming you want to be there.'

'You better believe it.'

'Did you find anything about the woman of the household?'

'Yeah, but not much. Charlotte's mother-in-law is Sadie Blankenship – been missing for twenty years. Her youngest son, Derek, was barely a year old at the time. Gary did tell everyone she ran off with another man but I found two of Sadie's old friends. They said they didn't know that Sadie had a boyfriend and never knew her to hang out in bars. They also said they hadn't heard from her since – and one of the women was still finding that hard to believe.'

'Any evidence Sadie is still alive?'

'We share the same suspicious thoughts, Lieutenant. I've been looking into that. Sadie didn't renew her Virginia driver's license so I put out a bulletin to all the states with her married name and maiden name to see if she got a new one. No record of her having any credit cards in her name – one of her friends said that Gary wouldn't have allowed that. Said Sadie didn't even have a checkbook, or access to the bank account. Only money she ever had was the cash she got from Gary.'

'Hopefully, somebody will turn up something. But this just isn't looking very good.'

'No, it isn't,' Jumbo said. 'Are we ready to roll?'

'Meet you in the parking lot in five. Maybe that house will be hiding something that will lead us to Sadie.'

TWENTY-SEVEN

Before leaving the Justice Center, Lucinda called Dispatch and arranged for uniformed backup. Two patrol cars sat in front of the row house when Lucinda and Jumbo pulled to the curb. Four officers stood on the sidewalk, one holding a small two-man ram to breach the front door.

'We don't think anyone is inside, but don't let your guard down – we could be wrong,' Lucinda said and headed up the stairs. She rang the bell, pounded on the door, shouted 'Police' and made multiple requests to open the door. When that failed, as she thought it would, she stepped off the porch to give the men room to batter the door. Two swings of the ram and they had access to the home.

Lucinda's nose twitched in the musty, stale air. She noted some slightly sour odor provided an undertone. She was relieved when she wasn't assaulted by the stench of decomposition.

Six flashlights pierced the darkness, the air so full of dust that the beacons looked like solid objects. The detectives and officers moved with caution through every room, checking closets, under furniture, anywhere a person could hide. Lucinda and Jumbo took the first floor. Two officers walked crablike up the stairs checking out that level as well as the attic crawl space. The two others went into the basement where they explored a finished family room, bathroom, laundry room and a large dank storage area with bare concrete block walls. The only sign of life were roaches scurrying back into the cover of darkness.

They all went back outside to await the crime-scene truck. When it arrived, Lucinda posted one uniform on the front door, another on the back. She told the other two they could leave after they helped the techs maneuver a diesel generator up the steps and into the house. The lights were carried in next. A videographer and still photographer followed shooting every corner of each room.

Lucinda hadn't needed to ask for that documentation, Marguerite just did it. She knew from experience that the lieutenant was demanding. Marguerite liked that in a detective; she hated the ones who tried to hurry her up or make her take short cuts. She and Lucinda both wanted a record of everything. Neither woman ever wanted sloppiness or negligence to set them up to be blindsided by a defense attorney in the courtroom.

When that task was completed, Marguerite and an assistant headed upstairs to look for any out-of-place fibers, gray hairs or locations where it might be useful to apply Luminal. Jumbo went with them to serve as an extra pair of eyes and to lend a hand where he could.

Another tech got busy dusting high probability fingerprint sites. Lucinda and the document specialist headed into the dining room where a large roll-top desk, bookcase and computer stand occupied one corner. It was disappointing that the computer was no longer there but when they lifted the lid on the desk, the amount of paper inside was staggering.

There was a high, sloppy stack of newspaper clippings, articles printed from the Internet, and small pamphlets all concerning an alleged connection between diet and Alzheimer's disease. It included pieces on the importance of blueberries, Himalayan goji berry juice, Vitamin E, spinach, olive oil, Vitamin C, co-enzyme Q10 and more in Alzheimer's prevention. On the right, a shorter stack was an assortment of alarmist manifestos claiming a conspiracy by the military-industrial complex, the Russians, the pharmaceutical companies – all of the usual suspects – along with dire warnings that the drugs we give our loved ones to treat high blood pressure and cholesterol were causing dementia; and other papers insisting that the increased incidence of dementia was the direct result of Aricept, Razadyne, Exelon and Memantine, the very pharmaceuticals doctors prescribed to help patients with Alzheimer's.

Lucinda moved to the bookcase while the document tech pulled open the file drawer. On the shelves, most of the space was occupied with older paperback science fiction by well-known authors like Robert Heinlein, Isaac Asimov and Poul Anderson, as well as an assortment of books with cheesy covers depicting rocket ships or aliens or unknown planets. Some of them were 'two-fer' books with double covers – read one story, flip it over and read the other. Interspersed irregularly were hard cover books with more relevance to the investigation: *The Anti-Alzheimer's Prescription*; *Drugs, Dementia and the National Institute for Health: A Conspiracy to Control Your Mind*; *The Chemical Warfare Experiment: The Military's Link to Dementia*; *Nutrition and Alzheimer's: You Are What You Eat*; *Exercise and Sleep: The Key to Staying Sharp into Your Eighties and Beyond*; and *Brain Food for Your Golden Years*.

Wouldn't it be nice, Lucinda thought, if dementia could be eliminated so easily? If eating right, exercising and getting enough sleep could protect you from all harm.

Jumbo hollered down the stairwell, interrupting her thoughts. 'Lieutenant. Spellman wants to Luminal and wants to know if you want to see it.'

'On my way,' she shouted back.

Marguerite met her at the top of the stairs. 'Maybe I'm getting a bit carried away, Lieutenant, but I won't feel right if I don't check it out.'

'What's got your radar blips sounding, Spellman?'

'Well, there are three bedrooms up here. Only one is carpeted. The other two have hardwood floors with throw rugs. It's been a long time since any of these rooms have been painted but the room with the carpet looks as if it's a little bit of a newer paint job. Now, I know that could be explained easily – it was the only room redecorated.'

'I'm not questioning your judgment, Spellman.'

'Still, I want to tell you the clincher. Come in here,' she said, nodding her head toward one of the smaller bedrooms. She pulled open a closet door and shined a flashlight inside of it. 'Look.'

The silver bar had only a few hangers on it: one held a blouse, another had a dress, the rest were empty. On the floor, a small pile of two or three garments next to a beat-up pair of shoes.

'Abandoned stuff from the looks of it, right?'

'Sure – just things the owner didn't want any longer,' Lucinda agreed.

'Right. It's the same thing in the other small bedroom except it has a few articles of clothing which are male.'

'And you have something different in the larger bedroom?'

'You betcha. In that bedroom, there are two closets,' Marguerite said as she walked across the hall. 'One of them contains a couple of pieces of men's stuff. But the other . . .' She pulled open the door of a packed closet. Clothes rammed tight on the rod, shoes piled high on the floor.

Marguerite flipped through the garments with blue gloved hands. 'Just look at this stuff: billowing maternity dresses, oversized shirts, stirrup pants, but these . . .' She bent down and picked up a pair of pink plastic shoes. 'If these jellies don't say Eighties, I don't know what does.'

Lucinda whispered, 'Sadie.'

Over her shoulder, Jumbo said, 'That's just what I thought, Lieutenant. And it looks like she didn't pack a bag.'

'Where do you want to spray, Spellman?' Lucinda asked.

'I want to do the headboard of the bed and the wall around it.'

'Do it.'

'If I find anything, I'll want to rip up the carpet and do the floor.'

'Fine.'

'I might even want to rip up the carpet if I don't find anything.'

'Go for it, Spellman. If the answer to what happened to Sadie Blankenship is here, I want to find it.'

Jumbo helped Marguerite hang a blackout cloth over the sole window in the room to eliminate the light from a lamp post in the alley. With the door shut, the lights switched off, Lucinda and Jumbo stood close enough that they could hear the other person breathe but could not see each other at all.

They heard the spray and smelled the salty tang of the chemical that always reminded Lucinda of the beach. The glow began. First, tiny specks twinkled on the headboard. Then the brightness spread on the wall, more evidence of high-speed splatter, then a huge, splotchy smear as if someone bleeding hit the wall and slid down to the floor.

Marguerite kept spraying, up to the ceiling where the splatter grew finer and finer and then stopped. While they watched, they heard the slow whirr-click of the camera on the tripod taking long exposure shots.

'Need help ripping up that carpet, Spellman?' Lucinda asked.

'The more the merrier,' Marguerite said. 'You both have gloves on, right?'

'Yes, ma'am,' Lucinda and Jumbo said in unison.

Marguerite flipped on the portable lights. With one person on each corner, the two forensic techs and the two detectives scooted the double bed to one side of the room. Marguerite pulled out a utility knife and made a two inch cut into the edge of the carpet. Jumbo grabbed that and pulled. When he loosened a big enough chunk, Lucinda latched on to it and tugged, too.

Marguerite and her assistant duplicated the effort on the other side of the room. Soon, they had a large rectangle of bare wood floor. Marguerite got down on her hands and knees and peered at the floor. 'Holy crap! I can still see the blood in the cracks of the boards. No need for Luminal here. All I need are some swabs.'

Lucinda joined her on the floor. 'And there's even some staining on the top of the flooring.'

'There's no way to date these bloodstains but they are nowhere near recent. Too much wear on the carpet, and there's even some rust on the carpet tacks,' Marguerite said.

'Maybe we can date the carpet. Jumbo, there's a tech going through the papers in the desk. Would you ask her to keep her eye out for a receipt?'

Jumbo nodded and left the room.

'Sorry, Lieutenant,' Marguerite said.

'Sorry? Sorry? You may have just solved a twenty-year-old homicide that no one even knew about.'

'But that's not why we're here. We haven't found anything to connect to your missing and dead old folks. We've found lots of hairs – but not one gray or white one in the bunch.'

'My disappointment in that is more than compensated by what we've found. And the clothing – if it's been worn since its last washing, you can pull DNA and knock out profiles of the whole family. If that's Sadie's blood and those are Sadie's clothes, samples from her children and her husband will pull it all together.'

'You want me to prioritize those profiles?'

'Definitely. Can you get Beth Ann Coynes to run them?'

'It will require sidestepping Doctor Ringo but that's nothing new for me,' Marguerite grinned.

'How's Audrey doing?'

Marguerite shrugged. 'She's a little mellower since her double mastectomy – talks about realizing the value of living one day at a time quite a bit – but for the most part, she's still the dragon lady she's always been.'

'Has she had a recent follow-up?'

'Yep. No sign of cancer.'

'Good. Dragon lady or not, I hope her survival is complete and permanent. We've lost too many women already. Domestic homicide is a horrible thing but breast cancer is sneakier and it scares me even more.'

Lucinda went downstairs and returned to the dining room. 'Found a carpet receipt?'

'Not yet, Lieutenant,' the tech answered.

Jumbo looked up from an open file folder. 'Lieutenant, you've got to read these letters. There's a connection to River's Edge.'

'You're kidding?' she said reaching for the folder. She sat down at the dining-room table.

'They seem to be in chronological order. Copies of letters Gary Blankenship mailed and the original responses he received. A lot of his letters are nearly identical, just addressed to different people. If you read the first one all the way through, you can skim through bunches that follow. Do you think they could use me upstairs while you read?'

'If you don't mind bagging evidence, I'm sure they could.'

'No problem. Have fun.'

It was a well-worn manila folder with ragged edges with a tag labeled 'Mom'. The first letter, dated April 10, 2002, was addressed to: Administrator, River's Edge.

My mother is Mary Agnes Franklin Blankenship Hodges. She is being held in your lockdown Alzheimer's unit under false pretenses. She does not have Alzheimer's or any form of dementia. I realize she displays the symptoms of one of these brain maladies but it is artificially inflicted. My stepfather, Alvin Harold Hodges, has poisoned her with pharmaceuticals.

Before she came to stay with you, I argued with him on many occasions about the medication she was receiving and about her diet. He ignored all the information I provided him both orally and in written form. When he tricked you into taking my mother into your facility, he left all the articles and books I had given him on my front porch. I don't think he'd read any of it.

The reason he did not care is because he was trying to get rid of her. He wanted power of attorney over her assets and he wanted to date other women. Alvin Harold Hodges is an evil man. I warned my mother before she married him but she just thought I was jealous. He had fooled her and manipulated her so badly that she just thought I was jealous of sharing my mom with that man. I tried to object during the matrimonial ceremony but the pastor ignored me.

I did try to rescue my mother from her captivity last month but one of your misguided staff members would not listen to reason and had me evicted from the premises. I have not been allowed to visit her since.

Alvin Harold Hodges has put you in a position where you will be liable to face criminal charges. When he is arrested for attempted murder, you will also be charged for aiding and abetting him in his criminal activity and

for holding my mother against her will. I do not want
this to happen to you. That is why I am writing you now.
I want to give you the opportunity to do the right thing
before I contact law enforcement. Then, it will be too
late. You will end up in jail along with many of your
staff members. River's Edge will be forced out of
business. You will probably face civil action from your
stockholders. Please do not wait a minute longer.

Do the right thing. Let my mother out of your prison.
I am more than willing to care for her and I am confident that I can nurse her back to health. My children,
her grandchildren, are looking forward to seeing her
again and are eager to help me with her.

Lucinda knew the response Blankenship received to this letter
could not have pleased him. It was an invitation to a confer-
ence with a physician and other health care providers to
discuss his mother's physical and mental condition. It ended:
'Once you understand and accept that your mother does
need to be here, we will gladly reconsider the restriction on
visitation.'

The next letter was to the police chief explaining the situation outlined in the first letter as well as complaining about
the officer who refused to file a criminal report. He then wrote
to the state police, the state agency on ageing, and the
Alzheimer's Association – both the state chapter and the national
organization. He turned next to politicians, writing to repre-
sentatives and senators on the state level, followed by his federal
elected officials, the governor and even the president.

At the very back of the folder were two pieces of white paper
with no date, no address, no signature line – just an identical
message in caps. One was addressed to Alvin Harold Hodges,
the other to the administrator of River's Edge.

YOU HAVE KILLED MY MOTHER.
YOU WILL BURN IN HELL FOR HER MURDER.
YOU MAY BE IN HELL A WHOLE LOT SOONER
THAN YOU THINK.

Lucinda was stunned. She still wasn't sure how all of the puzzle
pieces fit together. But she sensed that these letters were the

key to the motive. Was Gary Blankenship responsible for three recent deaths in addition to the murder of his wife? And what about Alvin Harold Hodges? Was he still alive?

TWENTY-EIGHT

'I got it!' the tech shouted from her spot on the floor next to the file drawer.

Lucinda looked up from the file. 'The carpet receipt?'

'Yes. And it's dated twenty years, three months and two days ago. That's the time frame you're looking at, right?'

'Sure is.'

'It's for a roll of carpet, no installation, delivered to this address.'

'Thank you.'

'And that's not all. Here's a receipt for carpet tacks and strips from Home Depot.'

'Between you and Spellman, we've nailed this bastard. Good work.'

'Let's just hope the DA agrees with you.'

Lucinda rolled her eyes. She raised her right hand, reached across her body and crossed her heart with her index finger and held her hand upright again. 'I swear to you he won't get a moment's peace until he does.'

The tech chuckled.

Lucinda lowered her hand. 'First thing tomorrow morning – or rather this morning after the District Attorney gets into the office – I'm going to get a warrant for the arrest of Gary Blankenship for the murder of his wife.'

Lucinda set down the file on the dining-room table and stepped over to the desk. She pulled out a tall drawer inside the roll top and blinked her eyes at what was there. She reached in and pulled out a plastic bag with a twisted rubber band around its neck. Inside were acorns, dozens of acorns. Across the side of the bag, a black magic marker spelled out 'Donnie'. She plucked out a second bag. It, too, was filled with acorns but labeled 'Derek'. The third bag was identical except that it had 'Donna' written on it.

Acorns. What's with the acorns? Lucinda turned to the tech and said, 'Make sure you collect these bags of acorns and bring them in as evidence.'

'Acorns?' the tech said with raised eyebrows.

'Yeah. I don't know either. It's just weird enough that it might matter.'

Lucinda looked toward the doorway when she heard someone pounding down the stairs.

Jumbo came around the corner. 'His name rang a bell and the more I've thought about it, I'm pretty sure we have a missing persons report on him.'

'Whose name, Butler?'

'Alvin Harold Hodges. Being how it's the middle of the night, I can't get anyone to check on it for me. I'll need to go back in to pull the file and follow up. Got all the clothes bagged and ready to go so I thought now was as good a time as any.'

Lucinda reached into her pocket, grabbed her keys and tossed them to Jumbo. 'Here take my car and call me when you've got things nailed down.'

'You want me to come back for you?'

'No need. I'll get a ride from someone here.'

Jumbo was walking toward the front door when Lucinda shouted out, 'Hey, Butler. Remember it's my car and try not to drive like a man.'

Butler turned around, his eyes squinting, his mouth twisted, 'What?'

'Never mind,' Lucinda sighed, 'just try to be careful.'

On the floor, the tech tittered. 'They don't get it do they?'

Lucinda grinned. 'Never met a man who did.' She peered into the remaining little drawers in the interior of the desk but found nothing that piqued her interest. Grabbing a utility light with a long cord, she walked through an archway into the kitchen. Here the sour smell she noticed when she arrived grew more intense. She checked the refrigerator first. Fortunately, the shelves were nearly bare. Nonetheless, the lack of electricity and extended period of time since someone opened it, the odor it released was unpleasant but not the pungent aroma she sought.

On a counter she spotted an open carton of half-and-half beside a coffee maker. She lifted the container and took a whiff. The creamer had curdled and dried into a lumpy mass at the bottom but the smell was unmistakable. Culprit found.

An oily sheen of dried coffee sludge dirtied the bottom of the glass coffee carafe. It wasn't the blackened and crispy mess you find in a pot left heating too long. It appeared to have evaporated down with the passage of time, a series of dark rings marking the descending volume.

She opened a cabinet door and cringed at the large number of roaches that scurried into hiding behind cereal boxes, opened bags of flour, sugar and cornmeal. A vermin holiday feast behind closed doors. When she opened cabinets that contained pots, pans and dishes, she still saw the nasty buggers racing away but not in the great numbers present in the ones filled with food.

She pulled open a drawer piled high with stainless flatware and saw the unmistakable evidence of mice: little black droppings everywhere. She grinned. As much as she was repulsed by cockroaches, she thought the field mice that invaded kitchens every Fall rather cute. She knew that they needed to be eliminated but the necessity always infused her with regret. She accepted that her fondness for the little rodents was perverse, fueled by her negative feelings toward her aunt who loathed the annual mouse appearance in the farm house, where she lived after her parents died.

She continued through her inspection of the kitchen, finding a bent cookie sheet coated with dried crud in the oven, a lone acorn in the corner of the junk drawer and a dozen bottles of dish detergent wearing red 'reduced' stickers lined up under the sink. Nothing except the lone acorn seemed significant and she wasn't really sure about that. She knew, however, that Spellman would haul a lot of it in, just in case.

Her cellphone rang. It was Butler. 'Hodges was reported missing a little more than two years ago. The bad news is that the lead investigator in the case died of cancer right around Thanksgiving last year. But the good news is that he kept detailed notes.'

'Butler, you ought to get some rest. We need to dig through those reports and follow up on anything we can. But first, head home, grab a couple hours of sleep. I'll give you a call when I finish here and head back to the Justice Center.'

'Lieutenant, what about you?'

'I'm going to stretch out on the sofa while Spellman and her crew finish up the job. I'll be fine.'

Lucinda didn't think she could actually fall asleep, but once she was horizontal, she was gone. It was a fitful rest, though, as dark images of her mother, her father and Edgar Humphries stumbled through her dreams.

TWENTY-NINE

Lucinda bolted upright at the sound of Spellman's voice. Tattered vestiges of fear and anger hung like cobwebs over her consciousness. She sensed some unpleasantness troubled her sleep but when she tried to grab the memory of her dreams they darted away like roaches in the light of day.

'Sorry I startled you, Lieutenant.'

Lucinda shook her head. 'No problem, Spellman. What is it?'

'We've finished up, loaded all the evidence we needed into the truck. We're ready to leave. Do you want to ride with us?'

'No. You go on ahead. I'll seal the place up and get a ride in the patrol car.'

Lucinda stood and stretched, still feeling a bit uneasy about the demons that stalked her dreams. She shunted those thoughts aside, crossed the back door and front door with yellow crime scene tape and slid into the back seat of the patrol car.

On the way to the Justice Center, she called Jumbo Butler. 'I'm on my way back but don't rush – have some coffee, even breakfast if you want. I've got to see the DA about a warrant before I'll be able to sit down and go through the Hodges file with you.'

Walking into the building, she took the elevator to the fifth floor and walked into the office of District Attorney Michael Reed. He looked up from his computer and said, 'You look like hell.'

'Thank you, sir. That's just what every woman wants to hear first thing in the morning.'

'Did you get any sleep last night?'

'A little.'

'Speaking of looks, when's your next surgery?'

'Jeez, Reed, I don't have time for this. I need an arrest warrant.'

'Pierce. You need to take time for yourself. You were injured in the line of duty. The city owes you that time.'

Lucinda dropped into a chair in front of his desk. 'I am really not in the mood, Reed.'

'You could have used a little more sleep, couldn't you?'

'Please, I need an arrest warrant.'

'Who do you want to lock up on this fine spring morning?'

Lucinda presented her case against Gary Blankenship. 'So, can you get one of your ADAs to take care of the warrant?'

'You don't have a body, Pierce.'

'With all the forensic evidence of homicide in that bedroom, sir, we don't need a stinkin' body.'

'Call me old-fashioned, Pierce. But a homicide prosecution and a body just kind of go together in my mind.'

'You've won cases without it.'

'Sure. But it's never easy. And you've not spent any time looking for a body. Do that – me and the jury will be happy if you do.'

Lucinda sighed and looked out the window.

'You can bring Blankenship in on suspicion, Pierce. We can do a warrant later.'

'I want a warrant so that I can hold him and question him about the disappearance of his stepfather, too.'

'You can do that without a warrant.'

'I also suspect he had something to do with the death of three seniors with dementia.'

'What else? Did he kill Hoffa, too?'

Lucinda glared at him.

'Bring him in on suspicion and talk to him about anything and everything you want.'

'If he's not under arrest, it's too easy for him to walk away.'

'See how it goes. Call me if you need me.' Reed turned back to his computer.

'That's not all, sir.'

'What?' he said spinning back around.

'Evan Spencer. Dr Spencer.'

'What about him?'

She told him about finding the woman battered in her home and getting her transported to the hospital. 'The sheriff's department is looking for her son. They said they'll press charges with or without her cooperation.'

'That doesn't wipe out the charges against Spencer.'

'If those charges stand, sir, it will weaken the prosecution's case in the county. It gives the defense a reasonable doubt argument.'

'Still . . .'

Lucinda rose to her feet and pressed her palms on the desk and leaned toward him. 'Sir, I do not want to have to respond to a homicide scene and find that woman's body.'

'Steady, Pierce. Calm down. When they have the woman's son in custody, I'll review the Spencer case and consider dropping the charges. OK?'

'I suppose it will have to be, sir,' she said. 'Now, if you'll excuse me, I'll see what I can do despite the limitations you've imposed upon me.'

Back in her office, Lucinda contacted Dispatch to issue a BOLO – be on the look out – for Gary Blankenship. Finishing that, she went looking for Jumbo Butler. When she stepped into Missing Persons, he was on the phone.

'Hey, Lieutenant, just got off the phone with Hodges' daughter from his first marriage. She said we could come by this morning and talk to her about her dad and her stepmother's family. Said she always suspected Gary Blankenship had something to do with it.'

'That's no big surprise.'

'No, but she wasn't the only one – the lead detective brought Blankenship in for questioning three times and tried to get a search warrant for the house you just spent the night exploring. He, unfortunately, was told he didn't have just cause and never got inside.'

'Damn, Butler, this is just looking too freaking weird. If Blankenship did kill his wife, which seems likely, it probably was because she was about to leave him or for money. Do we know if she had a life insurance policy?'

'Yes, she did – a $50,000 policy she got at work. But Blankenship never made any attempt to collect it or to have her declared legally dead.'

'Scratch the money motive,' Lucinda said. 'She announces her plans to leave him – bam, she's dead. That's one motive. Now, for the sake of argument, let's say he killed his step-father Alvin Hodges. From his correspondence, the reason for that murder was revenge for causing his mother's death. That's a different kind of motive. But both have one thing in common – these were two people he knew, two people who were a part of his life.

'Then we have three dead seniors with little clues that seem to tie them together despite the differing means of death. But yet, if we tie them together, how do we connect the death of three strangers to Blankenship? Or should we even be trying? That brings us back to the license plate.'

'But, for all we know,' Jumbo interjected, 'the license plate was stolen from Blankenship and the white panel truck has nothing to do with him.'

'But then, there are the acorns.'

'There are a lot of oak trees in this old neighborhood.'

'Tree DNA? That means a forensic botanist. I hope I can find one who isn't too squeamish. Better get someone on that right away. But still – how can all of these deaths be caused by one doer? Killing family members *and* killing strangers?'

'It's too soon to have anything from toxicology on the three elderly folks?'

'We should have some preliminary results in today. Let's go talk to Blankenship's daughter. I sure hope she answers more questions than she asks.'

THIRTY

The home of Sarah Hodges was a townhouse in one of those new residential/retail communities that seemed to have popped up all across the country overnight. Her place looked out on a large green space. On the far side of the expanse of grass were two bocce courts across the side-walk from an Italian market and restaurant.

Sarah answered the door with a smile. She was a petite blonde in her forties with an armful of gold bracelets and

large gold hoop earrings. Lucinda felt like a freak of nature
towering over her.

After Jumbo made the introductions, she asked, 'When you
said you were bringing another detective, I expected to see
the man who interviewed me when I reported my father
missing.'

'Unfortunately, ma'am, he passed away last year. Lieutenant
Pierce is working on another case that seems to overlap because
of Gary Blankenship.'

'My stepbrother is crazy – in fact, I think everyone in my
stepmother's family is nuts, except for her. She was a little
eccentric but very nice. After I learned she had Alzheimer's,
I wasn't certain if the oddnesses I saw in her were early
symptoms or if she was just a little different from the rest
of us.'

'In what way?' Lucinda asked.

'She was very superstitious. The number thirteen really
bothered her. When the license plates for her new car came
in the mail from DMV, the last two digits were one and three.
Boy was she upset. She took them in and demanded a new
set. 666 made her nuts, too. Once we were shopping together
for Dad's birthday – she picked up those gold toe socks he
liked and the total came to $6.66. She gave the woman $7,
told her to keep the change and refused to accept the receipt.
She was strange, too, about black cats, broken mirrors, all
that usual stuff.'

'Did you notice anything else?'

Sarah laughed. 'She had the most peculiar fascination with
acorns.'

'Acorns?' Lucinda and Jumbo said in unison.

'On the one hand, she thought they were the most powerful
force in the universe. But then, she'd take them and make
silly things with them.'

'Silly things?' Lucinda asked.

'Yes. She'd paint faces on them – say they were wearing
little berets. Sometimes, she'd create little scenes using
construction paper, cardboard, pipe cleaners and balsa wood.
The most detailed one I remember was a classroom. Rows of
tiny desks with acorn-headed children in chairs. Their caps
were off and their berets all hung on a row of hooks on a
cardboard wall. She'd glued on little bits of yarn for hair on

all the acorns – except for one. That little boy was bald. She said he had leukemia and was undergoing chemotherapy. It was really odd. When she passed away, I helped Dad clean out her clothes and stuff. I found a whole drawer-full of acorns – some with painted faces, some still blank.'

'Do you know if Gary shared her fascination with acorns?'

'If he did, I never noticed. But I tried not to spend much time around him. As I said, he was crazy – dangerous crazy. He became particularly malignant toward my dad when my stepmother's illness became apparent. He ranted and raved about drugs causing the problem, insisting nothing was wrong with his mother. He shoved Dad around a few times – never seriously hurt him but he was a real bully.'

'What about Gary's children? Do you know them?'

'A little – most of them were living at home still when my dad went missing. I think the oldest, Don, had gotten married and moved out. The youngest boy, Derek, was in his last year of high school but the other two were in their twenties. They all seemed normal most of the time. But, at others, it was apparent that they swallowed their dad's world view whole. It made me wary of them.'

Jumbo asked, 'I read the report, but I'd like to hear from you about the last time you saw your dad.'

Sarah sighed and sunk a little deeper into the chair. 'When Dad and I were cleaning the house, he had me set aside some things for Gary. Some of it made sense – like a ruby ring Dad thought Donna should have and the little incense-burning log cabin that Derek loved. Lots of other little mementoes like that.' Sarah smiled softly and sighed again. 'But there were also these stacks and stacks of papers about pharmaceutical company and government conspiracies, the evils of the drugs used to slow down the progress of Alzheimer's and diet and nutrition as the answer to the disease.

'I said, "Dad, just throw this crap out." But he said that wouldn't be right. Gary gave it all to him and he really should give it back. When I left his house that day, it was the last time I saw him. But he called the next morning and said he was going over to Gary's to give all the stuff to him. I offered to help him and he pointed out that it wasn't a good idea since Gary and I didn't get along. He was right about that so I dropped it.

'I'll never forgive myself for that.' A tear slipped from Sarah's eye and rolled down her cheek. She wiped at it and sighed. 'I never spoke to, or saw, my dad after that morning.'

'Did you ask Gary about that?' Lucinda asked.

'Yes. He said Dad never came by that morning. In fact, he started accusing me of stealing the ruby ring that he claimed his mother promised to Donna. He called me over and over threatening me over that piece of jewelry. When I had enough, I changed my phone number. Then, he started sending me nasty letters. I moved here about 19 months ago and for a couple of weeks, I marked all his mail "return to sender". And then it stopped.'

'Did he mention anything about your dad in those conversations or letters?'

'Not much, but when he did, he talked about him as if he were dead.'

Lucinda and Jumbo exchanged a glance and Lucinda said, 'Do you think he was?'

'Not at first,' she sobbed. 'But I came to believe, and I still believe, that Gary killed Dad.'

Jumbo stood up and put an arm around her shoulder. She sniffed hard, straightened up and said, 'Thank you. I'm OK now. Anything else?'

Lucinda asked, 'Do you know how your dad and stepmother met?'

She grinned. 'Oh yes. At a covered dish supper at the church. He fell in love with her corn casserole and then he fell in love with Mary Agnes. They dated for a while until Dad was able to convince her that the family would get along just fine if she lived a few miles away.'

'The family?'

'Gary and his kids. She'd moved in with them when Gary's wife ran off with another man. It worked fine while the kids were still little. She shared a room with Donna for years. But it became uncomfortable when Donna became a teenager – every 13-year-old wants her privacy and like most girls her age, her stuff was consuming every inch of available space. Still, Gary wasn't happy when Mary Agnes told him she was getting married and moving out. He tried to force her to stay there and Dad had to intervene.'

'What about the kids – how did they react to her leaving?'

'There were a lot of tears. Donna was happy about getting her own room but when the reality of Grandma moving out actually hit her, she was devastated. They called her every day, even after they were grown. Never forgot a birthday or a Mother's day. They adored her and she cherished them.'

'Were your dad and stepmother happy together?' Lucinda asked.

'Oh yes. They were very much in love – it was cute to see them together. That is, until Mary Agnes started losing it. And even then, she always recognized Dad, called him her "Alvinator". But by the time she went into the lockdown unit, she didn't seem to understand their relationship any longer. He was simply "Alvinator", that man who visited her.'

'And when she died?'

'My dad was devastated. Putting her away was the most difficult decision he ever made. He visited her every single day – no matter how angry she got, no matter if she ignored him. Those days broke his heart but he never stopped going to see her. And never stopped worrying if he'd made the wrong decision.'

'What about Gary – how did he react to her death?'

'He made me so angry. My poor dad was dragging around an undeserved bucketful of guilt and old Gary just had to pour more into the pail. The funeral service was a disaster. The minister was talking about Mary Agnes and all she had done for the church and how she touched so many lives when Gary let out a wail. Herding his kids in front of him, he rushed to the front and threw himself on top of the casket moaning and crying. He made all the children kiss their grandmother. All three of the kids were crying – but it didn't seem like tears of grief. It looked more like terror, as if they were afraid of their father and what he was doing.

'It got worse at the graveside. The minister was reading scripture as he stood beside the casket sitting on a metal frame above the grave. Gary walked up, knocked the Bible out of his hands. It hit the dirt and slid down into the hole under the coffin. Gary went into a rant about how my father, the doctors and the government killed Mary Agnes. He paced back and forth waving his arms, bumping into people and he just wouldn't shut up. They police were called. They cuffed him and put him in the back of the patrol car – but I don't think

they arrested him. I think they let him go after the service
was over and everyone else had left the cemetery. Like I said,
Gary is crazy.'

'One more thing, Ms Hodges,' Lucinda said. 'You mentioned
that Sadie Blankenship abandoned her family to run off with
another man. Do you know that to be a fact?'

'No. Not at all. That's just what Mary Agnes told me.'

'Did she give you a name? Did she offer any proof?'

'If she had any proof or knew who it was, she never
mentioned it to me, I don't think. Why? Do you think something happened to her, too?'

'I don't know, Ms Hodges. At this point, I simply don't
know anything with certainty.'

Back in the car, Jumbo said, 'Are you having doubts about
Sadie Blankenship?'

'No. That was just my answer for public consumption. I
am certain Gary killed her. I need to figure out what he did
with the body.'

'The acorns – from finding them in the home where Sadie
died to discovering them in Edgar's pockets – it all comes
together with the acorns.'

'But we still have the same problem,' Lucinda said. 'How
do these disparate deaths all tie to one perpetrator?'

'Maybe it's not one. Maybe these three recent deaths and
disappearances are the responsibility of one of Gary's kids –
or all of them.'

'Yeah, that thought had crossed my mind, too. I had
Research do a background check on the three children, but
they found nothing. Not even a speeding ticket.'

'Wouldn't be the first time that a criminal was never caught
until he committed murder.'

'True. But here's what doesn't make sense to me. There is
every indication that the kids loved their grandmother and if
they loved her, why would they kill someone just like her? It
doesn't make sense.'

'Neither do the acorns when you really get down to it.'

Lucinda's cell rang. 'Pierce.'

The voice on the line said, 'She's taken all the money out
of our joint checking account, she's changed the locks on the
doors, she won't answer the phone.'

'Who is this?'

'Sorry. Kendlesohn. Eli Kendlesohn. And I'm pretty sure my wife killed my mother.'

THIRTY-ONE

Earlier that day, Eli Kendlesohn sipped coffee in the kitchen while he read the newspaper. He didn't speak to his wife when she came into the room. He didn't acknowledge her when she sat down across from him at the breakfast table.

She placed her hand on top of the newspaper and pressed down. 'Eli, we need to talk.'

Eli looked at her and then back at his newspaper. He pretended to read but they both knew that it was now far too crumpled for him to decipher a word.

'Eli. Look at me.'

Eli picked up his coffee cup and took a gulp without lifting his eyes.

'Merciful heavens, Eli. You are a stubborn man. My mother warned me. God rest her soul.'

Eli couldn't continue his self-imposed silence any longer. 'Oh, God rest *your* mother's soul but mine can just be burned to ashes and dumped into the ocean.'

'Don't get hysterical, Eli. It was just an expression. But now that you are paying attention, I want to inform you of the dinner party Saturday night.'

'A dinner party?'

'Yes. Just a small one. I've invited three couples.'

'Three couples? Saturday night? Here?'

'I could add a fourth couple if there's someone at work you want me to invite.'

'My mother's funeral is on Friday.'

'Oh, good. Then it won't interfere.'

'We can't have a dinner party the day after my mother's funeral.'

'Oh, don't be old-fashioned, Eli. I haven't been able to entertain in my home for months because of your mother's behavior and then for even more time because she was missing and you didn't feel up to it. And we have racked up a long list of social obligations as a result. We need to get started as soon as possible.'

Eli jerked to his feet and backed away from his wife. 'You are evil. You did it, didn't you?'

'What's wrong with you? What are you talking about?'

'You killed my mother.'

Rachael rose to her feet. 'Don't be ridiculous, Eli. You are acting like a child.'

'Was I next, Rachael? Did you plan to kill me before or after the dinner party? Maybe over dessert?'

'I can't believe you would dare to speak to me this way. Just get out. Get out of this house. I can't bear the sight of you.'

'Fine. Just don't expect me at your dinner party.'

'You're no longer invited.'

'Fine,' Eli said, walking out of the kitchen and into the garage.

The drive to the office calmed Eli. Once at his desk, he called the director confirming that everything was in order for his mother's funeral. He asked about the death certificate and autopsy report. The director referred him to the pathologist in Norfolk.

He reached in his pocket for his cellphone to make the long-distance call. It wasn't there. He checked all of his pockets, his briefcase, and the top of his desk. He went down into the parking garage and searched in his car. Back in his office, he called home. His wife didn't answer. He called her cell but got no response on that phone either.

He gave up and called the morgue using the office line. 'The death certificate has been released,' he was told. 'The cause of death was drowning. However, the autopsy report is not ready yet.'

'Why not?' he asked.

'For one, we are running toxicology tests – all the standard ones as well as analyzing for the presence of her prescription medications. Secondly, there are concerns about the water in her lungs. Preliminary results indicate that it was not the same as the water in the pond where her body was found.'

'What? What does that mean?'

'She died somewhere else, Mr Kendlesohn. We are analyzing the water to attempt to learn where that happened.'

Rachael did it – I know she did it. Did she drown Mom in the tub? The pool? Where? That heartless bitch. I'll make her tell me. I need to go home for my cellphone anyway. I'll make her tell me now.

On the way home, he stopped at the ATM outside his bank to replenish his cash. He was irritated when the machine insisted that the account was closed. He parked the car, walked inside, filled out a withdrawal slip and stood at the white line waiting for the first available teller.

When he stepped up and handed over his slip, the clerk tapped into her computer and said, 'I'm sorry, sir. But this account is closed.'

'Impossible.'

She checked again. 'Yes, sir, Rachael Kendlesohn closed it this morning. She transferred the funds in this account over to another bank.'

'What about the savings account?'

'It's not in your name, sir. Doesn't appear it ever has been. I can't withdraw any money from an account that does not have your name on it.'

He stared at her, struggling to maintain his composure. He knew it wasn't her fault but he still had the irrational urge to yell at her. He exhaled deeply and said, 'No, of course you can't. This is not your problem, it's mine.'

'I'm very sorry, sir.'

He nodded at her and spun on his heels and left the bank. Back in his car, he pounded a palm against the steering wheel. 'Damn it! Damn it! Damn that bitch to Hell!'

He tore out of the parking lot, squealing his wheels as he turned on to the road. Pulling into the driveway of his home, he got out of the car, leaving the door wide open as he strode up the sidewalk. He slid his key in the lock but it wouldn't turn. He pulled it out, looked at it and stuck it in again. He tried to force it but it still didn't work.

He stomped back to his car, grabbed the garage door remote and punched in his code. Nothing. He threw the remote down on the passenger seat and went up to the keypad on the garage itself. He punched in the code again. Still nothing.

He was incredulous. *The bitch had been busy. Closing the bank account, changing the locks and the code.* He couldn't help being impressed with her efficiency. He went back to the front door, pressed the door bell and held it in for thirty seconds without letting up. Then he pressed it a dozen times for short intervals. He banged on the door with both fists. 'I know you're in there, Rachael,' he shouted.

He walked around to the back, peering in windows on the way. He didn't catch a glimpse of his wife and assumed she must be upstairs. He checked the French doors on the patio, the back door leading to the kitchen. Both were locked and his keys worked in neither one. He picked up a rock from the edge of a flower bed. Before he smashed it through a pane of glass, though, he became appalled by what he was about to do and set the rock carefully back in place.

He went back to his car and reached in his pocket for his cell. 'Damn,' he said, remembering he didn't have it. He drove out of the neighborhood and stopped at a service station where he made the call to Lieutenant Pierce from a pay phone.

THIRTY-TWO

Eli Kendlesohn agreed to meet the detectives at the Justice Center. Jumbo called and made arrangements for Eli to be brought up to the interview room when he arrived. He was waiting there when Lucinda and Jumbo walked into the police department.

Lucinda didn't quite know what to think of this latest development. She didn't like Rachael Kendlesohn; kind of liked the idea of cuffing her and hauling her into the station. But it just didn't seem to fit with all they'd learned. And the man sitting across the table from her and Jumbo looked crazed. His hair stuck up in several directions as if he'd been trying to pull it out. His eyes had the glazed look she associated with someone who'd just been smoking pot. He fidgeted in his chair like a little boy afraid to ask the teacher to be excused to go down the hall.

'Mr Kendlesohn, are you OK?' Lucinda asked.

'Oh, yeah. I'm fine. Just fine. My mother's dead. Murdered. I have no money. I forgot my cellphone but can't get into my house to get it. I'm homeless now, too, I guess. Except for my car. I could live in my car. And, oh yeah, my wife is a murderer.'

'What makes you think that your wife killed your mother?'

'Come on, Lieutenant. Isn't that why you came to the house in the first place? You thought one of us killed Mom. Well, it wasn't me. I didn't want to believe it was that woman. But now I'm sure of it.'

'Why do you think your wife killed your mother?' Lucinda asked again.

'I had my suspicions last night when she complained about how much it would cost to bring my mother home for a funeral. But then this morning, I knew it.'

'What happened this morning?'

'She informed me about the dinner party. A dinner party! She's planned a dinner party. Can you believe that? For Saturday evening. I'm getting ready to go to work and she drops a dinner party on me. When I objected, she said now my mother is finally gone, things can get back to normal. That's when I knew it. She killed Mom so she could have a dinner party. I've put up with a lot from that woman over the years. But this time she's gone too far. I want her arrested. And I told her so. I told her I knew what she did. She didn't deny it.'

'How do you think she killed her, Mr Kendlesohn?'

'Drowned her. Drowned her in the bathtub. Or maybe the pool.'

'And why do you think that?'

'How do you suppose the body got out to that pond in the country?'

'I thought about that. She had to have help. I can't think of anyone we know socially who'd be willing to help her dispose of a body. I tried but I just can't imagine that even of the worst of them. So, I figured she must have hired someone. The gardener maybe. Or the pool guy. Or maybe the woman who cleans the house knew somebody who could help her. Maybe she even hired somebody to do the killing so she wouldn't have to get her hands dirty. Now that I think about it, it sounds like her. Never willing to do her own dirty work. Every mess she ever made was cleaned up by me or the housekeeper. She's so above it all. She can still get a life sentence if she didn't actually do it but hired someone to do it, can't she?'

'Yes, Mr Kendlesohn. But we can't charge her without any proof.'

'You can lock her up on suspicion, can't you?'

'We could bring her in for questioning, sir. But we can't arrest her based on the word of an estranged husband.'

'Well, get the proof and arrest her.'

'It's not that easy, sir. In fact, all our evidence right now is pointing in another direction.'

'Well, I sure can't get in the house and get the proof for you.'

Lucinda sighed. 'Excuse us for a moment, Mr Kendlesohn.' She turned to Jumbo and motioned to him to join her out in the hall.

'Listen,' she said, 'we've got to get the poor guy into the house to get his stuff. But I don't trust him not to flip out and start destroying things or taking his wife's personal property. And I can't trust her to behave either. You have the best rapport with her . . .'

'Say no more. I'll get a patrolman to drive me and Mr Kendlesohn over to the house. I'll sit with her while the officer keeps an eye on him.'

'That sounds like a plan – a good plan. Now, I've got to get back to work on the serious leads.'

Lucinda went into her office and opened her email. She scanned the list of senders and started opening anything from a staff member in the research department. They'd come up empty on the search for any property owned by Gary Blankenship or any of his children. And none of them had any addresses except for the row house she'd searched and a post-office box where the mail had been forwarded. She thought about getting a patrol officer to stake out the box but that could eat up a lot of man hours without getting any results. She decided to save that as a last resort.

There was a BOLO out on the white van, another on the old Nissan – using the same tag numbers in case the family was switching them back and forth between vehicles – and one for each of the Blankenships. She'd decided to circulate the old missing persons report for Sadie Blankenship to make the DA happy even though she was certain she saw the scene of her murder at the row house.

She called down to Research. 'I know I've been piling it on you guys for the last couple of days but I need your help again.'

'No problem, Lieutenant. Whatcha need?'

'I need a list of any white cargo vans reported stolen in the last eighteen months and please filter out any that have been recovered.'

'You are a lucky woman. About a dozen years ago, none of the vehicle registrations listed the color. The only ones that don't now are old cars that haven't been sold since the law changed. Still might be a long list – pretty common business vehicle. What else do you need?'

'I'm going to email you an ancient missing persons report. I need a list of all the unidentified bodies in the country that could possibly be a match for her. The last time she was seen was about twenty years and three months ago. Her husband told the detective that she ran off with another man. I think she was murdered and her body dumped nearby, so first check locally for any Jane Does that date back that far and then spread out the search because I could be wrong. Get back to me with the local results as soon as you have them.'

'Will do. Now knowing your penchant for starting with the easiest task first and escalating as we go along, I'm almost afraid to ask you what else you need.'

'Sorry. I know I'm asking a lot. But this last request, I'm not even sure you can do it. I'd like to have a list of everyone who lived on the block where she lived before she disappeared.'

'We can do it. It will take time. It's not on the computer but we can dig through the paper archives. Actually, this is easier than your second request – you're slipping, Lieutenant,' she said with a laugh.

'But I need one more thing about those neighbors: the most recent phone numbers and addresses. Can you dig that up, too?'

'We'll do our best, Lieutenant. Will get on it as soon as that report hits my email box.'

Lucinda hung up, scanned the report and sent it down to Research. She leaned back in her chair to think. The ringing of her desk phone brought her out of her reverie. 'Chief Deputy Hirschhorn on line three, Lieutenant.'

'Thanks,' she said and pressed in the button. 'This is Pierce. How can I help you, Chief?'

'I'm calling with good news, Lieutenant. We picked up your boy on the domestic violence case. The lady's still in the hospital but the old boy is behind bars.'

'That is good news. Is he talking at all?'

'That's the best part, ma'am. That little bastard admitted to beating up the old lady in the parking lot but he did it with a grin. I said to him, "You're looking mighty happy for someone who's about to go to prison." And he laughed at me and said, "My mom won't press charges." Then I laughed and said, "She doesn't have to, we can charge you with or without her help." Grin slid off the old boy's face real fast.'

'Thank you, Chief. I do have a favor to ask you, though.'

'Sure, what do you need?'

'Could you call DA Reed and tell him what happened? I'd really like him to hear the news from someone other than me.'

'DA giving you a hard time? They sure can be pissers sometimes. I'll let him know right away.'

'Before you go, what about the little girl?'

'Oh,' he sighed. 'Hannah Singley? We haven't found her yet. I'm not having good thoughts.'

'Hang on to any thread of hope you can find, Chief. And let me know when you find her.' Dead or alive, she thought but could not bear to speak those words aloud.

Lucinda thought about calling Evan Spencer at his office to tell him about the arrest but decided it would be more fun to deliver the news in person. She'd go over to his place when she left here for the day. It would give her a chance to see Charley; it'd been too long since she'd seen the girl. She thought about calling Jake Lovett to bounce the case back and forth with him. But she worried if she called him at the office, he'd feel obliged to report it. Then she'd have the local FBI jerks breathing down her neck over the attempted kidnapping and the other suspected abductions. She really liked Jake – more than liked him truth be told – but the rest of those Feebs? She'd like to give them all a hand basket and send them on their merry way.

THIRTY-THREE

Jumbo entered Lucinda's office and flopped into the chair by her desk with a huge sigh. 'I hope I never have to see that woman again for the rest of my life.'

'Didn't go too well?' Lucinda asked.

'Could have been worse, I suppose. There was a lot of yelling and shrieking, mostly on Rachael's part but Eli did lean over the balcony occasionally and holler out a zinger. It took all my powers of persuasion to keep her downstairs and under some semblance of control. For a while there, I thought I was going to have to sit on her.'

Lucinda grinned at the image he created in her mind: a leprechaun perched on a shrew. 'Have you given any more thought to Eli's accusations?'

'At moments of relative calm, I fired a few questions at her. I did get the sense that she was holding something back, hiding something from me. But I sure can't imagine her killing somebody. And I can't imagine anyone she'd know who'd be inclined to commit a crime for her or her money. She doesn't strike me as the kind of woman who inspires loyalty or devotion.'

'But she's lying about something?'

'Could be just a lie of omission – but, yeah, there's something there.'

'Maybe we ought to get busy looking for a connection between Rachael and the Blankenships.'

'Phone records?' Jumbo asked.

'I doubt I can get a warrant for the Kendlesohns' phones and with Eli locked out of the house, he can't provide them. Damn, I wish I'd thought of that while you all were still inside. I'll ask Eli to request copies from the phone company.'

'And I'll go down to Documents and see what they found at the Blankenship place.'

'As long as the family's been gone from that place, there won't be anything dating up to the time of Adele's disappearance. But I shouldn't have a problem getting a judge to sign a warrant for their records from that time until now.'

'If not, maybe we'll get lucky. Maybe there's a connection that dates back to when the Blankenships still lived in the house.'

'Maybe, but I'm not going to count on it. Let's get busy.'

It took Eli's gleeful cooperation and hours of paperwork and conversation, but finally they had all the records they needed. The documents for the landlines were useless since the calls between the two households were local. And there were no records of any of the Blankenships having cells. On the other hand, Eli and Rachael's cellphones were on a single plan. Eli had no trouble obtaining the records and those documents had every call listed: incoming and outgoing, local and long distance. The detectives went through the pages carefully, line by line, looking for any calls to the Blankenship home and verifying all the phone numbers on the list around the time of Adele's disappearance. When they finished, Lucinda dropped her head on her desk with a thud. 'Another dead end,' she said with a sigh.

'Rachael still could have called him on the landline.'

'Shoulda. Coulda. Lot of good that does us. The Blankenships haven't had a landline since they left the house. They had to have cells, but they must have been throwaways. Those damn things should be illegal.'

'I wouldn't hold my breath on that legislation,' Jumbo said.

'Have you seen Ted Branson today?' Lucinda asked, her mind suddenly on other things.

'Yeah, a little while earlier, he helped me out when I was going through the evidence looking for phone records, but I haven't seen him since. Why? Is he supposed to be doing something for the investigation?'

'No, we just started a conversation I'd like to finish but we never seem to be in the same place at the same time. Well, that will have to wait,' Lucinda said. 'In other dead ends, I heard back on the criminal background checks of the staff at River's Edge. A few traffic violations, a couple of college-era misdemeanors but not a single felony in the bunch – not one red flag, not even a pale pink one. Research is preparing a spreadsheet for the complete list with employment dates and job positions. We should get it in the morning. We're going to need to follow up with each one of them.'

'Is that really necessary? I mean, I know that River's Edge

keeps popping up but the investigation seems to be pointing in another direction.'

'Yes, it *seems* to be but what if there is an accomplice at River's Edge – someone who perhaps does nothing more than feed information to the Blankenships? That's a possibility but, I agree, the legwork will probably turn out to be a big fat waste of time, except for one thing: we can never close a door that the defense might open at trial. Every avenue needs to be followed to the end.'

'I think I'll stay in Missing Persons – we don't have trials, just successes and failures. And if the failures end in murder, we give them to you guys.'

'After all this afternoon's futility, it's time I switched gears and did something pleasant. I'm going to give someone else a bit of good news,' Lucinda said. 'If you think of anything, give me a call, anytime. Otherwise, I'll see you back here in the morning.'

In the lobby of the building where the Spencer family lived, Lucinda called up to the condo and Evan Spencer activated the elevator for her to go up to the top floor. The moment the lift's door slid open, she heard a squeal down the hall. Charley was running toward her at full speed. Lucinda embraced her, lifting the girl off the ground. She gave her a kiss on the forehead and set her back down.

'Thank you, thank you, thank you, Lucy! You get another star on your hero chart.'

'You already know?' Lucinda asked.

'You mean about you saving Daddy from jail?'

'Yes. I thought I was going to deliver the news.'

'Some man called for Daddy and told him that they were dropping the charges and it was all because of you.'

'I bet he didn't say that last part.'

'Well, no, but me and Daddy, we know – if it wasn't for you, he'd be a jailbird.'

Lucinda laughed. 'I doubt that, Charley.'

The eleven-year-old girl stopped walking and put her hands on her hips. 'You never give yourself enough credit, Lucy.'

A bitter-sweet thrill rushed through Lucinda's mind as she looked down at her young friend. *Still such a child despite the veneer of maturity granted by her intelligence and enhanced in the fire of tragedy. Soon, though, the transition will begin and where will we go from there? It will change our relationship and probably not for the better; not until she's made it through the rebellious rite of passage.* Lucinda sighed.

Charley cocked her head to the side. 'OK?'

'Yes, OK.' Lucinda smiled.

The door opened and Evan said, 'I cannot thank you enough, Lucinda.'

'Evan, this would have eventually worked out fine without me.'

'Maybe. But even if it did, it certainly would have dragged on a lot longer.'

Lucinda caught sight of Ruby, Charley's six-year-old sister, peering out from behind her father. 'Hi there, Ruby.'

'Hello, ma'am,' she said and then stuck the knuckle of her thumb sideways in her mouth and gnawed on it.

Lucinda crouched down to see her eye-to-eye. 'How are you doing in school, Ruby?'

One of her shoulders pulled up to her ear, 'I'm doing OK,' she mumbled.

Poor little thing. Is she always this shy? Is the pain always so obvious in her eyes? Or is it just me. Do I remind her of her mother's murder?

'OK?' Evan said. 'You're doing much better than OK, Ruby.'

The little girl squirmed; her discomfort obvious. Lucinda rose to her full height; getting down to the girl's level seemed to have made matters worse.

'Ruby has gotten excellent marks on her report card and she's started playing the violin. But she says she really wants to play the cello as soon as she's big enough, right, Ruby?'

She gave a tiny nod and shrunk back further. Charley patted her sister on the shoulder and Ruby offered up the hint of a smile. Charley turned to Lucinda and said, 'Oh, enough about Ruby. C'mere. Come to my room. I need to show you something.' She grabbed Lucinda's hand and tugged.

When they reached Charley's room, the door was shut and a note taped to it read: 'No Male People Allowed.'

'Are you already having problems with men?' Lucinda asked with a laugh.

'Don't be silly, Lucy. That's just to keep Daddy out. He

can't come in here while I'm working on his birthday present.'
She opened the door and shut it behind them.

'Look,' she said. 'I made the casts all by myself with plaster
of Paris and strips of newspaper. I had to throw a bunch of
them away before I got it right.'

An eighteen-inch-high skeleton hung from the hook of
a black metal stand. It was sat atop a block of wood with a
computer-generated label that read: 'No break too big or too
small, Dr Spencer fixes them all.' It wore three casts: one on
the right leg from knee to toes; another on the left arm hanging
in a blue fabric sling; and a third, bulb-shaped, stuck up on
the thumb of the right hand. The lower ribs were wrapped in
tiny strips of adhesive tape. The crowning glory of the whole
creation was the left hip: the socket was painted bright silver
to resemble an artificial joint.

'This is incredible, Charley.'

'I wanted to wire his jaw shut but I wasn't sure how to
do it without making a mess of the skull, so I didn't. But
I do need your help with one thing.'

'I doubt if I can do anything to improve on this.'

'Yes. Yes, you can. It will be a big surprise,' Charley giggled.
She carefully slipped the blue sling over the skull and off of
the arm and handed Lucinda a fine tip pen. 'Sign it. Autograph
his cast. Write as small as you can – he's got a little arm.
Then I'll put the sling back on so Daddy won't see it right
away. It'll be a big surprise.'

Lucinda pinched the pen between her fingers and with her
nose almost touching the cast, she spelled out her name on
the white surface. 'There you go.'

While Charley put the sling back in place, she said, 'You
know how I told you I liked that boy Shawn at school?'

'Yes.'

'Well, I don't like him anymore.'

'What happened?'

'We were reading *The Diary of Anne Frank* and the teacher
was talking about how those bad Nazi police busted into
people's homes and took them away to those prison camps.
And Shawn raised his hand and said, "My dad says if we're
not careful the police here will start doing that to us – to real
Americans."

'I said, "They will not. My best friend is a police officer

and she wouldn't do that – she wouldn't let anybody do that."
And he said, "Not now. But my dad says to watch out 'cause
those socialists want to take all our guns and when they do,
we're done for." And I said my dad said that you should never
listen to anybody who calls people names – he says they only
do that 'cause their ideas are stupid. And then Mrs Marsh
said, "I don't think your dad used that word, Charlotte" – she
always calls me that even though I told her I don't like it.
Then she says, "It's not right to call people stupid." Well, she
was right about one thing. Daddy didn't say "stupid". I forget
what word he used, but I'm sure it meant the same thing as
"stupid". Anyway, she told us to stop talking politics and get
back to history.

'And so I raised my hand and she called on me again but
told me to watch my language which kinda made me mad
since I wasn't gonna say "stupid" right after she told me not
to and I almost just didn't say anything but then I did. I
said that politics and history need to be together 'cause my
dad said that we need to learn from the dumb things people
did in the past, or else we'll do the same things all over again.
And she said that was right and then she said the same thing
– kind of different from the words I said but I think it was
exactly what Daddy said. Mrs Marsh said that was a famous
quote. But then she said we probably shouldn't talk politics
anyway.

'But I know the constitution says that I can talk about what
I want, but I didn't say anymore in class anyway. But maybe
somebody should talk to her about that. She moved here from
Bosnia and became a citizen. Maybe she doesn't know we
can do that here. Maybe she doesn't know we have rights.
Could you talk to her?'

'Well, Charley, I think she probably does know all about
the constitution and about the Bill of Rights, which is where
you'll find the part about Freedom of Speech. But have you
ever heard of this expression: there's a right place and a right
time for everything?'

'No.'

'I think that's what your teacher was telling you. She wasn't
saying you couldn't voice your opinions, she was just saying
that right then when you were talking about Anne Frank, it
wasn't the right time to be discussing today's politics.'

'Well, who gets to decide when the right time is?'

'In this case, your teacher, because it's her classroom, her place.'

'That's not fair. I'm an American, too. I've been an American longer than her.'

Lucinda was spared from mouthing a platitude by a knock on the door.

'Who is it?' Charley asked.

'It's your dad.'

'Oh, oh, go away. Don't come in here. You'll ruin everything!' She plastered her back on the door and braced her feet on the floor. 'Go away. Go away.'

'Hey, Charley, I'm not going to open the door. I just wanted to ask Lucinda if she wanted to stay for dinner.'

'Oh, Lucy, will you, will you, will you?' Charley pleaded.

Lucinda knew she should be focusing on the case, puzzling over the pieces, making plans. But the temptation to set it all aside for just a little while, to eat a sit-down dinner with other people in the comfort of their home was just too much. 'Yes,' she said, 'I'd be delighted.'

Ruby seemed more relaxed at the dinner table than she had appeared earlier but there was still a wariness wrapping around her, as if she were too keenly aware of the dangers lurking out in the world, too fearful they would invade her home again. When Lucinda smiled at her, Ruby would return the gesture but her smile was fleeting and her eyes skittered away too soon. Lucinda stayed until the girls both went to bed, enjoying watching the sisters interact with one another and with their father. As she was leaving, she asked Evan about Ruby.

'She's still seeing the psychologist every week,' Evan said. 'The therapist has every confidence in her progress, her recovery. But it's been three years and sometimes it seems non-existent to me. I guess I was hoping she'd be happy and bouncy like Charley by now, but she's not.'

'You know, Evan, at the dinner table, I was thinking that Ruby was very withdrawn and then I wondered if I was being fair to her. Maybe it's just that Charley is so naturally gregarious that any child would look like an introvert in comparison.'

'You may be right. And I still think you should move in with us.'

'Evan!' Lucinda bristled.

'No, not pressuring,' he said, throwing up his hands. 'I just think you understand the girls so well – maybe because of the trauma you share in common, maybe because you're a woman—'

'Or maybe,' Lucinda interrupted, 'because you have an idealized vision of me that I just could never live up to.'

'If I promise to behave, would you come by for dinner more often? I know you have a special relationship with Charley and I wouldn't want to take away from that but I'd really like Ruby to get to know you better, too.'

'I'll try, Evan. I really would love to spend more time with the girls. It's not always easy – I probably should have been working on the case instead of relaxing here tonight . . .'

'Sometimes, you need to do what you want to do and work be damned.'

Lucinda's cell rang. 'Speaking of the damned – duty calls.' She slipped out the door and pulled out her phone.

THIRTY-FOUR

'Pierce,' Lucinda said into her cell.

'Jumbo, here, Lieutenant.'

'What's up, Butler?'

'Want to give you a heads up. My captain called me, wanting to know if my missing person's cases have turned into homicide and abduction cases, why I was still involved.'

'What did you tell him?'

'The only thing I could think of to stay in the game – I said you asked for my assistance because of my expertise in missing person's cases since the evidence of abduction and murder is not clear in every case.'

'Good. I'll make the request official with my captain in the morning.'

'There was one other thing. He asked me why, since we were suspicious of abduction, the FBI weren't investigating.'

'Damn.'

'He said he's going to arrange a meeting with your captain in the morning.'

'Shit.'

'You haven't been keeping your captain up to date, have you?'

'Hell, no. I knew he'd want me to bring in the Feebs and I didn't want to – not these local jokers and I doubted if I'd get my way again in bringing in the one special agent I actually trust.'

'Why not?'

'He's located in the DC office and the Special Agent in Charge at his office doesn't want him to even think about anything but terrorism threats.'

'Is there any way that we can work terrorism into our list of possible scenarios?'

Lucinda laughed out loud. 'I knew there was a reason I liked you, Butler. You think of a way to do that, you let me know right away.'

Despite her anxieties about what the next day held on the bureaucratic front, the evening's activities at the Spencer house had calmed Lucinda enough to allow her to get the first good night's sleep she'd had since Edgar Humphries showed up on his son's front porch. She awoke rested and refreshed.

She went into work a little early hoping to get to her captain before he heard from Butler's supervisor. She'd only been there a few minutes, though, when Ted popped through her doorway.

'Ted, what are you doing in at this hour?'

'I was hoping to catch you at your desk so I could talk to you before the captain told you.'

Lucinda's stomach lurched. She pulled her eyelids shut with a wince. 'What now?'

'It's good news – well, I think it's good news. I gave my notice yesterday. The captain talked to my new boss at the Regional Computer Forensics Lab who persuaded him to let me go right away – today is my last day here.'

Lucinda blanched. 'Today?'

'Yes, today. I'm driving up tomorrow and moving in with Dad.'

'Tomorrow? What about Ellen? What about the kids?'

'The lab is going to cover the traveling expenses for all of us to get together up there or down here every weekend until

Ellen can sell the house and the kids can finish the school year. That will free me up financially to hire someone to stay with Dad twenty-four seven on the weekends I'm down here.'

'So you and Ellen are going to put your marriage back together?'

'Not really. We're going to stay together – we need each other to take care of the kids and take care of Dad. Ellen won't work outside of the home. And we'll have separate bedrooms. We're committed to making that work. We have our doubts that romance will ever be a part of our relationship again, but, for now, we're both content with that decision.'

'I'm very happy for you, Ted. It solves so many of your problems and gets you into the work you really love. And it's not going to be easy for either of you. I'm really glad for you, but, damn, I'm going to miss you.'

'I'll miss you, too, Lucinda. Always. I will never forget you,' Ted said. He shook his head hard. 'I knew this wouldn't be easy. But, listen, you need any computer forensics, I'm your guy. Your cases will jump to the top of my priority list every time.'

'I'll confiscate every computer I can,' she said with a smile.

'I'll get back to you with phone number, email address, street address, everything as soon as I know it.'

'Pierce!' a voice growled from the doorway.

Ted and Lucinda looked away from each other at Captain Holland scowling in the doorway, his arms crossed tight on his chest. 'Yes sir,' Lucinda said.

'My office. Now.' He walked back down the hall as Lucinda listened to the menacing tone of his retreating steps.

'I'm the one that's leaving,' Ted said. 'Why is he pissed at you?'

'I don't think he's mad about that, Ted. We have other issues. I've left him out of the loop. And, as you well know, that has a tendency to make him very grumpy.'

Lucinda forced a smile on to her face and injected as much perkiness as she could muster into her voice as she stepped into Holland's office and said, 'Yes, sir, what can I do for you?'

'Sit. Now.'

Lucinda slid into a chair across from him, her smile still in place. The effort made her lips ache and her pleasant expression had no impact on the captain's sour one.

'First, let's get the department business out of the way. I assume Branson told you his big news?'

'Yes sir.' She focused her eye on the top of his head. The red bristles of his brush cut seemed to vibrate with the anger she was certain lurked close to the surface.

'I want to replace him as soon as possible. I'll go through the interested and eligible candidates and get a list to you and the others for feedback, hopefully by this afternoon.'

'Robin Colter, sir.'

'What?'

'Sergeant Robin Colter. She's the best person to fill the vacancy. She's helped out in a number of cases. She'll start out running. You can save a lot of time – just give her an interview before you do anything else.'

'Obviously, you didn't notice my current state of displeasure,' Holland said, his face getting a little bit redder with every word he spoke. 'You come in here telling me what to do when quite frankly I am so pissed at you, I could spit.'

'Yes, sir. Uh, no, sir, I wasn't trying to tell you what to do. I was merely suggesting—'

'Shut up, Pierce. Despite my exasperation with you, I will take your suggestion under consideration. But I certainly would appreciate it if you would review the list I will send you anyway and inform me of your second and third choices.'

'Yes, sir. Of course, sir,' Lucinda said, her smile long gone.

'Now I understand you're dealing with the abductions of senior citizens and you haven't bothered contacting the FBI.'

'Sir, they are suspected abductions.'

'Don't finely chop this one, Lieutenant. You had a failed attempt.'

'We certainly did, sir. But it was only an attempted abduction—'

'Pierce, you are so trying my patience.'

'I am sorry, sir, but until we knew we had a successful kidnapping, I didn't want to waste the FBI's time, sir. I know their priorities are on national security and I didn't—'

'Bullshit, Pierce. You just didn't want them involved. You didn't want to give up any control. You think I'm stupid. I know how you work. Lone dog Pierce, nobody else can do anything right, can they?'

'Sir, no, with all respect, that is not true. Sergeant Butler has been by my side throughout this investigation. In fact, I'd like to make an official request to keep him working with me. And Sergeant Branson has assisted when asked. Research has been invaluable – and Forensics, well I can't say enough—'

'Stow it, Pierce. You know what I mean. Sure you usually play well within your own sandbox, but you don't play well with anyone else – in any jurisdiction or at any agency.'

'That's not accurate, either, sir—'

'Oh right. There's Special Agent Lovett. The one person from the outside that you can get along with – one exception does not change the rule, Pierce. I know how you operate and you know I know it. Now, get out of here and get to work. I want the FBI involved in your case. And I want it to happen today.'

Lucinda rose and walked toward the door.

'Is that clear, Pierce?'

She turned toward Holland, clenched her jaw and said, 'Yes, sir.'

She knew she had to do what he asked but she swore she wouldn't do it until the end of the day. The longer she could work without the Feebs, the better.

THIRTY-FIVE

Sherry blinked open her eyes that morning, awoken by bird song. The awareness that she shouldn't be there hit her hard. She knew she had to get back to her daughter. *I should go now before anyone knows I am awake.*

She dressed, tied her shoes, grabbed her purse and turned the doorknob, gave it a hard tug and to her delight and amazement, this time it opened. She peered out, making sure no one was watching. As fast as she could move, she scurried back behind her bungalow and into the woods. She followed the same trail she'd taken before and once again found herself at the gate. She examined the padlock holding it shut.

How to get to the other side? She knew at one time, she'd have scaled the fence and dropped down on the other side without a hitch. But now, even if she could get up the fence, she'd probably tumble off and break her hip.

She remembered early in the day seeing Donnie and his brother Derek driving the van up to the cafeteria and unloading food. They had to go somewhere to get those supplies, which meant they had to leave the property. *Maybe that's when I could get out? I know it's always early in the morning. But is it every morning? I don't know.*

After thinking it through, she was certain those deliveries were her best opportunity to get away. Somehow. She wasn't sure how she'd get through without being seen but she knew she had to try. She sat down on a rock hidden by trees and shrubs but with a clear view of the gate. She clung to her mental clarity. It was difficult to maintain focus, to keep track of where she was and why she was there.

She wasn't sure of how long she waited before hearing the distinctive sound of the van tires crunching over the gravel surface of the drive. She struggled through the wispy strands of fog that created a barrier between her and the ability to reason.

She pinched her arm to keep on track and memorize each movement, every action, everything. The van stopped at the gate. Derek got out of the cab. He walked over to a rock, lifted it and pulled out a key. He inserted it into the padlock, opened it and slid it out of one half of the hasp, leaving it hang from the other, the key still attached. He pushed open the gate and got back into the van.

She was tempted to make a run for it then but she realized that Derek was certain to see any movement. *Getting out unnoticed will be easier when he is on the other side.* He pulled through the gate and stopped the van again. He pushed the gate shut. But she didn't see him touch the padlock although his body was blocking the view. *Did he take the key with him?*

She waited until he turned on to the road and drove out of sight, then she walked over to the gate. He had fastened the padlock again but he hadn't taken the key – it still protruded from the end of the lock. Her heart raced. Her breath choked. She knew it was time to act but for a moment the shock of it all made her incapable of moving. Then, with shaky hands, she reached for the key.

It took three tries for her to click it open. She slipped it out of the hasp and held it in her hand, eased open the gate and put the padlock back in place. *Free. Free. What was that song about being free? The one they sang at marches?* She heard it in her head but the words were muffled and indistinct.

She'd been standing there less than a minute but she feared it was much longer. Panic rose, and with it, its surly companions, a swelling sense of doom and the relentless drumbeat of despair. Her heart pounded. Her lungs starved. She gulped down air, tried and failed to smooth out her breathing. *I need to hide.*

She went up to the road and, turning to the right, walked as fast as she could. Her jagged breathing stole some of her energy with every step. She ducked behind a clump of wild shrubs. She needed to collect herself before she went any further. She sat down on a fallen tree trunk.

Time passed, her sense of purpose faded but her heart and breathing rates calmed. Her head drooped as she drifted away from conscious awareness.

The sound of her name brought her to full alert. 'Sherry, Miss Sherry,' the voice called. She almost cried out, 'I'm here – right here,' but slapped her hands over her mouth before the words escaped.

'Miss Sherry, it's your good friend Don. Miss Sherry, I'm worried about you. Come out, come out. Where are you hiding, Miss Sherry?'

She listened quietly as the voice drew closer and closer. Then it moved away, further, further, the sound of it became a whisper. She pushed up on her feet. She broke from her cover with caution, peering around a tree and down at the gate – no one was there. But beside the gate was something she'd never noticed before – a metal pole, a tall, rusted pole.

Her eyes travelled up the length of it. It formed an L and held a sign. It was faded and difficult to read. She couldn't understand why she felt such a desperate need to decipher and remember what it said but she followed the instinct. After a few attempts, she succeeded, the top line read: Sleepy Hollow. In smaller print below that: Motel, Lodge, Camping.

A smaller sign hung below that, one end attached to the bottom with a chain link, the other end swinging free. It read: No vacancy. Sherry began her mantra, 'Sleepy Hollow. Motel, Lodge, Camping. No Vacancy. Sleepy Hollow. Motel, Lodge, Camping. No Vacancy.' She kept repeating those words as she trudged up the road. As she walked, though, she dropped pieces of her mantra without noticing. By the time she'd gone half a mile, her chant was reduced to two words: 'Sleepy Hollow'.

She looked back over her shoulder at the sound of every vehicle that approached her from behind. Nothing alarmed her until she passed the one-mile mark. Then she saw it. A white van. She ducked into the undergrowth and hid behind a tree. She stopped chanting and listened. It sounded as if the van slowed as it came near. She held her breath. If it stopped and someone got out and someone came to get her, she knew she couldn't outrun any one of them – and if two of them came after her . . .? Tears slipped from her eyes as she prayed for deliverance.

Then she realized she could hear nothing. Not the sound of the motor. Not the sound of footsteps. *Did the van continue on down the road? Or was it waiting for her to come out of hiding? Or was Mr Don nearby, creeping up on her without a sound?*

She trembled, squeezed her eyes shut and tried to make herself small.

THIRTY-SIX

D on inhaled through his nostrils until his lungs could hold no more and then he blew the air out of his mouth in a sharp, short gust. Wrapping his hand around the door knob, he opened the door to his father's office, stepping inside, his heart thudding with trepidation.

As usual, his father was huddled over his computer, pounding on the keys. Mounds of papers and opened books covered his desk. He mumbled while in the throes of composition. Don never could understand him when he was writing.

He often wondered if he was saying the words as he typed or if he was cursing his tormentors as he tapped away.

His father wrote letters all the time to government officials, bureaucrats, newspapers. He thought they were all idiots but he wrote to them anyway – demanding letters that usually went unanswered. When his father did get a response back, it was typically a form letter, firing his father's anger even more.

Gary also authored lengthy rants that he read aloud to Don, Derek and Donna, usually late at night and into the wee hours of the morning. They had to stand at attention while he read – just as Don did now. Shoulders back, gut in, head steady. He didn't dare speak until his father acknowledged his presence.

Gary raised his head and cast fevered eyes in his oldest son's direction. 'What now, boy?'

Don grimaced. He hated that his father still called him 'boy'. He was thirty years old and his father still treated him like a child. He swallowed hard and said, 'Dad, I can't find Sherry Gibeck.'

'What do you mean, you can't find her?'

'She didn't show up for breakfast. Donna went down to her bungalow to fetch her but her door was unlocked – Donna said she's sure she locked it last night but some of the locks just aren't holding any more and need to be replaced. Anyway, Sherry wasn't inside so I went out looking for her by the gate where I found her the other day but she wasn't there either.'

'She was out by the gate the other day?'

'Yeah.'

'And you didn't see fit to tell me about that?'

'It didn't seem like a big deal, Dad. She came right back with me. She hasn't been acting any squirrelier than usual. I didn't think much of it.'

'You got shit for brains, boy. You're stupider than your mother.'

Don wanted to speak up in his mother's defense but he choked down the words. He'd learned the hard way that it didn't sit well with his father if he said anything nice about her. Gary yelled, hit him and came up with ever more derogatory phrases to describe her: whore of Babylon being his current favorite. As he stood in front of the desk, feeling small and insignificant in his father's presence, Don couldn't blame his mother for leaving that bastard but he sure wished she'd taken him with her when she left. *I can't forgive her for that.*

'Have you checked the pond?'

'Yes, sir.'

'You sure she hasn't fallen in?'

'I didn't see any signs of it.'

'Yeah, well, you didn't see any the last time either, did you? Go get your brother and sister. We have work to do.'

THIRTY-SEVEN

Lucinda paced in the tiny space of her office cubicle and then reached for the phone. She called the morgue, hoping for answers. She smiled when Dr Sam answered the call. 'Are you ever planning to retire, Doc Sam?'

'They won't let me go. Nobody else will put up with you,' he growled back at her.

She laughed. 'I was calling to see if you had any information on Edgar Humphries' toxicology results.'

'Patience is not a virtue you even try to cultivate, is it? I don't have the full report yet but I did get a call. There is no evidence of any of his prescription medications in his body.'

'Do you think that factored in his death?'

'No, Pierce. I know it did. The man needed those drugs. Not having them caused his death. I guess, in a way, that makes it a natural death. But if someone kidnapped him and kept him from the medical care he needed, I'd call that homicide. Not sure how it will read in my final report. When I figure it out, I'll let you know.'

Lucinda disconnected the call and punched in the numbers for the morgue in Norfolk. She sat on hold, waiting for nearly five minutes.

'Make it quick. I've got a backlog of bodies this morning,' the forensic pathologist said.

'I was calling to see if you had any results on the water analysis or toxicology.'

'That woman did not drown in the pond where they found her. She did not die in a bathtub or swimming pool – I'd lean toward calling homicide if she did. But the water in her lungs was from a naturally existing source – just not the one where her body was found. But there were no signs of struggle on her body anywhere, leaving me pretty flummoxed. Definitely not ready to file a final report.'

'Drugs in her body?'

'Nothing that was prescribed – not even in trace amounts. Nothing suspicious either. Same for the old guy. But I still think his was an accidental death. You're going to have to figure out how the both of them ended up out there in that pond. Gotta run.'

Jumbo sat down in the chair beside Lucinda's desk while she talked. When she hung up, he said, 'Didn't sound like good news.'

'No, it wasn't. But I wouldn't call it bad news, either. It's just baffling. Three deaths with no signs of homicide other than where the bodies were found. That in and of itself sounds like foul play to me. But how can I prove it? And if they were killed, why were they killed?'

'Maybe they were a bit more trouble than the abductors counted on?'

'Reasonable. But why were they abducted in the first place? No ransom demands. No claims of responsibility to deliver a message. Why?'

'The Blankenships seeking revenge on River's Edge?' Jumbo offered.

'It makes sense up to a point, but some things don't fit. For starters, the place has a long waiting list, knocking a few people off of that is not going to hurt them financially, so how do they get any satisfaction. And, if revenge were the motive, you'd think they'd kill the victims right away; but they kept them for months.'

'The other thing that perplexes me,' Lucinda added after a pause, 'are the contradictions. Edgar Humphries appears to have died simply because he didn't take his pills and his body was left where it was sure to be found. On the other hand, Francis DeLong and Adele Kendlesohn were dumped where they might have never been found. He died of non-suicidal self-inflicted injury and she drowned, but we don't know where.

'It's making my head ache. There's something odd going on here that is beyond the stretch of my imagination. Some twisted reason that probably won't make sense even when we know what it is. And how does the disappearance of Gary Blankenship's wife and stepfather figure in to all of this?'

Jumbo shrugged and shook his head as the phone on Lucinda's desk intruded on their conversation. 'Pierce,' Lucinda said as she picked up the receiver.

'Lieutenant, a patrol officer spotted the white van you're looking for.'

'Where?'

'In the Colonial Heights subdivision on Independence Way.'

'Abandoned?' Lucinda asked.

'No. There's a man sitting in the driver's seat.'

'Did patrol approach him?'

'No, they pulled around the corner out of sight and called it in.'

'Good. Send out enough patrol vehicles to block every road out of the neighborhood. I'm on my way.'

In the car, with Jumbo sitting beside her, Lucinda flipped on her flashing lights and tore across town. Her passenger paled at the speed of her driving and the abruptness of her turns. He braced himself against the dashboard, his fingertips turning white.

Before pulling through the brick pillars on either side of the main entrance to the community, Lucinda flipped off her lights and slowed down to a normal driving speed. She approached Independence Way, turned on to the street and drove past the van, pulling into a driveway two houses away.

She stepped out of the car, closed the door and walked at a casual pace toward the back of the house. Then she raced over to the next house, through two backyards and stopped behind the house directly in front of the van. She spoke into her radio. 'I'm about to approach the van. Stay on high alert. Be prepared to move in on this location at my command, but also be ready to move out and block him if he runs. And have stop sticks ready to deploy if he gets really reckless.'

Lucinda calmed her breath, peeked around the corner and

walked slowly beside the house attempting to appear as if she had just come out the back door and was strolling toward the sidewalk on her way up the street to visit a neighbor. Although she kept the van in view, she took care not to look directly at the driver's face. She was halfway to the street when the engine cranked.

She shouted, 'He's running,' into the radio and pulled out her gun as she raced toward the vehicle. 'Police, Mr Blankenship! Mr Blankenship, turn off the engine!'

The van pulled away from the curb and took off at a high rate of speed. Lucinda ran back to her car, leaped inside and backed up while still pulling the door shut. She spun around and headed after the van. Up ahead, she saw him turn left. 'He just turned up Paul Revere. Somebody put out a stop stick.'

The patrol car that originally spotted the van had joined the chase, pulling in behind the van and ahead of Lucinda. She hollered again, 'Where's the stop stick?'

'It's on Paul Revere just before the intersection with Constitution. He's approaching. He's half a block away. He . . . shit, he spotted it.'

Lucinda pulled into the middle of the street to see around the patrol car ahead of her. The van swerved up over a curb, across the grass, bisected the driveway, clipped the rear end of a Mini, spinning it at an angle, and then spit dirt as it tore through a flower bed and swerved on to Constitution Avenue.

'Pick up the stick! Pick up the stick!' Lucinda screeched into the radio. The officers moved into action immediately but too late for the patrol car ahead of Lucinda. He went flying over the stick, puncturing his tires, leaving bits of rubber in the road. Lucinda was ready to swerve into a front yard to avoid the obstacle but was spared that adventure by the quick response of the patrolmen. They cleared enough of the roadway to allow her to squeeze past into the intersection. She flew by, an officer's astonished face just inches away.

She turned the corner and saw an arcing trail of decapitated daffodils and mud tracks on the pavement. She pressed down the accelerator to lessen the distance between her car and her target.

The van jerked off of Constitution and up on to a ramp, rocking a little to one side with the abruptness of the motion. He merged on the highway with Lucinda close to his tail. For

miles ahead, patrol cars from the police, the sheriff's department and the state troopers converged on the highway blocking
off ramps and trying to get traffic to the side of the road, out
of harm's way.

The van rocketed through the remaining traffic, using a
zigzag pattern that made it impossible for Lucinda to pull up
beside him. Behind her, a pack of patrol cars, sirens wailing,
grew in number with each passing signpost.

The driver was now in the far left lane. Lucinda pulled into
the lane to his right and tried to close the gap. Suddenly, the
van jerked across Lucinda's path, crossed the remaining two
lanes of traffic and entered the off ramp.

Lucinda braked and turned right. Her car shuddered, nearly
stalled and then surged forward, off the highway heading
into downtown. At the bottom of the ramp, the van kept
going against the light, horns blared, brakes shrieked, metal
grinded against metal. The driver's side of the van scraped
the rear end of a truck, forcing the fleeing vehicle up on its
right wheels. It continued forward at an angle; Lucinda didn't
think it could maintain the position for long without flopping
on its side.

Just as it started to go over, the passenger side scraped
against the concrete abutment running along the up ramp to the
highway. The van bounced down on four wheels and plowed
forward into the grassy hill beside the underpass. Lucinda
slammed on her brakes, sending her rear end into the beginning
of a spin. The car jerked to a stop, throwing Jumbo forward, his
head just inches from collision with the dashboard.

'Holy shit!' he swore.

'Call for an ambulance!' she shouted as she jumped out of
her car and ran to the van. She inhaled the stench of exhaust
fumes, burnt rubber and fresh-churned earth. She heard the
sirens approaching, impatient horns blaring, the slapping of
her feet on the asphalt.

Reaching the van, she jerked open the driver's door with
one hand while she pulled her gun with the other. The driver
didn't move. She stepped up on the side board, reached
for his neck. She found a pulse. She put her fingers in front
of his mouth and felt his breath. *Thank God*. Still he just hung
limp, his seat belt all that kept him from collapsing on his
side.

Gently, she placed a hand on his shoulder. 'Mr Blankenship,' she said. 'Are you Mr Blankenship?' She got no response. 'Don? Don Blankenship? Are you Don Blankenship? Derek?' she said and saw a flutter in his eyelashes. *The younger son.* 'Hang in there, Derek. Help is on the way.' *And don't die. Whatever you do don't die.*

She stepped down and looked through the maze of spinning lights, hoping to see an ambulance peel out of the pack. She shouted into the radio, 'Where the hell is the ambulance?'

'Less than a mile away, Lieutenant. Are you OK?'

'Why wouldn't I be?' she spit out.

She stepped back up on the running board. 'Derek. Derek. Can you hear me?'

His lids opened to small slits. He gave a nearly imperceptible nod.

'The ambulance is almost here. You're going to be fine.'

His lips smacked. 'Hurts,' he rasped.

'I see the ambulance. Help is here. Coming this way. They'll take care of your pain.' She stepped back to make way for the emergency medical personnel. She ran both hands through her hair as she walked back to her car. She leaned her rump against the hood and watched the activity at the van.

She heard the car door open, and then Jumbo was by her side. 'Hey,' he said.

'Hey, Butler.'

'I was thinking . . .'

'What's that?'

'Maybe after what we've just been through, you could start calling me Jumbo – all my friends do.'

Lucinda's head dropped back as she laughed. 'Yeah, you would think I would, wouldn't you?'

THIRTY-EIGHT

Terrified and paranoid, Sherry did not move until the urge to pee overcame her caution. She stepped back a little deeper into the wild growth on the roadside, blushing a bright red the moment she pulled down her pants. Squatting she felt vulnerable and immodest. When she finished, it hit her: no toilet paper, no tissue. She thought about ripping off a leaf, but she'd spent her life in the city, she'd heard of poison ivy but didn't know what it looked like. Instead she bounced in place for a moment then pulled up her slacks. She wrinkled up her nose with distaste at the damp spot left on her underpants.

She couldn't remember how she managed to get into the bushes on the side of the road but one thought remained anchored in her mind: she had to find her daughter. She high-stepped through the undergrowth until she reached the mowed swatch next to the pavement where she walked at a slow but steady pace.

The road was not well traveled but every car seemed one too many and she cringed as each one whooshed past her. Reaching a bridge, she stopped. When she crossed it, she'd be exposed with no easy place to hide. She located the midway point and picked out a mark nearest that spot and kept her eyes on it. *If I need to run before I reach that point, I have to turn around.* She ratcheted up her courage and crossed the bridge with a pounding heart.

She grew hungry as she traveled down the road but the grumbling in her stomach was far more tolerable than the dryness that spread from her mouth down into her throat. Her tongue felt like a big wad of partially chewed squid – she wished she could spit it out. She had to find water soon. She continued forward on the road that never seemed to end.

A car slowed beside her. She panicked and ran into the bushes again, ducked behind a tree. The car, though, didn't stop as Sherry feared. She exhaled her relief when she realized the driver had no interest in her. It was just making a turn off the road up ahead. She couldn't see a street sign. *Maybe there was a store or a house or a school up there – someplace I could get a glass of water.*

She moved her tired legs as fast as she could. *How long have I been walking? How far have I gone?* She was painfully conscious of the weight of her feet and the effort it took to lift and move them forward. *What if there's nothing there? What if I'm hurrying to nowhere?* Her lower lip quivered. Tears formed in her eyes. She shook off the threatened crying jag; she had no time for it now.

At long last, she reached the spot where the car turned off

the road: a paved entrance to a gas station and convenience store. It was an old place that appeared a bit down on its luck; nonetheless, the sight of it gave her a fresh burst of energy. She hurried across the lot and into the front door. She stepped up to the counter and forced her dry mouth to form words. 'Could I have a glass of water, please?'

The man behind the counter said, 'The bottled water is in the back along the wall,' and turned to another customer. When he counted out that man's change, he turned back to Sherry who stood in the same spot, blinking her eyes and clutching a purse to her chest. 'Ma'am, did you hear me? Did you understand me?'

'I really need some water,' she squeaked.

He rolled his eyes, stepped from behind the counter, walked to the back and plucked a bottle out of the refrigerator case. Getting back to the cash register, he punched in the price and said, 'That's ninety-four cents after tax.'

Sherry just stuck out her hand, reaching for the water.

'Ma'am, you've got to pay for it first.'

'Please,' she said.

'Hand me your purse,' he said, reaching his hand toward her. 'I'll get the money out for you.'

Sherry stepped back, clutched her purse more tightly to her chest and shook her head.

'OK, lady. Calm down. Here,' he said, stretching across the counter with the bottle. 'Take it. It's yours.'

She stepped forward, jerked it from his hand and twisted off the cap. She upended the bottle gulping hard and fast.

'Hey, lady. Easy there. You're going to hurt yourself.' He grabbed the folding chair from behind the counter and set it down beside her. 'Here. Sit. Drink slow and easy. Are you hungry, too?'

Sherry looked up at him and nodded.

'OK. You stay right here. I'll see what I can rustle open for ya, OK?' She watched as he turned his back to her and raised a thin, flat object to his ear. When he whispered into the object, she thought he was talking to himself.

Returning to Sherry, he held up a candy bar, a pack of peanut butter crackers and a bag of pretzels. 'Does any of this look good to you?'

She pointed to the crackers. He gave them to her and

watched her eat. She gnawed on the edges like a squirrel. When she finished the first one, she took a huge gulp of water. After the second one, the water was gone. He got her another bottle and asked, 'You got a name?'

Sherry bit her lower lip, nodded her head and said, 'Sherry.'

'You got a last name, you know, like a family name?'

Her eyes darted back and forth in their sockets as she struggled to comprehend the question and find the answer. 'Gibeck,' she said.

'Well, Ms Gibeck, you from around these parts?'

She shook her head.

'Where you from?'

Sherry shrugged.

'Where'd you come from? I mean, like when you started your walk that brought you here?'

She furrowed her brow, but it relaxed as she remembered. 'Hollow,' she said.

'The hollow? Which hollow?'

She shook her head.

Chief Deputy Hirschhorn walked through the front door and toward Sherry. She jumped up from the chair and darted behind a row of shelves.

'She scares pretty easy, Chief.'

'Did you get a name?'

'Yeah, Sherry. Sherry Gibeck.'

Hirschhorn walked softly to the end of the aisle and whispered, 'Ms Gibeck? Sherry? I'm a deputy with the sheriff's department. I'd like to help you find what you're looking for. You want to ride in my car back to the station?' He eased around the shelf and stood, with his hands loose at his sides, smiling at her.

She pressed her back against the shelf, knocking off a few cans that hit the floor and made her jump. She sobbed out, 'I need to find my daughter.'

'OK. I can help you with that,' he said stepping closer. 'Just give me your hand and we'll go find her. Before we leave, do you owe that nice fella any money for your drink and stuff?'

She nodded her head and handed him her purse.

He opened it up but there was nothing inside but a pile of acorns. He closed it, handed it back to her and said, 'Thank you, ma'am.'

Hirschhorn pulled a five out of his wallet and slapped it on the counter.

'No need for that, Chief.'

'Don't worry about it. Just take it,' he said and led Sherry out of the store and into his car. He strapped her in the front seat and finally, she gave him a smile.

THIRTY-NINE

A uniformed officer stood by the entrance to the operating room. Another was positioned in front of the double doors leading out of the wing of surgical suites. Lucinda and Jumbo slumped in chairs in the waiting room across the hall. Lucinda wasn't sure what they were doing to Derek behind those closed doors but it certainly was taking longer than she thought it would.

Jumbo's cell phone rang and he stood up and walked out into the hall. When he returned he was grinning as wide as his mouth could stretch.

Lucinda bit her tongue. She wanted to ask if he finally found the pot of gold. Instead she said, 'Good news?'

'The best. The sheriff's department just picked up Sherry Gibeck.'

'Sherry Gibeck?'

'Joan Culpepper's mother. She just wandered into a convenience store asking for a glass of water.'

'She's been missing since December and she just now asks for water? Do they have any idea of where she's been?'

'Chief Deputy Hirschhorn – he told me to say hello by the way and to let you know they found Hannah Singley.'

'Where did they find her? Is she OK?'

'She was dehydrated and hungry but otherwise doing fine. She'd gotten up early, went for a walk and got lost. She eventually found her way to the elementary school and fell asleep on the loading dock by the cafeteria. The head cook spotted her there, fixed her a bite of breakfast and called the sheriff.'

'That sure is good news. OK, was there anything else about Sherry Gibeck?

'Yes. Hirschhorn said that whenever she's asked where she's been, she just says, "hollow". But when he asks which hollow, she just looks confused. But she knew her name and he found her on the Silver Alert list and gave me a call. I'm going to run out there and pick her up and take her home. Hopefully, she'll remember something more on the ride back.'

'Keep in touch,' Lucinda said. She sat still for as long as she could, then rose and paced the room. It seemed to be bothering some of the other people in the waiting room so she stepped out into the hallway and went back and forth out there. Finally, a doctor in green scrubs called out her name. 'Derek Blankenship is in recovery now,' he said. 'But he'll be moved to his room in an hour or two. He'll be a bit groggy at first but as long as he doesn't get agitated, I don't see a problem with you talking to him as long as you promise to get out of the room if asked.'

Lucinda gave him her assurances and returned to the waiting room, taking a seat in the first available chair. She reined in her impatience by considering her approach with Derek. *How can I get the information I need without making him get overly excited?* She thought twenty-one-year-old Derek was involved in the abductions only because he was doing his father's bidding. She hoped her theory was right and she could appeal to the young man's conscience.

Ninety minutes after Lucinda talked to the doctor, a nurse arrived to escort her down the hall to Derek's room. A uniformed officer Lucinda knew sat in a chair by the door. She nodded to him as she passed. The nurse laid a hand on Lucinda's forearm and said, 'Keep him calm. We'll be monitoring the room and will end this interview immediately if we perceive a problem.'

The detective nodded and pushed open the door. Derek was propped up in bed with a spacey look in his eyes, but he smiled when she entered the room.

'Hello, Derek. I'm Detective Pierce. I want to ask you a few questions, is that all right?'

'Sure. You caught me red-handed. I shouldn't have taken off like that but I just panicked. I knew Dad wouldn't like it if I was spotted doing my job.'

'And what was your job, Derek?'

'I was keeping an eye on a house across the street, keeping

a log of the times people came and went from the home.
Making a schedule so my dad would be able to figure out
the best time to send my brother in to rescue this old lady
before she got locked up and brainwashed with drugs.'

'Rescue? Don't you mean kidnap?'

'Oh, no. You don't understand. She was going to be put in
this institution where she could never leave. We wanted to save
her from having her mind destroyed and take her to a place
where she could be free and enjoy her second childhood.'

Noticing Derek's distress, she regretted her accusatory question and backtracked. 'Derek, don't get upset. I simply want to
understand.'

'That's OK. A lot of people don't realize what goes on
in those places. They destroy people so that their heirs can
get their money.'

'Really?'

'Yeah, they did that to my dad's mom. Oh, but my dad was
all against it. It was her second husband that had her put in
there.'

'Is that what happened to your mother, too?'

'Oh no, my mother – jeez my mother. I never knew her but
I don't think she deserves to be called a mother. I was just a
baby when she ran off with that man.'

Lucinda decided to save her suspicions about what really
happened to his mother for later. Switching gears she asked,
'So this old lady you were watching on Independence Way,
once you figured out when to rescue her, where will you take
her?'

'Oh, I don't do the rescuing. That's my brother's job.'

'OK. Where would your brother take her?'

Derek bit his lower lip. 'I don't think Dad would want me
to tell you that. Maybe I shouldn't be answering your questions at all.'

'Derek, listen, I promise I won't ask that again.'

Derek worried his lip, sliding it side to side against his
teeth. 'I don't know.'

Before he could decide, Lucinda jumped in with another
question. 'Do you know an old lady named Sherry Gibeck?'

'Sherry. Did you find Sherry? Is she OK? She wandered
off this morning. My brother and sister were looking for her
when I left.'

'Yes. We did find her and she's OK. A detective is taking her home right now.'

'Oh man, that is so sad.' Derek shook his head. 'They'll mess up her head again. And she was doing so good – most of the time, anyway.'

'Did Edgar Humphries stay out at your place?'

'Oh, yeah. He was such a nice man. My sister Donna and me really liked him. He loved to tell stories and we loved to listen. And then he just died in his sleep. Donna found him in his bed like that.'

'And what happened to him after that?'

'Oh man, me and Donna got into a lot of trouble with Dad over what we did. He was so mad when we told him, he yelled at us for hours. Do you know how hard it is to stand at attention at two o'clock in the morning when someone is screaming in your face?'

'Derek, tell me what you and Donna did. I won't get angry.'

Derek sighed. 'Old Edgar was real special to me and Donna. Like a grandfather, you know? We thought he should go back to that old house he loved so much. He told us a lot of stories about that place and how he turned the whole backyard into a victory garden filled with vegetables during the war. It just didn't seem right to bury him out at our place. So we fixed him up real nice and took him back there. It seemed like the right thing to do.'

'I'm glad you did that, Derek. Now, what about Adele Kendlesohn? Did you know her and do you know what happened to her?'

'Adele, Adele, Adele,' he said shaking his head. 'Oh, that's right. Adele. I remember her,' he said slapping his hands across his mouth.

'Derek, we found her body. No sense in trying to cover it up.'

The young man hung his head. 'Oh, that just wasn't good. That wasn't right. I wish I had no part in that.'

'You wish you had no part in what, Derek?'

Derek sighed. 'Dad said that we had to get her body off the property because no one would believe we didn't hurt her. But we didn't, I swear. It was an accident.'

'What happened?' Lucinda said leaning forward in the chair and taking Derek's hand. 'You can tell me.'

'She fell out of the boat but nobody realized it right away.

As soon as we did, me and Don dove into the water, looking for her. We finally found her but it was too late. I wanted to bury her in the oak grove – she loved to lay on the ground up there and listen to the acorns fall out of the trees and on to the earth. She'd giggle whenever one of them would land on her. She was a sweet, funny, old lady.

'I wanted her to rest up there where the acorns could fall on her grave for all eternity. But Dad said we had to get rid of the body. So me and Don loaded her in the van and Don drove out to this place I'd never been before. I didn't want to dump her body in that pond but Don insisted that we had to do it. Said Dad would be pissed if we didn't. So I did.' Derek's brow furrowed and his mouth turned down. 'I'm really sorry about that. I know it wasn't right.'

'But you did it again, didn't you?'

'Yeah,' Derek exhaled forcefully. 'We put Francis in that pond, too. Man, he was a crazy one. We rescued that one too late. His mind was already ruined. He beat his head against the wall. He did it a lot. But this time, we didn't get to him soon enough. He knocked himself out. We carried him to the room and watched over him. Donna stayed in his room for two whole days, listening to him moan in his sleep. But he never woke up again. Don and me took him out to that same pond. When we got back, I told Dad I wasn't ever going to do that again.'

'What did your dad say?'

'He said, "You will if I tell you to, boy." I didn't argue with him. There was no percentage in that. I just shut up and figured I'd deal with it when I had to but I wasn't dumping any poor old people out there in the middle of nowhere again. It just isn't right.'

'How many others do you having staying out there, Derek?'

He bit on his lip again and said, 'Mmm, let's see. I guess we have about thirteen, maybe fourteen guests out there now. Two cabins are empty – so, yeah, fourteen.'

'How many passed away while staying with you?'

'Oh, I'm not sure about that. Never kept count.' Squinting his eyes, he said, 'I think there's about eight crosses up in the plot. But that doesn't count those other three we talked about.'

Lucinda's cell rang. She glanced at the screen, saw it was Jumbo. 'Just a minute, Derek, I need to take this call.'

'When I got Sherry Gibeck home, Ms Culpepper asked her where she'd been and she said, "Sleepy Hollow",' Jumbo said. 'We thought she was talking about the old story about the headless rider; but she said, "No. That's what the sign said."'

'I'll ask Derek about that,' Lucinda said. 'Call Chief Deputy Hirschhorn and see if it means anything to him.'

Derek raised his eyebrows and asked, 'You'll ask me about what?'

'Sleepy Hollow. Does that mean anything to you?'

Derek blanched but didn't say a word.

'It does, doesn't it? Is that where you're keeping those people?'

Derek pursed his lips but still said nothing.

'You abducted those people and took them to Sleepy Hollow, didn't you? Where is that, Derek?'

'You said you wouldn't ask that again.'

'Things have changed, Derek. If you don't want to end up in jail, you might want to answer my question.'

Derek's breathing got quicker. His face began to flush.

'What if I told you that your mother didn't abandon you, Derek? She died. In the bedroom of the house where you grew up.'

'No. That's not true!'

'We think it is, Derek. And we think your father killed her.'

'You lie! You're trying to trick me!'

The door to the room burst open. Two nurses ran through the door. 'Detective, you are going to have to leave,' one of them ordered.

'No, I'm not lying, Derek. We checked that room. We found the evidence. There's blood everywhere.'

'No! No! No!' Derek shrieked.

'Detective, leave now, or I'm calling security.'

'I can show you the blood, Derek. It's still deep in the floor-boards. Your mother's blood, Derek.'

The nurse shouted into the intercom, 'Room 335. Now! Hurry!'

'It's a conspiracy – you all are trying to stop my dad. He wants to save people and you just don't like that, do you?' Derek yelled.

One nurse put her hands on his shoulders, trying to push

him back on to the mattress. 'Mr Blankenship, please, you must calm down.'

'Get out of here, Detective,' the other nurse said as she drew a clear liquid from a bottle into a syringe and then plunged the needle into Derek's IV line.

'We're going to find them, Derek. Your father, your brother, your sister – and put them all in jail for a long time.'

Two armed guards burst through the door. Lucinda threw up her hands in a gesture of surrender. When one of them grabbed her upper arm, she shrugged him off. 'Don't you touch me.'

He reached for her again. She pulled back and shouted out to the officer outside the door, 'Officer. Officer Bennett.' She ignored the ring of her cellphone.

Bennett was at her side in seconds, one hand on his holstered gun, the other in the security guard's chest. 'Back off. The lieutenant was just leaving. There's no need for you here.'

Lucinda gave Bennett a nod of appreciation and walked past him, out the door.

FORTY

Lucinda pulled out her cell as she walked down the hall. She noted the missed call was from Jumbo Butler but before she could press redial, her phone rang again.

'Hey, Lieutenant. Chief Deputy Hirschhorn. Calling to see if you're coming out here.'

'Coming out where?' she said, stopping and leaning against the hallway wall.

'Oh, you haven't talked to that little Jumbo fella?'

'Sergeant Butler? No. About what?'

'Now that you mention him, you know, you shoulda warned me that he didn't live up to his name. We're just country folk out here and we take things kinda literal like. I mean, when I was headin' out to the front desk, I was fixing to introduce myself to some big guy like myself, but all that was waiting for me was a little red-headed runt.'

Lucinda laughed. 'Not an appreciator of irony, Deputy?'

'Actually,' he said with a chuckle, 'it's the best laugh I've had all week. Anyway, here's what's goin' on: Jumbo called me and said Ms Sherry mentioned a place called Sleepy Hollow. I told him it didn't ring any bells for me. But when I got off the phone, something was naggin' at the back of my mind. So I asked the dispatcher. And she said, "Wasn't there a motel and camping grounds out off of Highway 60 with that name?" Damned if there wasn't, Lieutenant.

'Used to be a prosperous place before they built the inter-state. Didn't have so much business after that. Then, the old couple that ran it died about thirty years back and it's been sitting empty. The sign's just been fadin' and rustin' ever since, but it's still standin'. I drove out and the gate's padlocked but there's a lot of fresh tire tracks in and outta there. Thought it was worth checkin' out.

'Anyway, I figured we oughta play it safe. I'm gatherin' up some deputies and the state's sendin' over some troopers. Jumbo should be on his way – he thinks some folks called the Blankenships might be holed up out there. Thought you might want to come along, too.'

Lucinda pulled away from the wall, walking fast down the hall. 'Tell me how to find it and I'll be there.' She bolted through the hospital doors and ran across the carport, memo-rizing the directions as she rushed to her car.

Driving out of town, her mind was a jumble of thoughts trying to pull together everything she knew to forge it into a solid clear picture. No matter how she tried, though, nothing was as tidy as she liked. She refused, at this point, to entertain the idea that she was now engaged in a wild goose chase and that all she'd find out in the country was disappointment.

She couldn't miss the closed service station Hirschhorn had picked for the gathering spot if she tried. Even if she'd been the first one to arrive, she thought she'd have recognized the deteriorating building with its caved-in roof and crooked sign advertising gas for 129.9 a gallon. As it was now, the normally vacant corner lot was packed with vehicles: state troopers in pick-up trucks, six brown, marked, Sheriff's Department cars, a couple of unmarked and emergency medical vehicles from two different volunteer fire departments. In between and around them, people bustled, checked guns, loaded up with ammunition, prepared for the worst.

Lucinda slid out of the car. Hirschhorn approached her and

said, 'Listen, I know this is my jurisdiction and not yours. But I've been talkin' a bit more to Jumbo and it looks like this might all be a part of a bigger investigation with your name on it. So I'd like the two of us to lead this operation together.'

'The state guys OK with that?' Lucinda asked.

'Yeah. They keep telling me they're just here to provide support. State ain't as bad as the Feds but I still don't trust them all that much.'

'I hear ya, Chief. I'm under orders to get the Feebs involved in this case before the day is over.'

Hirschhorn looked at his watch and grinned. 'Business day's almost over, Lieutenant.'

'Yeah. I'm real worried,' she said with a yawn and a roll of her eyes.

Hirschhorn snorted. 'I can tell. OK. What do you think we ought to do? My boys are itchin' to bust through the gate and bust some heads. But considering the possibility that we might have more old folks in there . . .'

'I think probably thirteen of them, Deputy.'

'That many?' Hirschhorn asked. 'How many bad guys?'

'I suspect Gary Blankenship and two of his adult children are in there. But I don't know if there is anyone else and I'm not sure if they're armed.'

'You thinking we need to do a little spyin' first – maybe just the two of us?'

'Sounds good to me,' Lucinda agreed.

Hirschhorn stepped up on the concrete platform that once held gas pumps. Swinging his arm in the air, he shouted, 'Hey, y'all.'

Bodies formed a circle around him. 'The Lieutenant and I are going to slip inside the gates and get a feel for the lay of the land.'

The mostly male crowd shuffled in place, mumbling where they stood.

'I know, I know. Y'all are all juiced up and ready to go but we have a possibility of thirteen hostages in there and we need to figure it out before we go bustin' in and get some of them killed.' He stepped down and walked to Lucinda. With a jerk of his head, he said, 'My car's over there.'

'Oh no, I'm driving,' she said turning on her heel and walking toward her car.

'But . . .' Hirschhorn started and then thought better of it. He retrieved his shotgun and shells from his car and got into the passenger's seat in Lucinda's vehicle. After they'd gone a mile, the chief deputy pointed across the road to a gated drive. 'That's it.'

Lucinda drove a few yards beyond it, made a U-turn and parked on the grass shoulder on the same side of the road. She got a rifle and ammunition from the trunk of the car and they walked to the gate. 'Up and over?' she asked.

'Sounds good to me.'

Lucinda handed her Winchester to Hirschhorn, and scaled the fence. Once back on the ground, she reached through the small gap where the gate met a post. He passed her rifle to her and then handed her his shotgun. As soon as he was into the property, Lucinda pointed to a trail leading through the woods.

When they reached the end of the path, they stood behind and a little above a brick bungalow, the last one in a horse-shoe string wrapping to their left around a large pond. Lucinda didn't think the motel looked all that bad at all considering the amount of time the property had been abandoned and neglected. From her elevated vantage point, she saw an obvious sign of repair on the cheap: green shingle patches stood out from the originally black roofs.

She realized the barge-like boat in the water was moving slowly around the edge but she found it difficult to believe what she was seeing. A donkey or mule – she wasn't sure which – walked along a dirt path running around the circum-ference of the pond. It was attached to the boat by an appa-ratus that reminded Lucinda of a photograph of the Erie Canal she'd seen in her high school history book.

To her far right, she spotted a hill with eight crosses just as Derek had described. Closer up was what appeared to be a small wooden Ferris wheel with four seats. A large black rubber belt connected the base of the contraption to a hori-zontal wagon-wheel-like hub with a harness built into the end of one of its spokes.

Next to that strange amusement ride was something even odder: a short, wooden pole, dark with creosote, was connected to a much taller pole with a double line of cable – like an old, tenement clothesline strung between two buildings. Hanging from the cable was a seat, just like the ones on the

Ferris wheel. A crank attached to the shorter pole appeared to be a mechanism to move the seat back and forth between the poles.

'What the hell is this?' Hirschhorn exclaimed.

'Appears to be a poor man's Disneyland to me,' Lucinda said. 'Look over there!' She pointed to the front of the larger, center building where a lone figure emerged. It walked up to the pond, out on to a small, low dock and waved. About a dozen hands poked out from under the boat's roof, waving back. 'I wonder how many more people are inside that building.'

'I wonder exactly who is on that boat,' the deputy added.

'We can't answer my question without going in.'

'And we can't answer mine until they all disembark, but we have no idea of knowin' how many times they'll circle that pond. And dusk will be here in an hour or so.'

'We need to get everyone down here, then,' Lucinda said. 'Get them to gear up and come on foot. Unusual traffic sounds might drift down into the valley and warn them that we're coming.'

Hirschhorn called the officer he left in charge of the group and issued orders, while he and Lucinda retraced their steps back to the gate. Five minutes after they reached the fence, they heard the rhythmic footsteps of the unit on the move in their direction. Soon, the uniforms were there, scaling the fence.

One state trooper stood with his back to the gate on the inside of the compound. He held a rifle across his chest and wore a Buckingham Palace guard expression on his face. A sniper from the sheriff's department planted himself behind a large tree, ready to pick off anyone who threatened the trooper – on foot or in a vehicle.

Two men remained with Hirschhorn, Lucinda and Jumbo. The rest spread out behind the motel from one end to the other. After a discussion long enough to rub Lucinda's small portion of patience down to a nub, they reached a decision. The two people who looked the least threatening – Lucinda and Jumbo – would walk down the drive. The remaining three would watch their backs.

As the two approached the buildings, Lucinda said, 'Smile, Jumbo, as if your life depended on it 'cause it very well might.' With every step, it grew more difficult for her to maintain a casual pace. She itched to draw her weapon and order everyone to the ground.

They walked closer to the pond, passing the end bungalow, entering the horseshoe. A shout echoed from the water, the words indistinct but the panic evident. A woman emerged from the center building. Stopped. Moved towards them. Lucinda raised an arm and waved in her direction.

The woman hesitated, then returned the gesture. She continued toward Lucinda and Jumbo. When she got within shouting distance, she yelled, 'May I help you?'

Lucinda took long strides in her direction. Jumbo struggled to keep up with her. The moment Lucinda felt she could speak in a normal voice and still be heard, she said, 'Donna? Donna Blankenship?'

Donna stopped, turned and ran back inside. Lucinda broke into a run and followed her. More shouts rang out from the boat. Lucinda heard a splash in the water as she reached the door. She pulled on it but it was locked.

Hearing footsteps on the wooden dock, she turned. A young man in dripping clothes ran up the hill toward her. Jumbo turned back to confront him. A shot rang out. Jumbo crumpled to the ground.

Lucinda pulled her weapon and went down in a crouch running for the cover of a park bench in front of the bungalows. Another shot sent dirt flying yards in front of her. She ducked behind the bench and called out on the radio, 'Officer down. Repeat. Officer down.'

Before she finished speaking, the team was already in motion, converging on her location. Hirschhorn and the trooper and deputy with him, took up positions and aimed their weapons at the covered barge. They held their fire as the shouting from the water was replaced by sobbing and whimpering.

Lucinda heard a crash and the grind of metal and worried about the source of the sound until she heard a siren approaching down the hill. She mumbled a prayer for Jumbo and turned her focus back to the wet man; she thought it was Don, making his way toward her. He didn't appear to have a weapon. When he reached a point that placed him between her and the boat, she rose to her feet, her gun pointing straight at him. 'Put your hands on top of your head. Lace your fingers together. And drop to your knees.'

He paused looking to his left and right then dropped in front of her, hands in the air.

Two deputies hurried in to pull Jumbo out of harm. Bullets hit the dirt around them as they moved the injured officer back up the drive and out of sight. The emergency vehicles filled the air with their desperate wails as they responded to the scene from their bivouac a mile up the road.

Lucinda shouted, 'Don? Don Blankenship?' at the man on the ground.

He nodded.

'Hands on top of your head.'

He complied and Lucinda stepped behind, grabbing one arm at a time, pulling it down and snapping on handcuffs. A loud crash made them both jerk in the direction of the center building where two deputies breeched the front door. Lucinda heard muffled shouting from inside. Then she heard a bullet sing as it passed her ear.

She grabbed the cuffs, jerked Don to his feet and dragged him behind the bench and forced him back on to the ground. Pinned in place, she boiled with anger. She pulled back on the cuffs, causing Don to yelp. 'Who's on the boat, Don?'

'The guests.'

'Who else, Don?' she said tugging again.

'My dad.'

'Gary Blankenship?'

'Yes.'

'How many hostages does your dad have?'

'They're not hostages, they're—'

'I don't give a damn what you call them, Don. Your dad is shooting at us. He could shoot his passengers. I want to rescue those people before they end up dead.'

'I don't want them to die. We rescued them so that their brains wouldn't die.'

'Don't want to hear it, Don. And we don't want to shoot your father but we will if we have to.'

'No, don't. He won't kill those people.'

'Oh, really, Don. Did you know he killed your mother?'

'No, no, she left us.'

'No, she didn't, Don. Where did he bury her body? You were ten years old. You must remember.'

'I can't. I can't.'

'Look,' she said pointing toward the center building where two uniformed officers emerged on either side of a handcuffed woman. 'Is that your sister Donna?'

Don nodded and whimpered, 'Yes.'

'We've already got Derek in custody.'

Don looked at her with wide eyes.

'Now. How are we going to get your dad off that boat without anyone dying?'

'Harvey won't stop till he gets to the dock.'

'Harvey?'

'The mule. We trained him. We wanted to make sure if anyone hooked him up to the boat and took off, Harvey'd always bring them back safely.'

'Can your father make Harvey keep going?'

'Not from inside the boat. You have to actually grab the harness and pull on him to get him going again.'

'How can we get your dad off of that boat?'

'I can talk to him. Me and Donna can talk to him. We can get out on the dock when he pulls up. We can tell him to give up, the dream's over.'

Lucinda knew it was a risky move but she also was aware that it would be near impossible to pick off Gary in a boat with a roof without injuring one of the other passengers. She radioed Hirschhorn. He agreed. With Gary's attention on Lucinda's hiding place, the deputy was able to make his way around the far side of the pond to where Donna was seated on another bench in front of the center building.

Looping his hand around her cuffs, he brought her to her feet and marched her toward the dock. 'Blankenship,' he shouted at the boat. 'Your son and daughter want to talk to you.'

That was Lucinda's cue to rise up and come out of cover with Don. She led him to the dock. Arrayed around them, all the others aimed their weapons at the barge.

The boat was just a few yards away. Donna spoke first. 'Dad, it's hopeless. When Harvey stops, just step out and turn yourself in.'

There was no response from Gary. 'Dad,' Don said. 'They've got Derek. They know everything. Don't make this any worse.'

Shots rang out again. Donna tumbled off the dock. Lucinda grabbed Don and rolled into the water on the opposite side, screaming, 'Hold your fire!' before she sunk beneath the surface.

She popped up sputtering and pulled Don under the dock itself. Once he shook the water out of his eyes, he lunged toward the other side. She jerked him back in anger and then she understood. Donna lay face down in the water, red tingeing the water around her. Lucinda pushed Don back, grabbed Donna's foot and pulled her under cover. Flipping her over, she saw the injury: a bullet hole right through the temple on the left side of her head.

Lucinda shook her head at Don and pushed the body away. Trapped as she was beneath the wood planks, Lucinda couldn't see much of the barge except for the underside of it as it cut through the water. She could hear the passengers, though. Quiet sobbing from some. Murmured words of comfort from others. One man said, 'What? What? What?' over and over again.

She heard 'Shut up,' snarled by an angry voice.

'What? What? Wha—' The voice cut off at the sound of a hard slap. A thump of what sounded like a body falling down. A wail ringing out. And then the angry voice hollering, 'I have demands.'

With those words, the barge came to a stop at the dock. Lucinda peered out toward the shore. The mule stood stock still in his harness, staring straight ahead.

'Yah, yah, Harvey! Go! Giddyup!' Gary shouted from the barge.

Harvey's ears twitched but he didn't move.

'See,' Don said, 'I told you he wouldn't move.'

Lucinda heard a voice over a megaphone call out, 'Gary Blankenship. You are surrounded. Come out now.'

'Come and get me,' Gary retorted and fired another shot.

'Send out your hostages, Blankenship. And then we can talk.'

'Talking's never done a damn bit of good,' he answered, firing again.

'Da-a-a-a-a-ad!' Don screamed. 'You killed Donna! You killed my sister! You killed her! Your daughter! You killed her!'

'You want to be next, boy?'

'I'll show them where the bodies are, Dad!'

'Not if you're dead, you won't,' Gary said and fired into the wooden planks of the dock until his gun clicked dry. None of his shots landed on either of the hidden targets.

'Missed me, Dad!' Don shouted as Lucinda shook him in an attempt to keep him quiet. *Why couldn't he pretend to be dead?* 'Don't egg him on,' she hissed at him.

Lucinda heard a quiet splash and saw a body in a wetsuit glide past her underwater. It moved around to the far side of the boat.

Another bullet smacked into the dock above their heads. 'I got a whole case of ammo, boy. I'll shoot this dock to nothin' if I have to.' Three more shots hit the wooden boards and zinged into the water. A loud grunt followed by sounds of a struggle. Feet banged the boards above her head.

Voices cried out sounding confused and terrified. An angry voice rent the air with a string of profanities. Someone sloshed into the water and peered under the dock. 'You can come out now, Lieutenant.'

Hirschhorn reached under the dock to give her a hand. Lucinda took his hand and grabbed Don's elbow to pull him along. They dripped on the shore line watching a sullen, cursing Gary Blankenship being led away, followed by twelve frightened senior citizens being escorted slowly up the dock.

Patrol cars poured down the drive as reinforcements arrived. A van painted with the state seal and marked as the property of the Virginia Department for Aging pulled to a stop. The doors opened and a team of eight social workers climbed out and walked straight to the senior citizens huddled by the side of a bungalow.

'Where's the other one?' Lucinda asked. 'There should be thirteen.'

'Old Fred wasn't feeling too good,' Don said. 'He went back to his room after supper to lie down – he's in bungalow six.'

'Let's go check on him.'

They trudged past the center building and knocked on the door marked 'six'.

'Come in,' a shaky voice shouted.

Lucinda looked at Don. 'You want to go get him?'

Don nodded.

'Don't do anything stupid, OK?' Lucinda said unfastening his cuffs.

Don shook his head. He and Lucinda walked into the bungalow. She leaned against the wall beside the door. He approached the man in the bed. 'Hi there, Mr Fred,' Don said.

'Mr Don?' Fred said.

'Yes, sir. It's me. I know you're not feeling too well but you really need to get up and get dressed. We gotta go for a ride.'

'A ride?' Fred said, a trace of excitement in his voice.

'Yes, sir. Here, let me help you get up,' Don said grasping the old man's hand and putting his other arm around his shoulder. 'Let's put on that blue plaid shirt you like so much and those navy-blue Dockers. You'll look right spiffy.' Don helped him dress and combed his hair across his bald spot. 'Now, sit down on the bed and I'll put on your shoes.' He helped the old man ease on to the mattress, slid the shoes on his feet and tied them tight.

Lucinda shook her head. She couldn't understand the total waste. *Don was so kind and gentle. They'd chew him up in prison. And Jumbo? Please God don't let him die. Damn that Gary Blankenship. Damn him to hell.*

Don led the old man to the social workers then turned his back to Lucinda with his hands behind him. She put the cuffs back on his wrists with a sigh.

Turning him over to a deputy, she watched as he was loaded into the back seat. The sun was gone now. She pulled out her flashlight to shine her path on the way to the center building. She flipped on the lights when she walked through the door. Display cases on the far wall were filled with dioramas of acorn people involved in various activities. A kitchen scene with an acorn lady wearing a skirt and apron as she worked in front of the stove, her acorn family seated at a table with teensy plates and forks in front of them. In another, an old-time wood log fort with buckskin-clad acorns stationed up on the walls, teensy rifles aimed outward and acorn Indians on foot or riding plastic horses ranged around the stockade outside.

There were many more little acorn scenes, but Lucinda turned away and walked over to a big white board labeled: Today's Activities. Below the heading was a list:

7 AM: Breakfast – pancakes and sausage

10 AM: The Great Acorn Hunt – meet by the flagpole for a hike into the oak grove

Noon: Lunch – Lasagna and salad

4:30 PM: Early Supper Tonight! Pork chops, parsley potatoes and lima beans

5:30 PM: Sunset Cruise – meet at the dock for a fun-filled ride into the sunset.

She stared at the schedule shaking her head. *Unbelievable. The Blankenships are totally nuts. How could they possibly think they'd get away with this?*

Her reverie was broken by the quiet squeak of an opening door. She turned and saw Chief Deputy Hirschhorn entering the room. 'Hey, Lieutenant,' he said.

'Hey, Chief. Any word on Jumbo?'

'Nope. Not yet. He was talkin' when they loaded him into the ambulance. That's good news.'

'Yeah. If only I hadn't gotten him involved in this mess.'

'He wanted to be involved in this mess, remember?'

'But he doesn't chase down killers. That's my job.'

'You gotta let that one go, Lieutenant.'

'Don't know if I can.'

'You feelin' guilty isn't gonna help Jumbo one little bit.'

Lucinda shrugged. 'What do you think of this place?'

'Little bit bizarre for me. Not quite my idea of a happy retirement home. I'm not sure if it all makes sense.'

'It doesn't, Deputy. Not a bit of sense.'

'I've got guards posted by the gate and the state has a forensic team on the way. The state's taking over now and they want you to go to headquarters and give them a statement.'

Lucinda sighed. 'They always want something and, dammit, I want to get to the hospital to check on Jumbo.'

'That's not all they want, Lieutenant. Apparently, Don Blankenship says he'll sign away his right to attorney and tell the whole story if he can talk to you.'

Lucinda's shoulders slumped. 'It's already been a long day, Deputy.'

'You can say that again. I'll give you a call just as soon as I hear anythin' 'bout Jumbo.'

'I'll keep my cell on – no matter what I'm doing.'

'I've got a man waitin' to give you a lift up to your car if you're done here.'

'I guess I am – there's just something bugging me. Something that feels undone.'

'Maybe Don will have the answers.'

'Maybe he will,' she shrugged.

FORTY-ONE

Driving over to state police headquarters, Lucinda called Jake. She ran down the events of the afternoon. After Jake congratulated her on a job well done, she said, 'Nonetheless, Captain Holland is still going to be pissed. I disobeyed a direct order.'

'What did you do?' Jake asked.

'He told me that because of the abductions, I needed to get the FBI involved and I needed to do it today. I never did call and there's no sense to do it now.'

'Tell Holland you did call the FBI.'

'I can't lie to my captain, Jake – especially not to cover my own butt.'

'Who do you think you're talking to, Lucinda?'

'Oh. Right. You're FBI. Hadn't thought of that.'

'And didn't you say that the state took over the case?'

'Yes. Ahhh – sure – it would be presumptuous of me to call in the FBI on a state case, wouldn't it?' Lucinda said with a grin.

'You betcha,' Jake said.

'Well, I might survive my next encounter with the captain after all.'

'You're really going to have to get over your aversion to working with the FBI or I might start taking it personal.'

'C'mon, Jake. You know I view you differently than any other *special* agent. I actually think you are kind of special.'

'What do you think of Special Agent in Charge Dixon in our local office down your way?'

'He's one of the worst, Jake. Arrogant. Pushy. Grasping. And I don't think he likes women detectives.'

'He's retiring next month.'

'Oh, really. Doubt if it will make much of a difference. What officious SOB will be taking his place?'

'That officious SOB will be me.'

'What?'

'Me – Special Agent in Charge Jake Lovett, at your service, ma'am.'

'You're moving here?'

'Yes.'

'When?'

'In four weeks. Do you think my office could expect more cooperation from you in the future, Lieutenant?'

'As long as the promotion doesn't go to your head *Mister Special* Agent in Charge,' Lucinda said with a laugh. 'Jake, I've got to run. Just got to the state trooper barracks. I'm really excited about your move. Talk to you soon.'

She was escorted to the interrogation room by a trooper who explained the audio and video recording capabilities. 'I'll be in the observation room. If you need anything, just let me know.'

When she entered, Don raised his head up from his folded arms resting on the table. 'Thanks for coming, Lieutenant.'

'Are they treating you OK, Mr Blankenship?'

Don winced. 'Please. Call me Don. My dad is Mr Blankenship and I really don't want to be reminded of that fact.'

'Because he shot your sister?'

'Yes and no. That's when it all hit me. Everything he was doing was wrong. I'd had my doubts before but I brushed them away. But when I saw her with that bullet in her head, it was as if – well, you know that old hymn "Amazing Grace"?'

Lucinda nodded.

'It's got a line in it: "I once was blind but now I see". That's how it feels, Lieutenant. When Donna died, everything came into focus.'

'Everything?'

'Yeah. Starting with my mother. There was a lot of fighting going on between her and dad right before she left. Mostly about my grandmother. Dad wanted her to move in with us after Grandfather died. Mom insisted there was no room in the house for another person. She wanted to find a place for her nearby. The night before Mom left, I heard her telling Dad that if he brought his mother into the house, she was leaving and taking the kids with her.

'Then, the next morning, she was gone. Dad said she was a tramp and she ran off with another man. And then, we never heard from her – no phone calls, no letters, no birthday cards. It hurt a lot. Grandmother was a big comfort to us all. But she kept telling us to forget our mother. Pretty soon, we did put her out of our minds. It was easier for Derek. He didn't remember her.'

'Don, I don't think she left you. We found evidence of massive amounts of blood in your parents' bedroom.'

He winced as he brushed his hair off his forehead and said, 'Yeah. It hurts to hear you say that but it tracks with what I've been thinking. My grandmother lived with us until she got married again to a guy named Alvin Hodges. He seemed nice enough but I never got to see much of him since my dad was violently opposed to the marriage and furious that his mother moved out of the house. He blamed Hodges for all of it.

'Then Grandmother started showing signs of Alzheimer's. Hodges took care of her at home for a while until it got too much for him. He put her in a lockdown unit at River's Edge. My dad was beside himself. He ranted and raved that Hodges had poisoned her. He said there was a conspiracy between Hodges and the staff at the Alzheimer's place to destroy her mind with drugs. He had piles and piles of articles and books to prove it.

'He sent a lot of that stuff to Hodges before he put grand-mother away. One day, I came home and it was all piled up on his desk along with all the other stuff he'd accumulated. I asked him where it came from and he said that Hodges dumped it all on the front porch without even ringing the doorbell.

'That night, I woke up hearing a noise in the backyard that sounded like metal against rock or brick. I got up, went downstairs and on to the back porch. Dad had a shovel in his hand and was throwing dirt on a spot by the fence. I hollered down and asked him what he was doing in the backyard in the middle of the night.

'He said, "One of you damned kids left the gate open and

some damn stray wandered in here digging the place up. I'm
shoveling the dirt back. I shoulda made y'all get your lazy
asses out of bed and do it." I told him I was sorry. And he
said, "You better be, boy."' Don's hands flexed and folded
into tight fists. 'I hate it when he calls me "boy". I asked him
but he just won't stop.'

'What are you thinking, Don?'

'I'm thinking that Dad was probably burying Alvin Hodges
in the backyard. Dad stopped calling and yelling at him on
the phone. In fact, he totally stopped talking about him. I'm
thinking Hodges did bring over those papers and books but
Dad never let him leave. And if he did that, maybe he did kill
our mother. Maybe she's back there, too. Maybe she never
left us after all,' he said, struggling to maintain control of his
emotions.

Lucinda's heart raced. *This is enough to get a search warrant
to tear up every inch of that yard. Maybe Sadie and Alvin
would finally get the justice they deserved.* 'Thank you, Don.
I know it had to be difficult to talk about that. Can I ask you
questions about what is going on now?'

He nodded. 'Yeah. I'd like to think about something else.'

'How did this whole thing get started out at Sleepy Hollow?'

'After Grandmother died, Dad grew obsessed with River's
Edge. Kept saying that he had to do something to keep them
from poisoning old people. He said that dementia was a label
they put on the elderly who just grew tired of it all and wanted
to relive their childhoods. He thought if you gave them a
place where they could be children again, where their bodies
were free of pharmaceutical poisons, then their minds would
heal.

'One day, he came home all excited saying he found the
perfect place. We all went out there to check it out. We fixed
up our rooms, a bathroom and the kitchen and moved in. We
got busy on the rest of the place – fixing up the rides, making
the bungalows livable. Then Dad went spying at River's Edge.
He parked on the edge of their lot. Said he found the perfect
spot under some trees where the light was dimmer, the sun
didn't bake the car and he had a clear view of the front door.
He said he was looking for people who were ready to put
their parents into jail. He could pick them out 'cause they
arrived with an old person and when they left they still had

the senior citizen with them. When he spotted a likely prospect, he'd follow that person all the way home. Nobody ever seemed to spot that they had a tail.

'He'd spend days watching the house and suddenly he'd come back with a new resident – a guest, he'd say. After we had about six or seven of them, Dad trained Derek to do the spying or stalking or whatever you'd call it. Then, Derek scouted the rest with Dad doing the pick-ups until all the bungalows were full.

'When the first death happened – a poor old lady died in her sleep clutching a teddy bear – Dad trained me to do the pick-ups. He called them rescues and he had me convinced. I saw myself as a hero for a while. I thought we were working in the service of a noble cause and never wavered in that conviction. Not until Dad made us dispose of the first body. I wanted to bury Adele on the hill with the others. But he wouldn't hear of it. I should have listened to Derek – he argued against it, he begged me not to dump her in the middle of nowhere. But I did what Dad told me to do like some stinkin' robot. Then, I did it again with that crazy guy, Francis DeLong.' Don dropped his head to the table and sighed.

Lucinda reached across to him and patted his shoulder. 'I think that's enough for today, Don. The prosecutor will want to talk to you tomorrow to hammer out a deal. And I'll be back at some point to let you know what we find in the backyard.'

Lucinda flipped off the audio, leaned forward, turning her face away from the camera. 'Don, get an attorney to guide you through the plea bargain.' She stood up and left the room.

As she stepped into the hall, a trooper was at her elbow guiding her in the opposite direction of the exit. 'This way, Lieutenant. The captain is ready to take your statement.'

'Excuse me,' she said, shrugging off his hand. 'It's been a long day. I need to arrange for cadaver dogs and an excavation team and I need to get to the hospital.'

'You'll have to talk to the captain about that, Lieutenant.'

Lucinda strode ahead of the trooper down the hall and threw open a door marked Captain P.L. Johnson. 'Sir, I need a couple of cadaver dogs and personnel experienced with the excavation of bodies to search the Blankenships' backyard tomorrow morning.'

'You certainly do. I was informed of that by the trooper monitoring your interview and have already gotten the ball rolling. They'll all be on-site at daybreak. Now, if you please have a seat, I'd like to get your statement about today's events.'

Lucinda remained standing. 'Captain, it's been a long, freakin' day. I've been shot at and dunked in water. I haven't had a bite to eat since I gobbled down a pitiful container of yogurt at 6 o'clock this morning. My partner is in the hospital with a gunshot wound. And I've gotten enough information from Don Blankenship to keep you busy for days. My body is beat. My brain is fried. It can wait until tomorrow.'

'We still need your statement, Lieutenant.'

She glared at him without saying a word.

'OK. OK. It can wait until morning.'

'Make that afternoon. Since your people are digging up a backyard in my jurisdiction, I need to be there.'

'I'd rather take care of this matter first thing in the morning, Lieutenant,' the captain said rising to his feet.

She grinned and straightened her posture when she realized he was shorter than her. *Tactical error, Captain.* 'No can do, sir. I'll be out here soon as I can. Thank you for your patience.' She turned and walked through the doorway.

Looking back, she added, 'Oh, yeah, don't screw with Don Blankenship, OK? Don't knock him around, badger him or give him a hard time. Give him a nice, warm meal, get a trooper to pick something up for him if you can't fix it here. OK?'

'All right, Lieutenant. No need to be a smart ass. We'll take good care of your boy.'

'Don't call him a boy – his dad did that. He hates it. I don't want him pissed off when I get back here. And I don't want to waste time listening to him bitch about you.'

'Do we need to give him a pillow and tuck him in, too?'

'Why don't you toss in a lullaby while you're at it, Captain? See you tomorrow.'

Back in her car, Lucinda paused before starting the engine. *Why is it I piss off captains wherever I go?* She turned the key in the ignition. *Face it, girl, you don't really care.* She pulled out of the parking lot and raced to the hospital.

FORTY-TWO

She was halfway to the hospital when her cell rang. 'Hey, Lieutenant. It's Hirschhorn. Jumbo's doing fine. In fact, he's asking for you.'

'Thanks for calling, Chief,' she said and pressed down on the accelerator. She muttered a prayer of thanks as she raced through the night.

When she arrived, she jerked to a stop along a yellow-painted curb and ran inside. Stepping into his room, she doubted what Hirschhorn had said. She stifled a gasp. Wires and tubes ran from Jumbo's body to equipment and apparatus on both sides. His eyes were closed and his small face too pale. His red hair stuck out in every direction like a visible aura around his head.

She approached his bed as quietly as she could and slipped her hand into his. Eyelids blinked and he turned to look in her direction. 'Lieutenant!' He smiled big, color rushing into his face and his eyes danced with pleasure.

She returned his smile, 'Hey there, Jumbo. You gave me a big scare. You shouldn't have stepped into the line of fire.'

Jumbo shrugged. 'What can I say? There was a guy heading straight for you. What else could I do? But he wasn't the one that shot me, was he?'

'No. The shot came from the boat. It was serious, Jumbo, but no main arteries were hit. They say you're going to be all right. It'll just take some time.'

'I'm not complaining. I get a paid vacation from work just in time for the baseball season openers. And I now have an interesting scar I can show my grandchildren one day. But, I tell ya, Lieutenant, homicide is not for me. A little too much agitation and high-speed action. I like Missing Persons where steady on wins the day.'

'Still, I bet our caseloads will intersect again,' Lucinda said. 'And, hey, did you notice I am calling you Jumbo now?'

He nodded. 'Yes, I did, Lieutenant. Thank you.'

'Well, don't you think it's time you called me Lucinda?'

'Yeah, well you would think I would, wouldn't ya?' he said with a laugh.

'Using my own words against me?' Lucinda chuckled. She answered all of his questions about what happened after he was shot and laid out the plans for the next day. Noticing the heaviness in his eyelids, she said goodnight, promising to come back the next day as soon as work allowed.

Lucinda slid the key into her apartment door wondering how her cat would react to her long absence that day; would he pout or be glad to see her? Chester didn't leave any doubt the moment she stepped inside. He ran up to her, sat at her feet and meowed. Then, he went berserk. He dashed through the kitchen, circled around the living-room furniture, raced to the bedroom, skidded into the wall with a thump and galloped back up the hall, making chirping noises that sounded more bird-like than feline. He screeched to a halt beside his food bowl.

Laughing, Lucinda plucked a tin out of the pantry and piled the food into his dish. He snarled as he gobbled it down. She was flat out too tired to prepare anything for herself. She settled for an apple and a chunk of Cheddar and carried them back to her room to eat while she dressed for bed.

The events of the day and the tasks scheduled for tomorrow were enough to keep her mind churning, but those thoughts were overridden by the persistent worry that something was missing. It was as if she'd completed a large panoramic jigsaw puzzle but an irregular shape defined a vacant space in the middle of the sky.

She returned to the kitchen to dispose of the apple core and found Chester on the counter rubbing his chin against the container of treats. 'OK, fella, I can take a hint,' she said, lifting him to the floor and placing a couple of treats at his feet.

She picked up her telephone to check her voicemail. A couple of messages from Captain Holland were first; she skipped over them without listening. She paid attention, though, when she heard Charley Spencer's voice. 'Lucy, Lucy, I saw this really cool place on the news. It was in the woods and I couldn't figure out everything on accounta the pictures were shot from an airplane or helicopter or something. But it looked like there was a Ferris wheel and a boat and then they put up an arrow beside this little person on the ground and they said it was you. Was it you, Lucy? I really—' The message cut off.

The next one was from Charley, too. 'I guess I talked too long. But, anyway, I want to go out there and see that place. Would you take me, Lucy? I saw Rambo at a PTA meeting. I asked him when he was going to fix your nose. He said he was waiting on you. You need to do that, Lucy. Oh, it's gonna cut off again. Call me or—'

In the bathroom, Lucinda brushed her teeth and stared at her reflection. She dreaded another surgery but hated that side of her face. She reached into a drawer and pulled out a photograph she called her reminder picture. It had been taken right after the incident and before she had any plastic surgery.

A sunken place where one of her eyes should have been. A shredded eyebrow, a convex cheekbone. Half a mouth with no discernible lips. And her nose – one side nice, normal, the other twisted and shrunken. She held the photo beside her face and looked back into the mirror. 'You've come a long way, baby,' she said out loud and barked out a bitter laugh at her inadvertent theft of a cigarette advertising slogan.

Sighing, she put the picture back in the drawer. *Later. Now I've got bodies to find.* She slid under the sheets. In seconds, Chester was lying on her chest purring like a mad man. She stroked his head. 'So tell me, Chester? What am I missing? What "i" did I forget to dot?'

'Meow,' Chester said.

'Oh, really. It's the "t"? I dotted all the "i's" but forgot to cross a "t"? Thank you, Chester. That's good to know.'

She closed her eyes and focused on the vibration from Chester's incessant purr. Quicker than she thought possible, she was asleep.

The alarm clock rang way too early. She almost hit the snooze button but then remembered she had to be at the Blankenships' row house before dawn for the search of the backyard. She groaned as she pushed herself out of bed.

Lucinda used the back porch of the Blankenship home as an observation platform. An officer and his cadaver dog, a black and white border collie named Sally, stepped through the back gate. She immediately went to one corner, sniffed the ground and eased herself down. Her paws stretched in front of her, her head resting on them, looking like a canine portrait of grief.

Sally's handler released her from her position and urged her to continue the search. The next spot that brought her to a state of alert was by the fence, midway up the yard. Lucinda thought that fit the description of the spot where Don said his father had been shoveling dirt in the middle of the night.

Lucinda, expecting to locate two bodies in the yard, was surprised when Sally alerted them again to the ground directly under the wooden porch steps. Leaving that suspicious spot, Sally searched the yard for another fifteen minutes without hitting on any other locations. She exited and another handler entered the yard leading Stanley, a short-haired brown mutt. Stanley hit on the same three spots, sitting at each one with his head held high as if honoring the dead with his erect posture.

Stanley was led out and the three members of the forensic anthropology team entered the yard suited up in Tyvec suits, booties, masks and latex gloves and carrying tile rods. At each spot, they carefully probed the ground and at every one, they nodded.

Beginning excavation at the site in the far corner, they uncovered the body of a woman in an advanced state of decomposition. The sweet, sickly smell drifted through the air, up to Lucinda, making her stomach churn. Lucinda doubted it was the body of Sadie Blankenship – after twenty years, she shouldn't be much more than bones. *Who was she then?*

Beside the fence at the midpoint, they found – as Lucinda expected they would – the body of a man. The odor of his decomposition, though fainter than the woman's, still sent a rush of nausea up Lucinda's throat.

The team moved to the site under the porch steps. Lucinda went halfway down the open stairs and kneeled backward on a tread and looked through the steps to watch the specialists at work. The first sign of success was the uncovering of the unmistakable white curve of a skull. The team now worked

with brushes and small picks and trowels. The unveiling was
so slow and magical; it appeared to be an act of creativity,
reminding Lucinda of the time she watched a sculptor carving
an otter out of a chunk of wood.

The forensic anthropologist leading the team stood and
lowered her mask. 'Lieutenant, it's a skeleton of a woman.
At first glance, she appears to be somewhere between her
mid-twenties and early forties. I can let you know more after
an in-depth study of her bones.'

Lucinda felt a fullness and buzz in the left side of her chest
accompanied by a melodious surge of sorrow and victory. She
checked to make sure she was not needed at the site any longer
and walked into the house. She went upstairs to the master
bedroom and stared at the missing floorboards and cut-out
carpet where the blood evidence was found. 'Thank you,
Sadie,' she whispered to the empty room. 'Justice is coming
– won't be long now.'

She walked down the stairs and out the front door. She
looked up and down the street amazed that the world seemed
oblivious to the enormity of the discovery in their midst.

FORTY-THREE

When Lucinda arrived at the state police headquarters, she was greeted by Tara Osborne, the state
prosecutor assigned to Don Blankenship's case.
Tara's pixie face appeared even smaller than usual, obscured
as it was by the black square frames of her glasses. Her curly
light-brown hair was fastened in a barrette at her neck but
stray strands poked out in every direction.

'Lieutenant, we have a problem,' Tara said.

'What's that, ma'am?'

'Everything was going fine until I presented Don with the
list of charges that required a guilty plea. He balked but won't
say why.'

'No explanation at all?' Lucinda asked.

'He just said that it needed to be changed. Then he asked
if you were coming out here today.'

'OK. I've got to talk to him about what we found in the backyard. I'll see what the problem is with the charging document. Can I have a copy?'

Tara turned over the list and Lucinda walked into the interview room.

'Good afternoon, Lieutenant,' Don greeted her.

'Hello, Don. The prosecutor tells me that there's a problem with the deal.'

'First, tell me what you found this morning, please?'

Lucinda inhaled long and slow. 'OK.' She described finding what she believed to be the body of Alvin Hodges and the skeleton of Don's mother. 'But, Don, there was a third body found – a woman's body. Do you know anything about that?'

Don's brow furrowed. 'Another body? Who is it?'

'I was hoping you could tell me.'

Don's eyes drifted from side to side as he thought. He shook his head. 'No idea, Lieutenant. I don't have a clue. I can't think of anyone else we knew who went missing.'

'Will you keep thinking about that and get in touch with me if anything drifts up from your memory?'

'Of course, Lieutenant. Are you positive that the skeleton you found is my mother?'

'I'm pretty sure, Don, but I won't know with certainty until the forensic anthropologist makes a formal identification.'

'How will she do that?'

'Hopefully, they'll be able to ID her with dental records. If not, I suppose we will have to extract DNA and take it from there.'

Don sighed. 'Have you told Derek yet?'

'No.'

'He's not going to believe you at first. He'll probably call you a liar and insist that Dad couldn't have killed her. He doesn't remember Mom. It'll be different for him. His loyalty will be with Dad. But don't hold that against him. He can't help it.'

Lucinda nodded and said, 'Now, what was your problem with the prosecutor?'

'I showed her all of the people that my dad kidnapped and she put the rest of them as counts on my list of abduction charges. But one of them shouldn't be there.'

Lucinda looked down at the document she got from the

prosecutor, laid it on the table and spun it around. 'Which one, Don?'

He placed his finger on a name and said, 'Adele Kendlesohn.'

'OK. Who abducted her?'

'No one.'

'Don't play games with me, Don,' Lucinda said, folding her arms across her chest and pushing her chair back with a push of her foot. 'We found her body, remember? You admitted to dumping her body in that pond.'

'I'm not playing games, I swear. And yes, I did dump her body and I admit to the abuse of a corpse charge in connection with her. But that lady was not abducted.'

Damn it. What is this? Another con? Has he been playing me? Through clenched teeth, she said, 'You're confusing me, Don, and I don't like being confused. Explain yourself.'

'We were paid to pick her up and we've been paid every month to take care of her.'

'What?'

'To be honest, I think that's why Dad made us dump her. He didn't want those checks to stop.'

The missing piece of blue sky clicked into the firmament of Lucinda's imagined jigsaw puzzle. *Rachael Kendlesohn bothered me from the start. I knew she was lying to me. I knew she was hiding something.* 'Who sent you those checks?'

'The Kendlesohns.'

'Both of them?'

'I can't say for sure about Mr Kendlesohn. Dad only talked to his wife. And all the checks were signed 'Rachael Kendlesohn'.

'How did this happen? How did she know to contact your father?'

'Before we started running the place out at Sleepy Hollow, Dad was a handyman and I was his assistant. Mrs Kendlesohn was one of our regular customers.'

'Doing what?'

'We cleaned gutters, power-washed the exterior of her house, maintained her pool, replaced light bulbs in ceiling fixtures, made little carpentry repairs, even hung pictures on the wall – stuff like that.'

'These regular monthly checks she sent, were they made out to your father?'

'Yeah and in the "for" line, she always wrote "home

maintenance" just like she did when we fixed the loose banister and everything else. Maybe she did that so her husband wouldn't know.'

That sounds just like her. Miserable shrew. 'Thank you, Don. I'm going to have to check out a few things to get confirmation on all of what you said, but it shouldn't take too long.'

In the hallway, she explained the situation to Tara and told her what she intended to do to follow up on the accuracy of the story.

'I don't think this should hold up our plea deal. I can just drop that charge for now. We can add it later if necessary.'

'Tell me, did Don hammer out this plea bargain with you or did he have a lawyer?'

'I wish it had just been the two of us. I think I could have gotten a tougher deal. Gotta hand it to him, the guy's got more remorse than a dozen defendants. But, yeah, he had an attorney with him this morning. But the lawyer left when we hit a standstill – apparently Don wouldn't explain the problem to him either. According to the rules laid down before we began negotiations, you're the only one who was allowed to talk to Don without his attorney. And the lawyer wasn't happy about that, but Don insisted. So after I get the document revised, I'll have to get him here before I can talk to Don. I'm still hoping I can get the deal done before the end of the day.'

'What's the offer?'

'I can't say I like it too much but the powers that be want to wrap up the father like a mummy. They think Don's testimony will do that. They pushed, I yielded,' Tara said with a frown.

'And?' Lucinda asked.

'Ten years, five of them suspended. Damn, with good behavior, he'll be out in three years or less.'

'Even that might break him in pieces too small to heal,' Lucinda said. She saw a quizzical look forming on Tara's face before she turned away. It made her smile. Always keep 'em guessing, she thought and her grin grew wider.

FORTY-FOUR

On the way downtown to Eli Kendlesohn's office building, Lucinda made two calls. The first was to Sergeant Robin Colter. Lucinda gave her the big picture in broad strokes and laid out the details directly related to the need for the Kendlesohn's bank records. Robin agreed to do everything she could to get a search warrant from a judge and get the needed information to her as soon as possible.

The second conversation was with Dispatch. After identifying herself, she asked, 'I need a pair of uniforms to pick up Rachael Kendlesohn and bring her in for questioning.'

'On what charge?'

'Right now, abduction – the abduction of Adele Kendlesohn. I'm not sure if we can make it stick but if we can't there's a statute involving the abandonment of a vulnerable elderly person that's a good back-up charge. Just stick her in a room when you get her to the Justice Center. I've got another stop to make but I'll be there to question her just as soon as I can.'

Lucinda pulled into a place clearly marked as a 'no parking' zone in Eli Kendlesohn's office car park. Riding up in the elevator, she thought about Eli. She didn't think he was involved but she couldn't eliminate it as a possibility just yet. She had to be as harsh and uncompromising with him as she would be with his wife a little later.

She approached the front desk of Kendlesohn and Wiseman Engineering, flashed her badge and said, 'I need to speak with Eli Kendlesohn right away, please.'

'I'm sorry, ma'am,' a perky young woman said. 'He's in a partners meeting and we do not disturb the partners.'

'Maybe you don't, but I will. Go tell him Detective Pierce is here. It is important. And it's about his mother.'

'I could lose my job if I interrupted them. I'd rather be arrested,' she said standing up and holding out two bony wrists.

'Oh good grief,' Lucinda said in one exhale. 'Sit down. Put your hands over your eyes. Now, count to ten.'

'One, two, three – hey wait a minute,' she said pulling her hands from her face.

But Lucinda was already on her way down the hall, opening closed doors as she went. When she hit the right one, a roomful of suits grew silent and stared in her direction. Behind her the receptionist grabbed and pulled one of her arms while squeaking, 'I'm sorry, sirs. I'm sorry, sirs. I told her she couldn't—'

'That's OK,' Eli said. 'It's Detective Pierce and I'm sure she's here to see me. If you gentlemen will excuse me.'

Eli joined Lucinda in the hall and walked her to his office. 'Not a woman in the room, Eli? I expected more of you.'

'Me, too, Detective. I'm just biding my time waiting for a couple of the old white dinosaurs to retire or die, then we can bring on new partners with an emphasis on women and minorities. We've actually lost some business because of our monochrome look. And sometimes an advantage in problem-solving. I'll be glad when those old farts are gone. Enough of my rant, what can I do for you today, Lieutenant?' he asked, gesturing to a pair of chairs inside his office door. Lucinda sat in one of them and Eli settled into the chair behind his desk.

'Tell me, Mr Kendlesohn, who handles the finances in your marriage?'

'Well, until I got tossed out of the house, we had it set up so that Rachael handled the day-to-day stuff: paying the bills, balancing accounts, transferring funds from checking to savings and vice versa. I took care of the long-term invest-ments: our stock portfolio, bonds, mutual funds, that kind of thing. Why?'

'Did you review the checking account statements or make yourself aware of the money going out of the checking account in any other way?'

'Well, I have on rare occasions, but it's been a really long time – I can't remember when I last looked at a statement.'

'Did you at any time look at your statement in paper form, in the bank or on-line since your mother's disappearance?'

'I don't think so. What's this all about?'

'Did you conspire with your wife to rid yourself of your mother?'

'What? What are you talking about? Are you saying my

suspicions were right? Are you saying Rachael killed my mother?'

'You became suspicious rather quickly, Mr Kendlesohn. Is it because you were her accomplice?'

'Accomplice? Accomplice to what?' he sputtered. 'Do you think I helped Rachael kill my mother?'

'If not, sir, why were you so quick to jump to the conclusion that Rachael killed your mother?'

'I was angry and worked up when I first mentioned that to you. But I found it hard to believe that someone I once loved could have done something so loathsome. My thinking has been going back and forth about that possibility for days. I've been trying to decide whether or not to call you and discuss it seriously. I keep changing my mind – back and forth. I finally decided that I was going to talk to my Rabbi first and hope he can help me make the right decision. I'm supposed to see him tomorrow morning. How am I going to tell him that I stood in the synagogue and exchanged vows with the woman who became my mother's killer?' The pitch of his voice rose with every word.

'Mr Kendlesohn, we have no reason to believe your mother was murdered.'

'Well, dammit, what is this all about then?' he said shooting to his feet.

'It is about the checks from your account to the man you hired.'

'Once again, Lieutenant, I need to ask you, what the hell are you talking about?'

'We should have a record of your banking transactions soon. The ledger will spell it all out clearly. It will show how you paid a nut job to take your mother and keep her out of sight.'

'You have lost your mind. I filed a missing persons report. I've been calling at least once every single week to press the police to look for her.'

'That would be a good cover-up, wouldn't it?'

'All I can tell you, Lieutenant, is that I don't know what you're talking about but if you think someone received payments to make my mother disappear, then you need to be looking at Rachael. Not me. In fact, if she did that to my mother, I am more than willing to testify against her at trial.'

Lucinda had seen enough. *I can't swear to his innocence*

but I believe in it. Unless the bank records tell another story, Eli is a victim. 'Relax, Mr Kendlesohn. Please, have a seat.'

He settled back in his chair and swallowed hard. 'I'm not sure if I'm ready to hear this or not. But I need to. What happened to my mother?'

'I've got someone obtaining a subpoena for your bank records right now, Mr Kendlesohn. So I don't have proof to show you at this moment. But I do have the statement of an accomplice. We think we know what happened. Your wife abandoned your mother at the mall and paid her handyman to pick her up and take her out to a strange, unlicensed home for the elderly. She continued to pay every month for her care.'

'She spent money on my mother? That doesn't sound like Rachael.'

'I believe she got a real discounted rate – don't think it would come anything near to what would be needed for a reputable facility.'

'That sounds like her. Did that handyman kill her?'

'We don't think so, sir. It appears she fell into a pond and, despite efforts to rescue her, she drowned.'

'Efforts to rescue her? Do you really believe that?'

'At this moment, sir, I do. The autopsy indicated that it was an accidental drowning and until proven otherwise, I tend to believe the corroborating statement from one of the sons of the man I think is responsible.'

'I'm the responsible one,' Eli said, his shoulders slumping as he spoke. 'I should have known. I should have gotten my mother away from Rachael before it was too late.'

'Eli, I know the guilt you're feeling is natural. But you did nothing wrong. Keep that appointment with your rabbi – you need him now as much as you did before. Your wife is being brought in for questioning – in fact, she may already be there. I'll do everything I can to get her to admit what she did.'

'I'll see my rabbi and I'm sure he'll agree with you about the guilt – not that it will make it go away. And it will also open me up to a lecture on hate. I really hate that woman I married. But I do have one immediate concern.'

'What's that?'

'Will you be keeping Rachael overnight?'

'I hope so, sir.'

'The dogs. Someone has to let them out and feed them. And I can't get into the house. She changed the locks.'

'That she did. I'll try to get the keys. If she refuses to allow me to give them to you, we will find a way to get inside. That I can promise.' *Oh yeah, just add breaking and entering to the list of my sins – the captain's gonna love me.*

On the way back to her car, she checked the voicemail on her cell: ten messages. Seven of them from Captain Holland. Two from Jumbo's captain. And one from Robin Colter – she listened to that one. 'The banking records are on your desk. I highlighted the checks to Gary Blankenship. And I have an interview with Captain Holland next week about an opening in Homicide. Thank you, Lieutenant.'

Good news all around. But Captain Holland? Does his interview with Colter mean he's not as mad at me as I thought? Nah, he's going to be pissed. Lucinda sighed as she pulled from the curb.

FORTY-FIVE

Lucinda held her breath as she walked past the captain's open door. She hoped to get past him to her desk and then to the interview room.

'Pierce!'

Lucinda cringed. 'Yes, sir, I'll be with you just as soon as—'

'Now, Pierce!'

'But sir, I have—'

'I don't care what you have. In here, now!'

Lucinda walked through the doorway. 'Sir, I—'

'Sit!'

She sat in the chair and struggled to keep her face expressionless.

'Did I or did I not tell you to bring the FBI into your investigation yesterday?'

'Yes, sir, you did.'

'Did you do that, Pierce?'

'No, sir. But the state took over the investigation and I would have been out of line to interfere—'

'As if being out of line ever bothered you before. And save it, Pierce. I heard from a state police commander. They didn't take over until very late in the day.'

'Yes, sir. But the case is solved. The bad guys behind bars. And I didn't shoot anyone.'

'But we do have a wounded officer, Pierce, and I've gotten grief from his captain and the commander about that.'

'I didn't shoot him, sir.'

'Well, thank the good Lord for miracles, Pierce. It certainly wouldn't have surprised me if you had.'

'Sir, that's not fair. I've never shot a fellow officer.'

'True, Pierce, but why do I think it's only a matter of time?'

Lucinda knew better than to respond to that provocation.

'You disobeyed a direct order, Pierce.'

'Yes, sir.'

'I should suspend you.'

'Yes, sir, but could you make it effective tomorrow? I have a few loose ends to tie up here.'

'You've got a lot of gall, Pierce. I can't believe you said that. For hours, I've been sitting here deciding whether to fire you or suspend you without pay for a month.'

'I'd prefer the suspension, sir.'

'You're not going to argue with me about a month-long suspension?'

'No, sir. I deserve it and I can put the time to good use – I need another surgical procedure.'

'If I didn't know you better, I'd think you just played the sympathy card, Pierce.'

'God forbid, sir.'

'God forbid indeed. I've muttered that a lot when thinking about you. But I can't suspend you, Pierce.'

Lucinda rose to her feet, her knees wobbling. 'You're firing me?'

'Oh, sit down, Pierce. No. I'm not firing you. I am not suspending you. And I will authorize any leave you need for surgery.'

Lucinda lowered down into the chair. Her eyes formed slits, suspicion sent zings of apprehension down her arms. She swallowed hard. 'Thank you, sir.'

'Don't thank me, Pierce. The police chief saw your little

operation on the news. So did the mayor. And I think about five councilmen. They all think you deserve a commendation. But then they don't have to work with you like I do.'

Lucinda sucked in her lips to prevent a grin from popping up on her face.

'There's just one thing that needs to end. And it needs to end now. At the very least, I expect an attitude transformation by the time you return from your medical leave. You have to get over this aversion to working with our local FBI office. I heard from the local SAC – he saw the news, too. He wanted to know why we hadn't asked for his assistance since we had multiple abductions. I told him it was an oversight. I don't think he believed me, Pierce. I do not want to be put in that position again. Is that clear?'

'Yes, sir, I will work on my attitude. And I can assure you that if you give me a month to make the transition, I will be more cooperative with the FBI.'

Holland narrowed his eyes. 'Why do I think there's something you're not telling me?'

Lucinda opened her eyes wide. 'I can't say, sir.'

Holland shook his head. 'Why do I put up with you?'

'Because I'm a good detective, sir?'

'Get out of here, Pierce.'

Lucinda didn't hesitate for a second. She bolted out of his office and into her own. As Colter promised, the file was on her desk. She flipped it open and paged through the ledgers. Scattered throughout the first two pages were transactions payable to Gary Blankenship, most of them under $500 – but a few were bigger – the highest one was for $1200. Then, in the month of Adele Kendlesohn's disappearance, there was a check for $5000 and additional payments on the first of every month after that for $1000. She picked up the file and headed down the hall.

Opening the door to the interview room, Lucinda said, 'Good afternoon, Mrs Kendlesohn.'

'Why am I here? I asked the officers and they deferred to you. So I expect an answer, now that you are finally here.'

'You have no idea why we brought you into the Justice Center?'

'One of the officers mentioned something about abduction, so I assume it is about my mother-in-law. Do you need me to press charges against those crazy people I saw on the news last night?'

'No, no, we've filed charges already. We don't need your help with that. In fact, right now, we're charging you.'

'Excuse me?'

'Why did you refer to the people we arrested as "those crazy people"?'

'Is that against the law now? Calling people crazy? Has political correctness run that amok? You must be joking.'

'Oh, no, Mrs Kendlesohn, I am not joking. Not at all. I just thought it was odd that you didn't refer to "those crazy people" by name.'

'I didn't catch the names on the news.'

'You didn't need to, did you? You already knew their names.'

'Oh my, Detective,' a wide-eyed Rachael said, one hand fluttering at her throat like a wounded bird. 'Are you saying that the people who took my poor mother-in-law were actually people I knew?'

Lucinda slammed the folder down on the table between them. She flipped it open to the page with the $5000 check and swung it around facing Rachael. Lucinda placed an index finger on the ledger entry. 'Cut the crap, Kendlesohn. You not only knew them. You paid them.'

'Oh my. Oh my, dear. That must have been my husband. You'll have to ask him about that check.'

Lucinda flipped through the file until she reached the copies of the actual checks. She hit the signature line with the tip of a finger. 'You're a liar, Rachael.'

'How outrageous! I want an attorney. And I want one now.'

'Can it, Rachael,' Lucinda said. She walked behind her, grabbed an arm and slapped on one side of the cuffs.

Rachael struggled, trying to keep her other hand away from Lucinda. 'How dare you? Do you know who I am? Do you know who I know? I'll call the mayor. You'll lose your job over this.'

Lucinda laughed out loud; she couldn't help it. After surviving Captain Holland's wrath, the idea of a threat from anyone else seemed ludicrous. Rachael stopped struggling and stared at Lucinda as if the detective had lost her mind. Lucinda slapped on the other cuff. She grabbed Rachael's purse and gave a light poke to one of the woman's shoulders and said, 'Let's go, girly.'

'How dare you!' her prisoner sputtered.

'Oh shut up. You invoked your right to remain silent – use it.'

Rachael continued to spout threats and insults all the way through the tunnel and up to the booking desk. Lucinda kept walking and laughing all the way.

At the desk, the booking deputy asked, 'What did you do? Arrest a comedian?'

'Not hardly,' Lucinda said, sliding the arrest warrant across the desk, 'but she cracks me up just the same.'

'Deputy,' Rachael said, 'I want to report this woman. She has arrested me under false pretenses and has not accorded me the respect a woman of my position deserves.'

The deputy leaned forward nodding, with a look of empathetic understanding on his face. 'Really, ma'am. I am so sorry. We always try to be polite to prostitutes.'

Rachael's mouth opened wide but no words came out, just short, hard pants of outrage..

'Lieutenant, is that her purse you're carrying?'

'Yes, it is. I would like the keys to her house, though. Rachael, could I give the keys to Eli so that he can take care of the dogs?'

'How dare you?' Rachael shrieked.

Lucinda turned to the deputy. 'I guess we'll have to break a window or bust down the door. Can't have those little dogs starving to death.'

'There's a law against that, Lieutenant,' the deputy said with a grin. 'In fact, I can call animal control right now and get the poor things taken to a shelter.'

'Take the keys. Take the damn keys. Give them to Eli. Tell him if anything happens to a hair on their heads, he's a dead man.'

'Oh, Rachael,' Lucinda said in a soft voice, 'I'm not an attorney but I must advise you not to say things like that. Threats against your husband's life won't sound good to the judge, particularly after what happened to your mother-in-law. In fact, when I tell him, he just might deny your bail and you'll have to make a whole new set of friends.'

'I want an attorney,' she sniffled. 'I want an attorney now.'

'I'm sure the deputy will let you call a lawyer as soon as you're booked. Won't you, deputy?'

'Sure will.'

'But first,' Lucinda continued, 'he's going to need the belt from your dress and your jewelry.'

'No!'

'Yes, ma'am. They've got to take your belt to keep you from harming yourself and they have to secure your jewelry to keep it from being stolen. Then they'll take your photograph and fingerprint you. After that, you'll be able to call your attorney, OK?'

'No, no, it's not OK,' Rachael cried.

A female deputy arrived at the desk. 'We can take it from here, Lieutenant.'

As Lucinda walked away, she heard Rachael's pleas. 'Detective, detective, don't leave me here. Detective, please!'

Lucinda knew she should feel some pity for a pampered sixty-something woman being locked up for the first time, but all she could think of was Adele, abandoned and thrown into strange surroundings where she drowned to death far from home.

FORTY-SIX

Back at the Justice Center, Lucinda went down to the morgue to see if any progress had been made on the identification of the remains found in the Blankenship backyard. She stopped first at Doc Sam's office. 'Hi, Doc.'

'Lieutenant. Good timing. Saved me some trouble.' He handed papers across his desk. 'This is the report from the forensic anthropologist. I haven't gotten to the death certificate yet but the cause of death was a gunshot wound to the head. And the skeleton was Sadie Blankenship – dental records confirmed that.'

'What about the male body?'

'Alvin Hodges, just as you suspected. And he was killed the same way.'

'And the third body?'

'Now that you mention it, Pierce, I'd like to make a request.'
'What's that?'
'It sure would be a lot easier on me if you find these damned
bodies one at a time.'
Lucinda smirked. 'I'll remember that in the future, Doc.'
'See that you do. Anyway, the third body. She wasn't shot.
She was strangled. The rope was still around her neck. And,
unfortunately, we don't know who she is. Came up empty in
the fingerprint database. Sent samples down to the lab for
DNA testing but I don't expect much from that. And her
pockets were empty.'
'Damn.'
'Ought to make a law – can't kill 'em and bury 'em without
ID.'
Lucinda left his office laughing. She called Robin Colter.
'Thanks, Colter. I really appreciated your help today. Can I
buy you a latte?'
'You most certainly can. Meet you by security?'

The two women expressed their mutual gratitude and walked
out of the building. As they started across the street, Robin
asked, 'What do you think my chances are?'
'I'd say—' Lucinda abruptly cut off as she saw a racing
car coming in their direction. She grabbed at Robin.
Simultaneously, Robin grabbed at her – both trying to push
the other out of the way. They almost cleared the car, but the
side mirror cut across Lucinda's upper arm. Both women hit
the ground, pushed themselves up and stared at the fleeing
pale blue, ancient, vintage Mercedes.
A patrol car parked at the curb took off in instant pursuit.
Lucinda called Dispatch. She described the incident, the
vehicle and requested more cars. Lucinda heard Robin on her
own phone asking for an ambulance and assumed it was an
over-abundance of caution.
The women watched as one, two, three, four marked vehicles flew out of the garage moving at high speed, the sound
of sirens fading as they moved further away. Officers carrying
barricades ran into the street, blocking it from traffic. An
approaching siren split the air, Lucinda looked toward the
sound wondering what it was.
An emergency vehicle screeched to a halt and a uniformed

paramedic jumped out with a bag and rushed toward Lucinda. The driver hopped out and went to the back of the vehicle.

'Lieutenant,' the paramedic said as he jogged toward her, 'let me take a look at that arm.'

Puzzled, Lucinda looked over at her left arm, saw the blood running down it and puddling on to the street. Suddenly, the pain registered. 'Damn,' she said.

The driver ran up pushing a gurney.

'No. No way. Nope. Do it here,' Lucinda said.

'OK, Lieutenant, just hop up on the stretcher sideways,' the paramedic said. 'I'll bandage you up in the street.'

As he cleaned up her injury, Lucinda observed the intensity of movement around the Justice Center. Beefy Captain Holland burst through the front doors, moving faster than she thought he should for a man of his size and age. He flew down the stairs, his feet barely touching the front steps.

'Pierce. Are you OK?'

'I'm fine, Captain. It's just a little cut,' Lucinda answered.

He looked at the pool of blood on the pavement and turned to the paramedic. 'Just a little cut?'

'Not exactly,' he said. 'But I've seen a lot worse. Probably should get a couple of stitches but the lieutenant doesn't want to go to the hospital.'

'Aw, c'mon. Do I really need stitches?' Lucinda objected.

'You're more likely to have a wider, permanent scar without them.'

'Oh please, look at my face. Does it look like a scar on my arm is going to bother me?'

'Whatever you say, Lieutenant,' the paramedic responded.

'You're certain the stitches aren't a medical necessity?' the captain asked.

'Yes, sir,' the paramedic said.

'Jeez, Pierce,' Holland griped, 'you go out on a wild-ass mission. Two people are shot, one person is dead. You were trapped behind a bench taking gun fire, shot at while you hid in the water under a pier. And now you get hit crossing the street in front of the cop shop?'

'Used up all my good luck, I'd guess,' Lucinda said with a shrug.

'Please don't move your arm, Lieutenant,' the paramedic asked.

'Sorry. Listen, Captain, this wasn't an accident. That car was coming straight at us with the pedal to the floor.'

'Is the whole Blankenship family accounted for?' he asked.

'Yes, sir. In jail, in hospital or dead.'

'What about the husband of the woman you just arrested?'

'Not likely.'

'Then, who?' Holland asked.

'Why do you assume I was the target, sir? Maybe someone was after Colter.'

'Colter? What do you think, Sergeant?' Holland asked.

'I don't know. She could be right. Or it could have been random anger – someone just wanting to run down a cop.'

'If it were random, wouldn't the driver have gone for someone in uniform?' Lucinda wondered aloud.

'Either of you dumped any boyfriends lately?'

The women looked at each other, rolled their eyes, and said, 'No,' in unison.

'Was anybody else working with the Blankenships, Pierce?'

'Not that I know of, but . . . The third body!' Lucinda said.

'Dead people can't drive,' Holland said.

'Yeah, but if someone else knows about that body . . .'

'You think?'

'It's possible. She wasn't shot, she was strangled. That tells me Gary Blankenship might not be good for that one. Could you call Jumbo's captain and see if they can find any missing women who might have a direct or indirect connection to the Blankenships?'

'He's not going to be thrilled to hear from me. But it'll probably help if I tell him you were a victim of a hit and run.'

'Thanks, Captain.'

A patrolman came running up. 'Lieutenant, they got him. They want to know if a man named Sandy Grisham means anything to you or Sergeant Colter.'

The women looked at each other and shook their heads.

'I'll give that name to Missing Persons,' Captain Holland said.

'I want to question that guy when they get him here,' Lucinda said.

'You sure about that, Pierce?' Holland asked. 'I can get someone else.'

'You better believe I want to face off with that guy. Try and stop me.'

'Take Colter into the interview with you. If she gets the job, watching you at work will be good experience.' The captain jogged back into the building, leaving both women smiling.

In the hallway outside of the interview room, Lucinda and Robin looked over the printout of Sandy Grisham's criminal record. Although the list was long, the offenses were minor; Sandy spent time in jail but never in prison.

Inside, a scrawny man in a blue denim shirt and black jeans sat in a chair, handcuffed to a U-bolt on the table. His mop of light-brown hair didn't look as if it had been touched by a comb or brush for a week or more. He smiled at the sight of the two women, revealing a missing upper tooth. 'Woo wee! Two women cops, God must love me lots.'

'We are the two people you attempted to kill today, Mr Grisham. I truly doubt that makes God happy,' Lucinda said as she sat down and leaned toward him with her arms crossed on the table.

'Hey, I lost control of the car,' he protested.

'Bullshit,' Lucinda said. 'I was there, remember. You veered straight toward us.'

'C'mon, c'mon, that's what happens, you know? You say to yourself, "Oh look, someone's in the road. Don't want to hit 'em." And damned if you don't steer right toward 'em without realizin' it.'

'Mr Grisham, you are facing some serious charges here. This isn't like one of your old beefs where they toss you in county lock-up for thirty days then send you home with a slap on your wrist.'

'You know, I didn't do all them things they said I did. In fact—' Grisham said, shaking his head.

Lucinda cut him off. 'I don't care about those petty crimes, Mr Grisham. All that concerns me now are the present charges: attempted murder, assault of an officer of the law, attempted assault of an officer, hit and run, resisting arrest, speeding, running red lights. That's just for starters, Mr Grisham. I imagine the district attorney will find creative ways to slap a few other charges on you over the next few days. Why did you try to run us over?'

'I missed you. I didn't run over either one of y'all.'

'That's because we moved, not because of anything you did, Mr Grisham.'

'How can you charge me with hit and run? I didn't even hit you.'

Lucinda stood. She removed the jacket she'd retrieved from her office before coming to the interview. Turning her left side to Grisham, she said, 'Explain that, then.' A bandage wrapped all the way around her arm. On both sides of it, the bruised area was growing darker. She slid back into her jacket and sat down. 'Well, Mr Grisham?'

'I did that?'

'Yes, sir. Didn't you notice the damage to your side mirror?'

'Didn't notice much of anything, to be honest; I just was trying to get home.'

'Just trying to get home? Do you normally drive seventy miles an hour through a residential neighborhood, Mr Grisham?'

'No. Not normally. I won't say I never done it before . . .'

'I should hope not. Because right in front of me it says you were going seventy-five miles an hour a couple of years ago when you drove past a suburban elementary school.'

'Yeah, somebody was pissed at me. I was just tryin' to get away.'

'That doesn't surprise me, Grisham. I'm beginning to get a little pissed at you myself.'

'C'mon, c'mon, I'm sorry I hurt your arm,' Sandy whined.

'Why, Grisham? Why did you point that car at us and try to run us down?'

'It weren't personal, honest.'

'Just tell me why.'

'I can't. I just can't. I would if it was just up to me. But it's not. So I just can't.'

Lucinda wanted to jerk that weasel up out of his chair and bang his head against the wall. Instead, she stared at him. He squirmed beneath her gaze. Thirty seconds of silence was all Sandy could tolerate. 'C'mon, c'mon, you know how it is, dontcha?'

A rap at the door caused a spark of anger to ignite inside Lucinda. She turned her head sharply toward it. Captain Holland's head stuck in and he motioned her out into the hall. Her anger dissipated in the hopes he had some information she could use.

'His daughter-in-law, Darlene Karnes Grisham, has been

missing for a couple of months. Most of her friends and neighbors thought she'd gotten fed up with supporting her abusive husband and just walked out. But maybe not,' Holland said.

'Is it her body in the morgue?' Lucinda asked.

'We think it is. Her driver's license photo looks like a match.'

'How about if I take our boy down to look at the body?'

'Might do the trick. She's pretty ripe. She's out in the isolation unit.'

'Tell a tech I'll be coming down for an ID,' Lucinda said.

As she returned to the room, Sandy said, 'This cop here needs some work. She didn't do the good cop thing too well while you were gone.'

Lucinda ignored him. 'Sergeant Colter, unlock the prisoner from the table and cuff his hands behind his back. We're going on a little field trip.'

Robin raised her eyebrows in an unspoken question and did as requested. The threesome went out of the police department and down the elevator to the basement. When they went through the stainless steel doors into the autopsy room, Sandy balked. 'I don't want to go in here. This place gives me the creeps. It's worse than a cemetery.'

Robin tugged on the chain between the cufflinks. 'Keep moving, Grisham.'

'We're just passing through,' Lucinda added.

They walked through the back door and across a concrete platform leading to a small, separate building butted against the wall of the bigger structure. A tech in a white jacket unlocked it as they approached. He pulled open the heavy insulated door. It made a popping sound as the seal released.

Sandy stopped at the doorway. 'Man, it really stinks in there.'

Robin manhandled him inside. 'If I have to put up with it, you can, too, Grisham.'

'Won't be here long, Grisham,' Lucinda assured him. 'We just need you to identify the body.'

Sandy squirmed as Robin dragged him closer to the sheet-draped stainless steel table in the middle of the room. Lucinda pulled down the top of the sheet, exposing the face. 'Look familiar, Grisham?'

Sandy turned his head away and closed his eyes. Lucinda grabbed his chin, twisting it toward the woman's body. She pushed down on the top of his head bringing him closer to her. He held his breath and squeezed his eyes tighter in response.

'Open your damn eyes,' Lucinda shouted. 'You can't hold your breath forever and you're not leaving here until you look at this body.'

Sandy's face turned red. His breath exploded out. When he inhaled, he made a disgusted sound and struggled. 'Get me out of here. Get me out of here.'

'Open your eyes, Grisham,' Lucinda demanded.

Sandy relented. He looked down at the dirt-stained face and sloughing skin. His shoulders jutted upward and he doubled over. Robin jerked him to the side of the room where he heaved up the contents of his stomach on to the floor.

'Who is she, Grisham?' Lucinda shouted over his retching. 'Who is she?'

'Get me out of here. Get me out of here and I'll tell you. Just, for God's sake, get me out of here.'

Lucinda dampened a paper towel and handed it to Robin who wiped Sandy's mouth. They led him back up to the interview room and cuffed him to the table. He sat, panting, his face ashen, beads of perspiration dotting his forehead.

'OK, Mr Grisham,' Lucinda said, 'who is she?'

Sandy sighed and shrugged without answering her question.

'Grisham, we can go back and have another look if you need to refresh your memory.'

'Dammit,' he spit out. 'It's my daughter-in-law.'

'Her name?'

'Darlene Grisham.'

'How did she end up in Gary Blankenship's backyard?'

'It's a long story.'

'I'm waiting, Grisham.'

'Well, it started about twenty years ago or so. Me and Gary were drinking and watching a game on the tee-vee. Sadie was ragging on him about something he was supposed to do. Gary got really pissed after a while. He got up and backhanded her, knocking her into a wall. Then instead of crying and saying she was sorry like she usually did, she sassed him.'

Lucinda bit her tongue. *Sassed him? Sassed him? She wanted to beat the crap out of him for even using that word.*

'Gary grabbed up a poker from by the wood stove and raised it up. Sadie ran for the stairs. Gary dropped the poker and chased after her. I just sat there until I heard the gunshot. Then I went upstairs. Gary had the gun in his hand. Sadie lay flat on the floor. "Did you kill her?" I asked. Gary just nodded.

'I don't remember how it all went after that but I know we buried her under the steps in the backyard and cleaned up the blood in the bedroom. Before I drove off, I said, "Gary, you owe me big time." He said, "Yep. Call on me anytime. And Sandy," he says, "did you know my tramp of a wife ran off with her boyfriend and abandoned her own kids. Can you imagine a woman who would walk out on her kids?" And that was that.'

'Not quite, Grisham. We did find Sadie's body right where you're saying. But we still have the other body – a far fresher corpse. How does that tie in?'

Sandy ran his fingers through his hair. 'I never called in that favor – never needed to. Not till a few months ago. My son came to me, real upset. He didn't mean to kill her. He was just tryin' to teach her a lesson, that's all. He just held on a little too long. It was an accident.

'That's when I thought of Gary and the favor he owed me. But I couldn't find him anywheres. That got me thinkin' about Sadie. All these years and nobody ever found her body. Seemed Gary's backyard was a mighty good place to hide Darlene's body, too. Gary was nowhere to be found and nobody else'd moved into the place. So me and Steve, that's my son, loaded her up and buried her in the corner by the fence. And thought that was the end of it.'

'Still, Grisham,' Lucinda pressed. 'You haven't explained why you tried to run us over.'

'That was pretty stupid. I shouldn't have listened to my boy. But he came to me all desperate. He showed me a picture of you he'd cut from the newspaper after you found the bodies. He said you'd figure it out. He said you had to be stopped.'

'Whose idea was it to use a vehicle to kill me?'

'It was mine,' Sandy said with a shrug. 'He wanted me to choke you to death or stab you or cut your throat. I couldn't do that kind of stuff. I never killed nobody. So I told him, maybe I could hit you with my car – it's old but it's a Mercedes, built solid, sure to do the trick.

'He said, "Perfect. It'll look like an accident." And here I am. And I'm sorry. On the long list of stupid things I've done, that one's right at the top.'

Lucinda sighed and rose to her feet. 'Sergeant Colter, take him over to the jail and book him. I'll go have a word with the DA.'

Lucinda went up to the fifth floor, briefed the DA and then walked down the stairs to her third-floor office. She picked up her phone and called the office of Dr Rambo Burns to schedule her next surgery.

EPILOGUE

Lucinda wore a broad white bandage from cheek to cheek across her nose when she picked up Charley Spencer. It fascinated the young girl no end. 'Can I look under it?'

'No. Dr Burns told me not to mess with it,' Lucinda said.

'But Rambo likes me. It'll be OK.'

'No it won't, Charley. Dr Burns particularly warned me about you. He told me to be on my guard and not let you talk me into taking it off.'

'He did not!'

'Yes he did, Charley.'

'Well, just wait till I see him again. What are we doing today, Lucy?'

'I thought it was about time my two best friends met each other.'

'You can't have two best friends, Lucy.'

'Oh yes you can if one of them is a girl and the other is a boy,' Lucinda said, making that rule up on the spot.

'You can do that?'

'You sure can,' Lucinda assured her.

'So you got a boyfriend?'

'Let's just say I have a friend who is a boy.'

'Do you kiss and stuff?'

Lucinda certainly didn't want to get anywhere near a discussion about sex with someone else's prepubescent child. She changed the subject. 'Jake is an FBI agent.'

'Really?'

'Yes. His official title is Special Agent in Charge.'

'Wow! That's a long title. I'll call him Jake.'

'I'm sure he'd like that.'

Lucinda pulled into a space at Riverside Park. 'I told Jake we'd meet him by the ice-cream stand.'

'Can we get ice cream?'

'Of course.'

Charley raced out of the car, straight to the stand and stopped in front of the only man there. 'Are you Jake?'

'Yes, I am.'

'I like your shoes,' she said noticing his turquoise Chucks.

'Thanks.'

'Is it part of your Special Agent uniform?'

'Not hardly.'

'Are they Special Agent in Charge shoes?'

'Nah, I just like them.'

Lucinda said, 'Charley, do you know what flavor you want?'

'I haven't looked yet.'

'Go pick one out. As soon as you decide, I'll place the order.'

Charley raced over to the display cases and peered down at the tubs, moving sideways across as she studied the contents.

'I'm not sure I know what to talk about with a young girl,' Jake said.

'Ask her about the news – what she likes to watch, what she reads,' Lucinda suggested.

'The news? She's just a little kid.'

'Trust me.'

After they sat at a picnic bench to eat their ice-cream cones, Jake said, 'Charley, Lucinda tells me you like to follow the news.'

'Of course I do. Don't you?'

'Yes, I do. Of course. Do you get your news on TV, in the newspaper . . .?'

'I like to get it from a bunch of places. Daddy says that way I can get the full picture. So I read the newspaper every day and I read *Newsweek* each Tuesday. Daddy said I could get a subscription to *Time*, too, for my birthday. I only read that once in a while now when I can talk somebody into buying me a copy. Would you buy me a copy, today?'

'Sure,' Jake chuckled. 'How about TV news? What do you like to watch?'

'I watch the local news and the network news every night unless I have too much homework. But my favorite is Rick Sanchez on CNN. He's really cute and funny. I like *Las Fotos*,' she said deepening her voice and mimicking Sanchez's accent. 'And Rick does good with the regular news and he tweets, too. I want an iPhone but Daddy says I'm not old enough. But I can only watch Rick's whole show during the summer break. And, sometimes, he's on vacation then. I wrote to him and gave him my schedule so that he'll work then when I can watch.'

'You sound like a very well-rounded and very busy person, Charley.'

'I have to be, Jake. I want to be a police officer when I grow up. I want to help some little girl someday just like Lucy helped me.'

Lucinda blinked and swallowed hard. She didn't want to cry in front of both of them.

'Jake, I need to talk to you about something serious,' Charley said. 'I mean, I know the news is serious. But this is personal serious.'

'What's that?'

'Lucy says that you are her best friend that's a boy.'

'I try to be, Charley.'

'Well, I'm her best friend that's a girl. And I think I've been her best friend longer than you have.'

'I think that's right.'

'OK. That makes me the boss friend. And I expect you to be good to her – all the time, even when you're in a bad mood. Promise?'

He looked over Charley's head and straight at Lucinda. 'I promise,' he said, using his index finger to make an X over his heart.

'Hope to die?' Charley asked.

Lucinda watched his eyes soften and grow moist as he scanned her face. 'I promise. And if I ever break that promise, I hope to die.'